SOHO ANGEL

THE SOHO SERIES BOOK THREE

SOHO ANGEL

THE SOHO SERIES BOOK THREE

GREG KEEN

THOMAS & MERCER

Text copyright © 2019 by Greg Keen

Published by Thomas & Mercer, Seattle

www.apub.com

Amazon, the Amazon logo, and Thomas & Mercer are trademarks of Amazon.com, Inc., or its affiliates.

ISBN-13: 9781542004107
ISBN-10: 1542004101

Cover design by @blacksheep-uk.com

Printed in the United States of America

For Mum

PROLOGUE

Kenny Gabriel wasn't what you thought when you thought private detective. His corduroy jacket, once probably black, was now an indeterminate colour. The jeans couldn't have cost much more than a tenner and his tousled grey hair needed a cut. During the time the man had been following him – getting on for two hours now – Kenny had smoked five cigarettes and eaten a slice of pizza bought from a kiosk by the station. It had been washed down with a can of Tango. He'd crossed the road and nearly been run down by a cab driver who hadn't seen him until it was almost too late. The cabbie had verbally abused Kenny and Kenny had abused him back. It was an entertaining interlude in an otherwise dull afternoon.

And yet maybe that was what made Kenny Gabriel good at his job, and it did seem from their research that he was good at his job. If no one noticed you, then you were already halfway to being successful. The man knew that from his own experience. He and Kenny had something in common – they blended into the crowd.

There were two of them in the business. One was a fat guy who looked a lot like B.B. King and didn't seem to get out much. The other was Kenny. The company was registered with the SIA, according to its website, and specialised in skip-tracing jobs. Usually that involved finding long-lost relatives, tenants who'd done a flit, or absent fathers who had reneged on child support orders. Not big-time exactly.

Kenny had popped a couple of pills shortly after the near miss with the taxi. Was he suffering from a hangover? He looked like a drinker but surely it was too late in the day for that to be the case. He'd been sneezing a fair bit, so perhaps Kenny had a cold or the flu coming on. There was a lot of it about, apparently.

Living on your own in middle age was sad. He'd read an article that claimed being single no longer carried the stigma it once had. Bullshit. If you were living on your own at Kenny's age then something had gone wrong in life.

The address was interesting. Kenny lived in Soho and living in Soho was expensive. Had been expensive for quite a while, in fact. Judging by the company's annual return, there was no way Kenny could be getting paid enough to rent a flat in Brewer Street. Perhaps he had a supplementary source of income.

He had decided that he quite liked Kenny. Maybe, if they were to meet under different circumstances, they would get on well together. His instructions were not to do anything today unless there was zero risk involved. Maybe a situation would arise and maybe it wouldn't. He would have to see how the rest of the day panned out.

And if it didn't happen then there was more than enough money available to engineer something. There had been a discussion as to whether Kenny needed to be killed or whether something very scary could be arranged to make him give up the case. In the end it was decided there was simply too much at stake.

Kenny Gabriel had to die.

ONE

OC Trace and Find was often approached to find a missing family member. Usually a couple of photographs and a description of the subject accompanied the briefing. In Emily Ridley's case, neither photos nor description were necessary. Half the nation knew when and, more significantly, with whom she had disappeared.

Emily's mother was sitting on one of the office sofas. On its opposite number were perched Odeerie and myself. The proprietor of OC Trace and Find had discarded the tracksuit he habitually wore for a double-breasted grey suit. The wall clock read 8.15. I had a hell of a headache, made unusual by the fact that alcohol hadn't passed my lips in six days. I sipped a lukewarm Nescafé and focused on the conversation.

'What exactly were you hoping for as a result of the investigation, Mrs Ridley?' Odeerie asked. 'Several organisations have attempted to locate Emily over the years.'

Pam Ridley had short iron-grey hair and a face latticed with lines and creases. She replied in an accent forged in one of the less fashionable London boroughs.

'They've tried to locate Castor Greaves. He was famous; Em wasn't. I want to know what happened to her, that's all.'

'You think that your daughter may still be alive?'

Pam Ridley shook her head. 'She'd have found a way to let me know if she was. Especially when her dad died. I want you to find out where she is.'

Odeerie nodded. The fat man was usually up for taking any job that paid the daily rate. I could understand his reluctance over this one. The chances of finding Emily Ridley in any condition after twenty-two years were slim, and her mother didn't look like a woman with the resources to fund a lengthy investigation.

'I've got the cash, if that's what you're worried about,' she said as though reading my mind. 'Uncle Rory left me a packet in his will.'

'I think Mr Charles was more thinking about the likelihood of a successful outcome,' I said, making my first proper contribution to proceedings. 'Emily was last seen in 1995, Mrs Ridley. If missing people don't turn up within the first six months, they frequently don't turn up at all.'

Pam Ridley's mouth tightened and she folded her arms.

'If you don't want my money then there's those that do,' she said, a comment that focused Odeerie's mind immediately.

'We're not saying that we don't want to help, Mrs Ridley,' he said, giving me a sideways look. 'Just that we're trying to understand your specific goals.'

'Well, you know now. Are you up for it or what?'

'Of course. We'll give you a new client form and take a retainer at the end of our meeting. As a matter of interest, what made you decide to approach OC Trace and Find?'

Pam nodded in my direction. 'Kenny found that girl who went missing a couple of years ago,' she said. 'And he sussed who killed Blimp Baxter.'

Although they had brought a fair degree of press interest, the cases in question hadn't been unqualified successes. This was a fact that Pam Ridley had overlooked, or was determined enough to ignore.

'You haven't had any contact with your daughter whatsoever since she was last seen at the Emporium club in Archer Street on the . . .' Odeerie consulted his notes. 'On the night of 19th July 1995?'

'Nope. Nothing at all.'

'What about the alleged sightings of Castor and Emily?'

'They're bogus.'

'There have been several photographs. The one in Goa did bear a very strong—'

'Have either of you got kids?' Pam interrupted. Odeerie and I shook our heads in unison. 'Well, the thing is that you've got a bond with them. When it's gone . . . when they've gone . . . you feel it in your guts.'

As if to emphasise the point, Pam Ridley patted her midriff.

'I knew that night something had happened to Em, without being told,' she said. 'And that I weren't going to see her again. Leastways not alive.'

'Have you any idea what might have happened to Emily, Mrs Ridley?' I asked.

'Murdered,' came the immediate reply.

The word hung in the air.

'Either that, or someone gave her drugs and she overdosed,' she added. 'Then they got rid of her body. It amounts to the same thing.'

'Was your daughter a regular drug user?' Odeerie asked.

Pam Ridley lost eye contact and shifted position on the sofa. 'She might have done a few things, but all the kids used to take stuff back then. That doesn't make her a bad person. She just fell in with the wrong crowd, is all.'

'Why d'you think Castor Greaves disappeared at the same time?' I asked.

'How should I know?' Pam said. 'All I wish is that my little girl never met him or his bloody rock band.' She glanced at the clock. 'Is that it? Only I've got to be at work by half nine . . .'

'I think that's sufficient information to be going on with,' Odeerie said, and heaved himself out of the sofa. He waddled over to a brushed aluminium desk, selected a new client form from a rack and made the return trip. 'Send this back to us with a bank transfer or a cheque for five hundred pounds and we'll get on with the job immediately, Mrs Ridley. You'll receive a weekly financial account along with a daily update.'

Our new client took the form and tucked it into her handbag. From the same bag she withdrew a bundle of fifties held together with an elastic band.

'Three thousand,' she said. 'When it's gone I'll send more.'

Most clients take months to pay their invoice, and bitch about my entirely justifiable, if not necessarily well-documented, expenses. It was the first time I could recall one paying up front in cash with an assurance of more to follow.

'Once we've reviewed the circumstances of your daughter's disappearance then we'll likely have more questions for you,' Odeerie said. 'And of course I'll give you a receipt for this . . .'

I helped Pam on with her coat. Uncle Rory may have left a packet, but his beneficiary hadn't been spending it on clothes. Her ancient sweater had multiple snags and the jeans could have come from the same budget rail as my own. 'What kind of work do you do, Mrs Ridley?' I asked when the manoeuvre was complete.

'Cleaner,' she said, which explained the outfit. 'I'm doing Professor Cranton this morning. The prof lives up in Belsize Park, so it's a bit of a trek.'

'Did Emily have any brothers and sisters?'

'No. Geoff and me wanted more, but it didn't turn out that way. Sometimes you've got to be grateful for what comes along in life, haven't you?'

'Yes,' I said. 'I suppose you do.'

Odeerie returned with a receipt. Pam shoved it into her pocket as though it were a Kleenex. 'You'll start on it straight away, then?' she asked.

'This morning,' Odeerie confirmed. 'Although you won't be a client officially until you've returned the form, Mrs Ridley. Kenny can pick it up. He might have a few more questions.'

'He's only working on this?'

Odeerie nodded. 'I'll pull Mr Gabriel off his current investigation and make him the lead operative on yours.'

As I was Odeerie's only 'operative' and my current 'investigation' involved counting the number of vehicles entering a car park in Hammersmith to work out whether the attendant was skimming the machine, this probably wouldn't prove too difficult.

'Nice to meet you, Kenny.' Pam Ridley and I shook hands. 'My swami said I'd encounter a man who would reveal a path that had been dark for many years.'

'Your what?'

'Swami Hari. He gives readings in Porteus Books. At least he used to, until it closed down. He does them over the phone these days.'

'And the swami thinks that man is me, Mrs Ridley?' I asked.

'Oh, yes,' she said. 'He's sure it is.'

As Odeerie hadn't been able to leave his flat/office for the best part of a decade, it fell to me to escort Pam Ridley to the front door of Albion Mansions. On my return, I pondered what she had said about being grateful for what comes along in life.

In a month I would turn fifty-nine. It was a time when most guys were putting their names down for the allotment or golf club where they could while away their retirement years. My pension plan wasn't likely to stretch to either, largely as I didn't have a pension plan. What

I did have was a job doing the legwork for an agoraphobic skip-tracer with an eating disorder, a flat on Brewer Street courtesy of an over-achieving brother, and the worst headache I'd had since Wimbledon won the FA Cup.

When I re-entered the office, Odeerie was munching a chocolate digestive. The banknotes had been subdivided into piles. 'D'you think we should be taking Pam's money?' I asked. 'Because I get the feeling she doesn't have that much of it.'

'You heard what she said about Uncle Rory.'

'All the same . . .'

'If she wants to spend her cash, it might as well be with us.'

Odeerie had a point. OC Trace and Find was going through one of its periodic lulls in business. My brother had waived the rent but didn't cover my utility bills.

'Aren't you meant to be on a diet?' I asked as he crunched into another biscuit. 'You know what the doctor said about your blood pressure.'

Odeerie sighed and put the biscuits into his drawer. He regrouped the notes and fastened the elastic around them before transferring the wad into an ancient cast-iron safe.

'We should start by reviewing the case,' he said after spinning the dial. 'Did you do your research?'

'I checked out Wikipedia, if that's what you mean.'

Odeerie looked at me expectantly.

'Castor Greaves went missing after Mean's last gig in '95. The band was about to release its third album but there had been a lot of tension amongst the members as to its musical direction. Castor was lead singer and had reportedly been heavily into drugs. Against expectations the gig turned out to be a total stormer with many critics rating it in their top ten of all time.'

'And which half of London seems to have seen.'

Odeerie had a point. If everyone who reckoned they were at Mean's last gig actually had been at Mean's last gig, then it would have needed to take place at Wembley Stadium as opposed to a modest venue in Soho.

'After the show,' I continued, 'Castor and the rest of the band and the crew have a small party to celebrate. At around one a.m., Castor's girlfriend, aspiring model Emily Ridley, says that she has to get up early for work and leaves. Five minutes later, Castor says that he's going to take a leak. When he doesn't return after twenty minutes, someone goes to find out where he is.'

'Someone?' Odeerie asked.

'Okay – Chop Montague, the bass player, goes to find out where he is. He's not in the toilets so the building is searched in case Castor has passed out, but he's nowhere to be found. Everyone assumes he's gone home. The party folds and the club's locked up for the night.'

'And neither Castor nor Emily are seen again.'

'Depending on who you believe. In the years that follow there are various alleged sightings of the couple as far apart as India and Iceland. People start wearing T-shirts with *I'm with Cas and Em* above their picture. Various theories appear in the press as to where they are and a couple of books are written about it.'

'What's *your* theory, Kenny?'

'Christ, I don't know. It's an urban legend, not someone using a dodgy key to rob a parking meter. Where do we start?'

'At the beginning,' Odeerie said. 'Like we always do.'

TWO

The journey from Albion Mansions on Meard Street to the Vesuvius club on Greek Street took ten minutes. April may be the cruellest month, but March can be a bastard too. The chill wind whistling down Bateman Street brought tears to my eyes.

It used to be that Soho at 8.45 a.m. was a fairly empty place, what with the clip joints and porno cinemas not opening up until noon. As most of these had become marketing agencies, or TV production companies, the place was crawling with execs clutching double-shot macchiatos on their way to the first meeting of the day.

The Vesuvius was a reminder of finer times. An expat Italian called Jack Rigatelli had opened the place in the late '60s. Jack's creative manifesto had been a simple one – a basement club in which 'members' could get pissed and/or play cards from when the pubs closed until dawn the following day.

Jack was no longer with us but the Vesuvius was. Its former manager had returned from Manchester to put the place back on its feet. Stephie hadn't made any dramatic changes, apart from opening up at lunchtime. This meant her second in command arrived early to sort the place out. I opened the door to find Whispering Nick pushing a vacuum cleaner around with the enthusiasm of a man sweeping for landmines.

'What are you doing here?' he asked after switching it off.

'And a very good morning to you too, Nick.'

He squinted at me. 'Not after booze, are you?'

'It's nine o'clock.'

'I know.'

That Nick fully expected me to knock back a large one for breakfast was irritating. 'I haven't had a drink for almost a week,' I said.

'Oh, yeah. That why you're never in here, then?'

'It's one of the reasons.'

'What are the others?'

'I've been busy with work. Which is why I wanted to talk to you . . .'

'It'll have to wait until I've had a brew,' he said. 'Fancy one?'

'A coffee would be great,' I said. 'Milk and two sugars.'

While Nick got busy in the small kitchen behind the bar, I took a seat next to the ancient fruit machine. I'd been frequenting the V for over forty years. Not much had changed for either of us. The club was still a dingy shebeen with nicotine-stained walls. I was still waiting for life to turn a corner. The only thing that was different since I'd last been in the V was that the framed poster of the 1982 Italian World Cup squad had been removed from the wall.

Nick returned with two steaming cups and laid them on the plastic gingham table cover. His voice box had been ruined when he was a kid. When the V is full, Nick uses a throat mic and speaker. As it was just the two of us, he remained unplugged.

'What have you been busy with, then?' was his first question.

'I'm working on something connected to the Emporium club.'

'To do with Cas Greaves?'

'What makes you say that?'

Nick blew on the surface of his tea and took a tentative sip. 'Because that's all anyone ever thinks about when they think about the Emporium.'

'It's connected to Cas in a roundabout way,' I admitted.

Nick chuckled. 'Gonna track him down, are you, Kenny?'

I parried the chuckle with one of my own.

'All I want to do is speak with someone who was around the night of Mean's last gig. Doesn't your uncle work at the Emporium?'

'Uncle Kris is the premises manager.'

'Was he there that night?'

'That's his claim to fame.'

'Any chance you could give me his number?'

'Sure,' Nick said. 'When d'you want a word?'

'Today if possible.'

Nick went over to the pegs at the side of the bar and removed a phone from his jacket. I sparked up my first Marlboro of the day. As well as knocking the booze on the head, I'd also cut down on Madam Nicotine. And Nick wasn't likely to invoke the smoking ban.

'What's happened to the footie poster?' I asked. 'You better not have chucked it out, Nick, or Jack'll come back from the grave to haunt you.'

'What you on about, Kenny?' Nick said, holding his phone to his ear.

'The Italian World Cup team, you've taken it . . .'

The poster was where it had always been. Dino Zoff, Franco Baresi, Bruno Conti and the rest of the team were staring down at me from the wall.

'Taken it where?' Nick asked.

'Nothing, Nick, just that . . . Nothing.'

'You sure you don't want a drink?' he asked.

'Positive,' I said.

I was halfway through my smoke, trying to understand how a poster could disappear and reappear in the space of thirty seconds. Nick was talking ten to the dozen in Greek. The street door opened and closed. Two sets of feet clattered down the stairs, and the real reason I hadn't been in the Vesuvius lately walked into the club.

◆ ◆ ◆

Two years after her husband died, Stephie Holtby turned up unannounced on my doorstep with a bottle of Stoli. After necking it, we went to bed and had the kind of uninhibited sex that people with half a bottle of vodka inside them generally do.

To assuage her guilt at betraying Don's memory, Stephie pretended that nothing had happened. Attempts on my part to discuss the situation were met with stony silence. Three weeks later, she arrived with another bottle and we went again.

Stephie looked ten years younger than her age and had a body honed by exercise and a vegetarian diet. I lived off Pot Noodles and supermarket Scotch and had begun to accept that the only attraction my body held would be for medical science.

For this reason I carried on with the charade. At least, I did until Stephie invited me to move up north with her. We were set for a happy-ever-after ending until I bottled things at the last moment. Stephie was understandably pissed off and I'd assumed that would be the last I saw of her. And then she came back. With a boyfriend in tow.

I hadn't met Jake Villiers, although I'd heard a fair bit about him. Sadly it all turned out to be true. He was fiftyish, with a lean physique, neatly cut dark hair and a jawline sharp enough to strike a match on. Had he been a character from the *Eagle*, Jake would have spent the morning test-piloting a prototype fighter plane before opening the batting for England with his best mate Dan Dare.

Worse than that, it seemed that everyone at the V thought that he and Stephie made the perfect couple. Worst of all, he was minted. Stephie had met Jake when she was working behind the bar of one of the thirty-three clubs, pubs and restaurants he owned around the country. She had moved back to London, as Jake lived in Richmond. They hadn't moved in together but apparently it was only a matter of time.

Obviously, I was as delighted for them as everyone else.

'Hi, Kenny,' Stephie said. 'How are you?'

'Great,' I said. I wondered if we were going to hug. We didn't hug.

'This is Jake,' Stephie said.

'Good to meet you, Ken,' Jake said. He was wearing a grey cashmere jacket over a black polo-neck sweater along with a pair of jeans and Chelsea boots. There was a whiff of muscular cologne about his person. We shook hands.

'Actually, it's Kenny.'

'I'm sorry?'

'Kenny. People call me Kenny.'

'Oh, right,' Jake said.

'Tell me Jake's watch is still here, Nick,' Stephie said. 'I forgot to take it home.'

Nick removed a small brown packet from the till and handed it to Stephie.

'It's guaranteed for a year,' she said, strapping something gold and slim to Jake's wrist. 'The guy said keep it away from water in future.'

'Thanks, sweetheart. And thanks for looking after it, Nick.'

If Nick had been a dog, I swear to God he'd have wagged his tail.

'Can we meet for lunch today, Jake?' Stephie asked.

A cloud passed over her boyfriend's face. 'I'd love to, Steph, but I've got to meet the builders at the Dulwich site.'

'Tonight?'

'Out with the guys from PDT.'

'Oh, yeah, I'd forgotten.'

'Why don't you and Kenny go to dinner?'

Stephie looked as though Jake had proposed a weekend crabbing in Great Yarmouth as a substitute for a fortnight's skiing in Val d'Isère.

'Kenny's probably got something on,' she said, almost hopefully.

'Nope,' I said. 'I'm free.'

'Good, that's sorted, then.' Jake consulted his recently repaired watch. 'I'd better be going,' he said, and cantered up the stairs like a man half my age.

'Where d'you want to meet, Kenny?' Stephie asked.

'Pizza Express on Dean Street?'

'Seven?'

I nodded.

'Uncle Kristos said that he could show you round this morning at eleven,' Nick said. 'Just turn up at the stage door and say you've got an appointment.'

◆ ◆ ◆

After leaving the Vesuvius, I took a short walk to Foyles in order to continue my research on Mean. According to Wikipedia, the main reference work was by one-time music journalist and hack-for-hire Saskia Reeves-Montgomery. Sure enough, there was a copy of *Play Like You Mean It* in the music section.

The first shot in the photo section showed the teenaged Mean Red Spiders. Lead singer Castor Greaves was slim, spotty and had a mullet hairdo. JJ Freeman was darker and chunkier. Despite his best efforts, Peter Owens looked as though he ought to be working in a bank, which is what he would jump ship to do four years later.

The pin-up of the four was Dean Allison. The Spiders' drummer was a couple of inches taller than his bandmates. He had the high cheekbones and piercing blue eyes of a professional model, and more of a pout on his lips than a snarl.

Successive photographs showed the Spiders rehearsing, onstage at various venues, and signing their first contract with Pergola Records. By this time, Gordon 'Chop' Montague had replaced Owens and the band had changed its name to Mean.

Even then Chop Montague's hair was receding. Now he was as bald as a cue ball. But when you're worth fifty million, who needs hair? After Castor went missing, Chop had carried on writing for himself and other artists, with huge success.

The final photograph I'd seen a thousand times. They were still selling T-shirts featuring it in Camden Market. Castor Greaves was staring directly into the camera; Emily Ridley had her head on his shoulder and was smiling dreamily.

Castor was a regular heroin user by then, but the photographer had caught him on a good day. Emily probably only had good days. Her blonde hair was cropped and she had the type of ethereal beauty that fashionistas trample over each other to get. Seventy-two hours later, she disappeared off the face of the earth.

All I had to do was find out why.

THREE

Archer Street is a two-hundred-yard stretch of road that joins Rupert Street to Great Windmill Street. Home to a couple of restaurants in which you or I would have to reserve a table in a previous life, it also boasts a design consultancy, a TV post-production company and, of course, the legendary Emporium club.

Hendrix played the Emporium, as did the Stones, the Clash and U2. It's a scheduled stop for every walking tour of Soho, and a place of sacred pilgrimage for Mean fans. Scrawled on and around the main door are hearts pierced by arrows, song lyrics, fan names, and a skull with a cigarette clenched between its teeth.

The stage door is less graffiti-ridden. It had just gone eleven when I pressed the intercom and announced that I had an appointment with Kristos Barberis. The woman left me waiting thirty seconds before pressing the release button. I opened the door and jogged Jake Villiers-style up two flights of stone steps to reception.

On the walls hung autographed pictures of the club's more famous acts. Notable by their absence were any of Mean. Behind a desk was a tall woman in her twenties who seemed concerned by the fact I was struggling to breathe.

'Kristos is on his way,' she said. 'Can I get you a glass of water?'

I shook my hand to indicate that wouldn't be necessary. Then I leant nonchalantly against one of the exposed brick walls and tried not to vomit.

Kris Barberis was a chubby man in his mid-sixties with a head of thick grey hair. Skinny brown jeans made his legs look like a pair of overstuffed sausages, and a denim shirt struggled to make it around his gut. The inverted silver cross hanging from the lobe of his left ear was about as trendy as a monocle.

'Hey, Kenny, my friend,' he said in a Greek inflection that forty years in the UK hadn't entirely erased. 'How you doing, mate?'

'I'm good, Kris,' I said. 'It's been a while.'

Kris grinned. 'Last time I visit the Vesuvius I spend the next two days in bed.' We shook hands. 'Nick said you want to look around the place? Still in the private detective racket?'

'Just about,' I said. The girl behind the desk looked up from her phone.

'Gonna find out what happened to Cas and Em?' Kris asked.

I shrugged and smiled. It did the trick.

'Well, you come to the right guy. You know I was here the night they disappeared?' He tapped me lightly on the chest. 'Just about the last person to see them both alive, mate.'

The receptionist's attention was straight back on the phone. I suspected she had heard Kris's claim to fame once or twice before.

'So Nick told me,' I said. 'I'd love to hear about it.'

A sigh from the girl, the significance of which wasn't lost on Kris.

'Probably best I tell you in Cas's dressing room,' he said.

The second floor had been modified to create eight separate rooms leading off the main hallway. Kristos led me to the furthest, and pulled a large set of keys from his pocket. He inserted one into the lock of dressing room 7 and grinned.

'Trust me, Kenny, everyone and his missus has had a go at working out how Cas and Em could have got out of here without being picked up on CCTV. No one's cracked it and no one will.'

At the far end of a room the size of a suburban garage was a long table with a plate-glass mirror above it. Rows of bulbs provided the light for make-up to be applied. A microwave sat at one end of the table, a washbasin at the other. There was a steady drip coming from one of the taps.

The rug had seen better days and the walls were unadorned plasterboard. Placed against one of them was a tatty blue corduroy sofa that looked to be the same vintage as the rug. There were three metal chairs and an empty clothes rail.

No ghostly giggling.

'So this is it,' Kristos said. 'Emily walks out of here at one a.m., and Castor about five minutes later. That's the last time anyone sees 'em.'

'Who was in the room?' I asked.

Kristos leant against the table and rubbed his chin.

'The band, plus me, Sweat Dog and Emily.'

'Sweat Dog?'

'Used to crew for Mean. Runs a tattoo joint in Muswell Hill now.'

I committed the name to memory. It wasn't difficult.

'Who was first to leave?'

'Dean Allison,' Kris said. 'Twenty minutes later, Emily said she had a modelling job in the morning and needed to get a good night's sleep.'

'Did you let them out?'

'Nah, the stage door was latched. You could open it from inside.'

'But not the outside?'

Kris shook his head. 'There were cameras above both exit doors and one on the stairs. You can see Dean leaving but there's no sign of Emily at all.'

'Could they have been faulty?'

'Nope, they were both tested. She didn't leave by the stage door or go into the auditorium. Neither did Castor. When he didn't come back, Chop went looking for him in case he'd passed out. Then we all searched the building. No sign of him anywhere.'

'Did you call the police?'

'Course not. We all thought he'd had a slash and figured that he might as well go home. It was only when Castor and Em didn't show up for a couple of days that anyone thought to check out the CCTV footage.'

'What was JJ Freeman like that night?'

'He and Cas were reminiscing about the old days while Chop was talking to anyone who'd listen about the next album. There was a real vibe in the room.'

'And Emily Ridley?'

Kris leant over and attempted unsuccessfully to stop the basin tap from dripping. 'Actually, she seemed a bit quiet,' he said. 'But that could have been because she was knackered. And obviously when you look back, you start imagining things.'

'The police must have been all over this place.'

'Not really. The guy in charge turned up with a couple of wooden-tops and had a nose round. That wasn't until a few days later, though.'

'DI Ronnie Mullen,' I said, recalling the investigating officer's name from my Wikipedia research. 'What was he like?'

Kris forgot about the tap. 'Didn't seem that interested, to be honest. Ronnie was coming up for retirement. He thought the whole thing was a publicity stunt.'

'And when it became clear it wasn't?'

'Not much happened. The whole Cas and Em thing has grown over the years. Back then the cops had better things to do than look for missing rock stars.'

'You must have had God-alone-knows how many investigators and journalists checking things out since, though.'

Kris shook his head. 'Bloke who owns the Emporium doesn't want cranks wandering round the place.'

'What's your theory about what happened?'

'Wormhole.'

'A what?'

'Tear in the space-time continuum. If you're unlucky enough to walk into one then it's over and out. There's loads of examples online, Kenny, but the government want to keep a lid on it in case of panic. I send you some links, if you like.'

'Can't wait, Kris. Any chance I could see the roof?'

'The roof?'

'Wasn't there something about a helicopter hovering overhead?'

Kris rolled his eyes. 'Trust me, there weren't no helicopter. People just hear about stuff afterwards and think they remember it too. There's a term for it . . .'

'False memory syndrome?'

'That's it. Take it from me, mate. Cas and Em are in the fourth dimension.'

'All the same, Kris, if I could take a look . . .'

My legs felt as though they were turning into plasticine, and the pain in my skull was pulsating. A gust of cold wind revived me to a degree, and I stepped out after Kris on to a tarmac roof covered in a layer of small stones. He closed the door behind us.

Several TV aerials had been tethered to a metal post that in turn had been lashed to a large chimney. There were five steel box-structures in a row. A tarpaulin had been wedged between a pair of boxes, one of which had been blackened by the elements.

I agreed with Kris that the helicopter theory was nonsense. The stories hadn't emerged until a couple of years after Cas and Em's disappearance. There had been a fire in Great Marlborough Street half a mile away that had been monitored by a helicopter. This was almost certainly the source of the 'black chopper' legend.

The building the Emporium abutted was a storey higher. You'd have to be an expert free climber or a straight-up magician to reach its rooftop without a ladder.

'What if they made it up there?' I asked Kris nevertheless. The wind snatched my words away. I repeated them with my mouth next to his left ear.

'How?' he asked, not unreasonably. 'And even if they did, the exit next door was padlocked, so they couldn't have got inside.'

'What are they?' I asked, pointing at the steel boxes.

'Run-off vents. Back in the day, the Emporium used to be a furniture showroom. That's where it got its name. Used to be a heating system that fed off a furnace in the basement. They ripped out the pipes and capped them years ago.'

I toed the tarpaulin in case it contained human remains that had lain undiscovered for twenty years. A shoal of silverfish scattered into cracks at the base of the chimney. In the interests of due diligence, I approached the roof's perimeter. I'm not fantastic with heights but the railings were sturdy enough, even if they were spattered with pigeon shit. Sixty feet below, Archer Street was getting on with its business.

In a window of the building opposite, a bearded hipster in a white suit was pruning a bonsai tree. Untamed brown hair fell to his shoulders. I was trying to work out what was familiar about the guy when he looked up as though I'd called his name. Steel granny glasses glinted in the light. He raised his hand and gave me a wave.

It was the last thing I saw before falling into a wormhole of my own.

FOUR

'Chances are it's nothing to worry about,' Dr Arbuthnot said, reclining in his chair. 'Although you were out for over a minute, so it's something we can't ignore. Also there are a few anomalies in your vision, and your right hand is significantly weaker than your left. I'd like to arrange an MRI scan in addition to the blood test.'

'How long will that take?' I asked.

'We should be able to schedule something for a couple of days. My PA will let you know this afternoon when the first slot is available.'

'If it does turn out to be something to worry about, what might be top of the list?' I asked. My brother's doctor laced his manicured fingers and pursed his lips.

'It could be a range of things.'

'Worst-case scenario?'

'Mr Gabriel . . .'

'Kenny.'

'Kenny, I think it's best that we wait for the blood work and the scan before we start discussing specifics. It really doesn't pay to jump the gun, in my experience.'

In his sixties, Dr Arbuthnot's retreating hair had retained its sandy-brown colour. His suit was made to measure and I suspected his reassuring smile had been too. On his pinkie was a heavy signet ring; wrapped around his wrist a Patek Philippe.

'All the same,' I said, 'I'd like to know.'

Dr Arbuthnot took a deep breath. 'Well, if you really must look on the darker side, then a tumour would be a possibility.'

The consulting room shimmered.

'A brain tumour?' I managed to say.

'I must stress that really would be the *absolute* worst-case scenario.'

'And if it were a tumour?'

'Should that be the situation, then treatment would depend on diagnosis. And for that reason, I really would advise against doing any online research.'

Arbuthnot took a surreptitious peek at his Patek.

'We'll have the blood work back in forty-eight hours, Kenny,' he said. 'Then we'll be in a situation to think about the next step. It's natural to be concerned, but try not to lose too much sleep. As I said, there are a number of things far more likely to be the cause of your passing out than . . . anything of a sinister nature.'

Arbuthnot stood up and we shook hands.

'How *is* your brother?' he asked.

'Fine,' I replied. 'He's in Hong Kong for work.'

'Do give Malcolm my regards.' Arbuthnot shepherded me across the thick pile carpet towards the door. 'Gaynor will make a follow-up appointment. If you do need to get in touch before then, for whatever reason, please don't hesitate.'

'Thanks again for seeing me at such short notice,' I said.

'Absolutely not a problem,' Arbuthnot replied.

The Trafalgar was a fairly unmolested Victorian boozer. A couple of snugs were intact, the carved oak bar surround looked to be original, and a bust of Nelson stared imperiously at me from a shelf above the fireplace. Had circumstances been different, I might have kicked back with my Scotch and enjoyed the ambience. As things were, I removed my phone from my pocket and googled *brain tumour*.

The news was mixed. If you have to have one, opt for a meningioma. It's usually benign and often doesn't require treatment. The one to swerve is a glioblastoma, almost always fatal with only three per cent of sufferers surviving more than five years. WebMD detailed up to eighty alternative diagnoses for my condition, including excessive caffeine use and nasal polyps.

Chances were that a decent decongestant spray and a good night's sleep would sort me out. The best thing to occupy myself with was work, not thoughts of invasive surgery, unsuccessful bouts of chemo, and being comforted in my final weeks by absolutely fucking no one. And yet it's one thing deciding that you're not going to think about something, another thing succeeding at it. It was a good ten minutes before I could turn off my phone and focus on the matter at hand.

I knew a fair bit about Chop Montague, because everyone knew a fair bit about Chop Montague. Less prominent were the other ex-members of Mean. Once again, Google enlightened me. Jean-Jacques 'JJ' Freeman was the owner of a music club in Dalston called the Junction. Its website claimed that it was 'the best blues venue in London', and open every night from six 'til late with live music Thursdays to Saturdays.

The proprietor was pictured with the house band. JJ's hair was shorter than it had been with Mean but remained as black as a raven's arsehole. He was bulkier and looked as though he spent a fair amount of time in the gym. By all accounts, JJ had been a bit tasty back in the day. Interviewing him might be interesting.

Dean Allison had forsaken the drums in favour of something called 'rogue taxidermy'. His Notting Hill shop was loved by the chattering classes and loathed by PETA. Its website featured creations constructed from the parts of several animals. Prominent was a pine marten sporting a fish's tail and a pair of bat wings stitched to its back. Even more delightful was the body of a rat fused to a lobster's shell.

Unfortunately, Dean had gone a bit too rogue for his own good. A police raid had discovered sixteen animals that were on the endangered species list in his workshop freezers, including a roloway monkey and a hawksbill turtle. Dean had pleaded ignorance and claimed that he had bought the animals from a dealer in good faith. A sceptical magistrate had handed down a fifteen-grand fine and a six-month suspended sentence.

I clicked on a video clip of Dean speaking at a lively press conference outside the magistrates' court. He expressed deep regret at having mistakenly purchased the animals and said that he found the trade in illegal species entirely repugnant.

Dean's cheekbones remained sharp, as did his piercing blue eyes. A dark suit sat well on his slim frame and an abundance of greying hair had been slicked down against his skull. An egg sailed through the air and splattered against the lapel of his jacket. Dean wiped it off with a disdainful expression and stalked out of shot.

Before leaving the pub, I tracked down an email address for Saskia Reeves-Montgomery, author of *Play Like You Mean It*. The best on offer had an 'info' prefix that didn't fill me with hope. Nevertheless, I sent a message to say that I was interested in Mean and would love to speak to her as soon as was convenient.

The transient optimism of booze dwindled as I trailed down Wimpole Street. I'd spent forty years smoking a pack a day and drinking the kind of Scotch you could run a lawnmower off. My meals arrived on the back of a moped or spent eight minutes in a microwave. Add to this an exercise regime that began and ended with *only walk if you absolutely have to, Kenny,* and I was living on borrowed time, regardless of what had poleaxed me on the Emporium's roof. Perhaps it was time to turn over a new leaf.

A cab pulled to a halt outside Flummery's Hotel. I was about to trot over and bag it when I recognised the passenger. Jake Villiers handed a note to the driver and waved away the change. He ascended the hotel steps, where a flunkey in a red jacket opened the ornate brass door for him. Jake looked like a man on a mission, which was probably the way Jake usually looked. Apart from the fact that four hours ago he had told Stephie that his mission lay in Dulwich and not at the snootiest boutique hotel in Marylebone.

Jake's plans may have changed. Instead of checking that the builders weren't behind schedule on his latest project, he could be meeting a business associate, his bank manager or taking tea with his Auntie Maude. And, of course, it was none of my business what he was up to. What I needed to do was go home, insert a tube of Sinex into each nostril and pray that I wasn't on the Reaper's to-do list for spring.

Ultimately, what decided me against this course of action was an abiding suspicion that Jake Villiers wasn't everything he seemed. Or was it that I hoped he wasn't? Either way, I let the cab drive off and approached the hotel entrance.

There were two reasons Flummery's employed a doorman. One of them was so that he could open it to people like Jake Villiers. The other was to make sure that it remained closed to people like me. For this reason, I bent down and appeared to pick something up from the gutter before mounting the steps.

'May I help you, sir?' the guy asked, as though he considered it unlikely.

'The man who just got out of the taxi dropped this,' I said, holding up my wallet. 'I'll nip in and return it to him if that's all right.'

'I'll take care of it, sir.'

The doorman extended a gloved hand.

'No offence, mate, but I really would like to give it to him personally.'

The doorman didn't appear thrilled at the idea of letting someone who looked like a destitute geography teacher into a hotel costing five hundred pounds a night. That I had indirectly questioned his honesty probably ratcheted up his scowl a few degrees.

'Or I could phone the manager,' I suggested. 'Obviously I'd have to say that you refused me admittance, though. What *is* your name, by the way?'

◆ ◆ ◆

Flummery's reception had a polished marble floor and oak-panelled walls. Two couches and three armchairs had been upholstered in refulgent cloth. A rococo clock stood on a plinth to my left, and a spectacular vase of lilies to my right. The queue at the desk was an advantage as it meant I could slip into the restaurant unhindered.

The room was four times the size of reception but less brilliantly lit. Presumably this was to promote the sense of privacy that Flummery's prided itself on. All the tables were taken and the sound of lunchtime chatter filled the air. The maître d' was on me before I could check whether any of the diners was Jake Villiers.

'Do we have a reservation, sir?' he asked.

'No,' I replied. 'Just popped in for a drink.'

Along one side of the restaurant was a cocktail bar. The staff mixed drinks for waiters to ferry to the tables or punters to consume at source. Its popularity meant it was a great spot to see if Jake was in the place, and, more importantly, who he was with.

Assuming the maître d' sanctioned it, that was.

'As you can see, we are *especially* busy today, sir,' he said.

'Maybe this would help . . .'

The twenty disappeared from my palm as though it had never been there. The maître d' focused his attention on another guest. I approached the bar and ordered a whisky sour. Jake was at a table about thirty feet away. Any worries I'd had that he might notice me proved unfounded. He was engrossed in conversation with a redhead who may not have been in the first flush but wasn't anyone's Auntie Maude.

Jake's glamorous companion said something that caused him to lean back in his chair. A waitress arrived. Jake consulted the woman, who nodded her agreement. The waitress departed. Jake and his companion rose from the table and headed for the door. Lunch had been scratched, apparently.

I followed them out of the dining room. If Jake saw me, I could always claim that I'd been having a drink with a potential client. They were waiting by the lift. Jake prodded a button that was already lit. The doors opened and they entered. I pretended to be absorbed in a rack of walking-tour guides until they closed.

Grabbing a guide, I approached the reception desk. The woman looked up from her computer screen with a welcoming smile.

'May I help you?'

'It's Harry from City Strolls.' I brandished the leaflet as though it were incontrovertible proof of identity. 'The lady who just got into the lift asked when Haunted Holborn starts. I'm afraid I gave her the wrong time.' I produced a biro and clicked the button. 'Would you mind if I left this?'

'Of course not,' the receptionist said, obligingly.

I poised the pen above the leaflet. 'God, I've forgotten her name. It's . . . Don't tell me . . .' I placed my hand on my forehead for a few seconds and muttered a curse. 'Nope, it's gone. Go on, then . . .'

'Oh, okay,' the receptionist said. 'I think it's . . .' She pressed a couple of keys on her laptop. 'Yes, Pauline Oakley.'

'Pauline. Of course.' I wrote on the leaflet, signed it *Harry* and handed it to the receptionist. 'Would you mind giving it to her when she comes down?'

'No problem,' she said.

FIVE

I've had a few jobs since I first arrived in Soho at the arse end of the seventies. Twenty-six, to be exact. When the last went west, I was introduced to Odeerie Charles, an agoraphobic skip-tracer looking for someone to do his legwork. Last year I'd nearly been shot in the head by a serial killer. Last month I was trying to photograph a former milkman who would rather a credit card company didn't have his new address. You can't beat a career with variety, as Odeerie frequently reminds me.

After getting back to the flat, I made a coffee and gave the fat man a call. 'Where the hell have you been?' was his first question.

'To see Nick's uncle, like we agreed.'

'That was hours ago!'

'I had to make an unscheduled visit to the doctor's.'

'Has the rash come back?'

'No, it hasn't.'

'What, then?'

'I'd rather not discuss it.'

'Suit yourself, Kenny,' Odeerie said after brief silence. 'But I wish you'd let me know about things in advance. I need to keep a proper time sheet for Pam Ridley. She said you can pick up the new client form tomorrow afternoon, by the way.'

'No problem,' I replied. 'Email me her address.'

'What did your friend's uncle have to say?'

'On the plus side, Kristos was there the night Emily and Castor went missing.'

'Well, that's something.'

'On the negative side, he thinks they fell into a black hole.'

'A what?'

'Kris hasn't a clue where they are, Odeerie. No one does, and we aren't going to find out either. You shouldn't be taking that poor woman's money. If we haven't found anything out in a couple of days then we should quit the job.'

'She'll go to someone else.'

'At least we'll have done the right thing.'

There was a bit of dead air. 'Let's get Pam signed up before we start thinking about getting rid of her,' Odeerie said eventually.

'Did you dig anything useful up?' I asked.

'The only concrete thing is the Goa photograph. At least one expert gave it an eighty per cent chance of it being Cas and Em.'

The picture had been taken in 2009 by a backpacker who had met a quiet English couple in their early thirties. The guy had posted the picture on Facebook along with a tongue-in-cheek comment as to how he'd been hanging with Cas and Em, only to find that half the world thought he might well have been doing precisely that.

Certainly the woman looked a lot like Emily Ridley. The guy had long hair and a straggly beard. It could have been Castor Greaves. It could have been Björn Borg. The whole thing provided the country with a few days of *are they or aren't they?* before going back to worrying about the recession.

'And that's the only evidence out there?' I asked.

'Well, there are the *People's Inquisitor* tapes. They published half a dozen tracks on their website by Castor Greaves. As far as anyone knows, they weren't recorded in his lifetime. Voice analysts are certain it's him. I can send you a file.'

'Okay,' I said. 'Odeerie, can I ask you something? It's not about the case; more a personal thing.'

'Go on . . .'

'Earlier I saw Jake Villiers go into Flummery's Hotel.'

'Who?'

'Stephie's boyfriend. He'd told her he was seeing some builders in Dulwich, so I followed him inside. He met this woman for lunch. At least, it looked as though they were going to have lunch, but they couldn't wait to get upstairs.'

'So what?'

'Obviously Jake's cheating on Stephie.'

'Maybe.'

'What d'you think I should do?'

The fat man sighed. 'Kenny, Stephie's moved on, and you need to move on too.'

'Just because we aren't together doesn't mean we aren't friends.'

'You've barely seen each other since she got back.'

'Yeah, but—'

'And Stephie isn't going to appreciate you destroying her relationship even if you *are* right about Jake. Get on with your own life and stop worrying about hers.'

My brother's company had bought the Brewer Street flat as a place where out-of-town clients could stay for a few days. As they usually preferred to rough it in the Four Seasons, my brother allowed me to live there rent-free. The sitting room walls have faded from utility-cream to nicotine-yellow and the springs in the sofas gave up the ghost around the same time as Michael Jackson. Malcolm had given me permission to redecorate but I hadn't quite got round to it.

After a cup of tea and a cheese sarnie, I opened Saskia Reeves-Montgomery's book at the point where Chop Montague replaced Peter Owens, who had been poached by that other fabulous band of hedonists commonly known as the NatWest. The print swam a bit before I could fully focus. Perhaps it was time to invest in reading glasses.

Chop's dad owned an engineering company and his mother had been a piano teacher. Their only child had shown musical ability from an early age and been accepted by the Royal College of Music. Gordon, as he was then known, had been prepped for a career as a professional pianist. That was until he entered the Blues Basement in Kentish Town and saw the Mean Red Spiders for the first time.

Getting to interview him would be tough and then some. Following Chop's surprise addition to the panel on *Moment in Time!*, most of Fleet Street was after the same thing. The best I could manage was a brief chat with his agent's PA's intern, to whom I gave my contact details. She didn't actually laugh out loud before saying that she would pass the message on, but I suspected it was an effort not to.

Next up, I put a call in to Still Life. Again I was disappointed. Dean Allison was busy in the workshop and didn't like being disturbed. He was scheduled to be in the Notting Hill shop tomorrow afternoon. Could I call back or visit in person?

I didn't expect the phone to even be answered at the Junction club, and was preparing for a recording when a gruff voice came on the line.

'Can I help you?'

'JJ Freeman, please.'

'Who's calling?'

'My name's Kenny Gabriel.'

'And what d'you want, Kenny Gabriel?'

Judging by the level of suspicion, I suspected I was talking to JJ in person.

'I'd like to speak to you about events leading to Emma Ridley's disappearance.'

'Oh, for Christ's sake, don't you people ever give up? It was twenty-odd years ago. Can't you find something else to write about?'

'I'm not a journalist, Mr Freeman. I'm working on behalf of Pam Ridley. She's trying to get some closure around her daughter's disappearance.'

'You know Em's dead, don't you?'

'Nevertheless, would it be possible for us to speak? Even if my conclusion is that Emily is probably deceased, it would be a comfort to her mother.'

Emotional blackmail doesn't always play well but, as far as JJ was concerned, it was the only game in town. 'Come to the club tonight,' he said.

'I'm afraid it might be difficult for me to—'

'If you wanna talk, be there. Otherwise forget about it.'

Fifteen minutes after my conversation with JJ, I received an email from Odeerie that had Pam Ridley's address and an audio file attached. I slotted my headphones into the jack and prepared to listen to what the *People's Inquisitor* was citing as proof that Castor Greaves was alive. There were seven songs in total. Two were half-decent; the other five sounded as though a pissed busker had improvised them.

The lyrics had been pored over in the hope they contained references to some event that had taken place after Castor's disappearance. Unfortunately they were mostly about the hard life and sad times of the singer. Living in luxury didn't sound much fun, although, for my money, it was definitely Castor Greaves behind the mic.

Of course, the songs had been recorded before Castor disappeared, which meant the real question was: who had sold them to the *Inquisitor*? They were rough, even for demos. Nevertheless, if someone had owned them legitimately, they could have been released in a 2CD collector's (also available on download and vinyl) edition that would have been catnip to diehard Mean fans.

As there was no way of answering this, my mind turned to the other big question of the moment: was there a tumour on my brain? For the last two decades I'd lived by the mantra that, starting tomorrow, everything was going to be completely different. If the scan found something ominous, there may not be many more tomorrows.

SIX

When I set off to meet Stephie the pavements of Brewer Street were teeming with office workers on their way to the Tube, confused tourists peering at smartphones, and developers debating which period building to carve into loft-style apartments next. The parish was once a dangerous place. Say the wrong thing to the wrong person and you could wind up stumbling into A&E with your ear wrapped in a handkerchief. The worst thing that's likely to happen now is that a barista forgets to stamp your loyalty card. The good old days have gone forever.

Pizza Express had been our preferred restaurant before Stephie decamped to Manchester. They did a competitively priced American Hot and there was usually some decent live jazz on offer in the basement. She was sitting by the window perusing a copy of the *Standard*, wearing a childlike frown of concentration.

Prior to seeing Stephie with Jake this morning, I'd run into her once before at the V. A roasting for not going to Manchester or keeping in touch was what I'd expected. What I got was a detached amiability that was far worse.

'Hope I haven't kept you waiting,' I said. Stephie shook her head and folded the paper. I took my place opposite her. 'How's your day been?'

'Okay. Tilly called in sick so I'll have to go back and help Nick, which I could do without. You in tonight?'

'I've got to be somewhere.'

'Oh yeah, and where's that?'

'The Junction club in Dalston. It's a work thing.'

'When you say *work*, I take it that you mean what you do for Odeerie, not . . . you know . . . real work.'

'That *is* real work.'

'If you say so, Kenny.'

A waiter arrived with a pair of menus. We ordered drinks, after which he departed. 'Nick said you were looking for Castor Greaves,' Stephie said.

'He's wrong. I'm looking for Emily Ridley.'

She looked up. 'You're being paid to do that?'

'Why wouldn't I be?'

'Well, I guess if someone's mug enough to give you money then you and Odeerie should fill your boots. I'm having a Caesar salad.'

'As a starter?'

'Uh-uh. I'm on a diet.'

'Why?'

Stephie smiled and looked back down at the menu. 'Oh, you know, spring's just around the corner. Got to make the effort, haven't you?'

Before I could reply, the waiter arrived with our drinks – a whisky and ginger ale for me, and a tonic water for Stephie. He said he'd be back to take our food orders and we clinked glasses.

'Welcome home,' I said.

'It's been nearly six months, Kenny.'

'I know, but this is the first time we've been alone.' I knocked back two-thirds of my waga. 'Actually, there's something I've been wanting to say for a while . . .'

Stephie's eyes narrowed. 'What's that?'

'About Manchester . . . It was a mistake.'

'Tell me about it. You always think that your hometown's going to be your hometown forever, but things change. Still, I'm back now.'

'What I meant was that I should have gone with you.'

Stephie looked directly at me. 'Why are you telling me this?'

A good question, and one for which I didn't have a definitive answer.

'I called a few times and hung up.'

'Oh, right, that was you, was it?'

'Yeah,' I said. 'That was me.'

The chatter of the other diners emphasised the silence between us. From the basement came the faint sound of someone running scales on a sax.

Stephie took a sip from her glass.

'I don't know what to say, Kenny. There's absolutely no need to apologise, but if that's what you're doing then apology accepted. If you're trying to say something else, then . . . well, obviously I'm with Jake now.'

'I know that,' I said. 'How did his thing turn out today?'

'What thing?'

'He said he was going to see the builders on his new project.'

'Oh, yeah.' Stephie smiled. 'Apparently it's really coming on. Why don't you come to the opening night? Jake would be delighted.'

'We'll see,' I said. 'Does he know about . . . you know.'

Stephie nodded. 'I thought I ought to tell him in case anyone else did. Not that he'd have a problem with that, but it's best to be totally up front.'

'And he didn't mind?'

'He doesn't see you as a threat, if that's what you mean. And Jake isn't at all possessive. That's why he suggested we have dinner together.'

I drained my waga and placed the glass on the table.

'Fantastic. I'm pleased for both of you.'

The waiter arrived. Stephie specified a low-calorie dressing on her Caesar. What with me not being too concerned about spring being just around the corner, I chose a Sloppy Giuseppe with dough balls on the side and a replacement waga.

'Going to Manchester was too much change for me,' I said. 'But if I—'

Stephie's raised hand stopped me mid-sentence.

'Water under the bridge, Kenny,' she said. 'And sixty-three isn't ancient these days. You've still got enough time to do something with your life.'

'I'm fifty-eight!'

'Even better, then. But you need to get on with it, because one day it really will be too late.'

The temptation to tell Stephie that I might well not see sixty was a strong one. Then again, my headache was marginally better. Admitting to someone that your brain tumour turned out to be a dust mite allergy isn't likely to impress.

'I'll bear it in mind,' I said. Stephie sat back in her chair.

'You're wasting your time searching for a dead woman, Kenny.'

'Emily Ridley isn't dead. She's missing.'

'And she isn't going be found. Not by you or anyone else.'

'How d'you know?' I asked.

Stephie shook her head and treated me to the kind of look that members of the Flat Earth Society probably have to get used to, and then checked her watch.

'Let's talk about something else,' she suggested.

We said goodbye at 7.45, which gave me more than enough time to make it to Dalston and the Junction club. The rest of our time at Pizza Express had been spent discussing what various members of the V were up to now, and Jake's latest business venture. That Stephie's eyes lit up when she spoke about him was what made me decide to do the right thing. At least, I thought it was the right thing at the time.

I asked for Jake's number, explained that Odeerie had a nephew looking for bar work. If Jake didn't have anything going then perhaps he would be able to point the fictional nephew in the right direction? Stephie was sure he'd be delighted to help.

I was standing outside Oxford Circus Tube station in a light drizzle when I made the call. Jake's phone rang a dozen times before he answered. 'Hello, Kenny,' he said after I'd identified myself. 'Aren't you meant to be having dinner with Stephie?'

'We've just finished,' I said.

'Great. Erm . . . Is everything all right?'

In the background I could hear the murmur of public conversation. For all I knew, Jake was back out on the town with Pauline Oakley.

'I was at Flummery's Hotel today,' I said. 'You looked as though you were about to have lunch with someone but the pair of you couldn't wait to get upstairs.'

'Why were you in Flummery's?' Jake said after a brief silence.

'Does it matter?'

'Probably not. Have you shared what you saw with Stephie?'

'No.'

'You wanted to tell me first?'

'That's right.'

'May I ask why?'

'Because it would be better if you broke it to Steph that you're having an affair rather than she hears it from me.'

'You think I'm having an affair?'

'Unless Pauline Oakley's a hooker.'

'My God, you even know her name. You're good, Kenny, but you've jumped to the wrong conclusion. Pauline isn't a hooker and she isn't my mistress either.'

'Who is she, then?'

'Can we meet tomorrow at my office?'

A bolt of pain shot from one temple to the other. A tumour giving my frontal lobes a kicking, or primal instinct broadcasting a warning?

'Why can't we talk right now?' I asked.

'I'm not a fan of phones, you never know who's listening,' Jake said, which was kind of interesting. We agreed a time and ended the call.

SEVEN

Kingsland Road runs from Old Street to Dalston, where it morphs into Kingsland High Street. It had been – and to a large extent still is – home to London's Turkish community. In the last few years artists and hipsters, priced out of Shoreditch, had started to colonise the place. Trendy bars and pop-up restaurants jostled for position with kebab shops and community centres. Half a dozen grizzled geezers were drinking glasses of tea outside the Ankara club, and a Rasta in a porkpie hat asked if I was interested in weed or pills. I wasn't, but it's always nice to be asked.

The Junction club was sandwiched between a pizza parlour and a halal butcher's. Its window had the club's name with *Open Late* stencilled above it in white letters. A chalkboard menu had been positioned to the left promoting blues-themed dishes. The centrepiece was a Flying V guitar rendered in blue and red neon.

'Sweet Home Chicago' hit me full blast when I opened the door. A bouncer demanded ten quid, in return for which he ink-stamped my hand with an image of Road Runner in full flight. At the far end of the room, an audience several rows deep surrounded a small stage. It was loud in the Junction and it was bloody hot.

I shouted into a barman's ear and asked whether JJ Freeman was in the club. The guy pointed towards the stage, indicating that his boss was currently engaged. I ordered a bottle of Lagunitas and began to insinuate my way through the crowd. After two minutes and several irritable looks, I was positioned in the front row.

The backdrop to the stage bore vintage promo posters for Muddy Waters, Howlin' Wolf, Sonny Boy Williamson and other blues luminaries. Above it hung an air-con unit that was either switched off or on the blink. Wall-mounted speakers took the feed from the amps and the mic, stationed behind which was JJ Freeman.

Now in his mid-forties, JJ had bulked up since his Mean days. I'd have said it was more from serious bench-pressing than consuming too many of the Hoochie Coochie burgers advertised on the Junction's menu. His shirtsleeves were rolled up to expose powerful forearms and his thighs could have belonged to a rugby prop forward.

Other members of the Blues Cardinals included a pale-faced drummer, a fat guy in a Hawaiian shirt on double bass, a woman on keyboards who was the spit of Annie Lennox, and a heavily bearded guitarist. They reached the end of 'Sweet Home' to enthusiastic applause and appreciative whistles.

'Thanks very much,' JJ said into the mic. 'Don't think I'll ever get tired of playing that one. Hope you feel the same way about listening to it.'

Several shouts indicated that that was the case, although half a dozen guys in suits sitting at one of several trestle tables didn't look too overjoyed.

'Okay, we're going to give you one more and then, after the break, the Chad Williams Band will be treating you to some very cool West Coast blues. You can order food from the bar, and there's more than enough time to wet your whistle.'

The drummer gave an impromptu roll and crashed his hi-hat.

'You looking forward to some whistle-wetting, Eddie?' JJ's pallid drummer nodded his head. 'Okay, I'm gonna let you decide what we finish with, then . . .'

Before the drummer could respond, there came a shout from the table of suits.

'Play "No Time Like Now".'

JJ's features hardened. 'You may not have noticed, my friend, but you're in a blues club in 2017, not a rock gig in the long-ago land of 1995.'

'I couldn't give a fuck,' came the answer. 'I wanna hear "No Time Like Now".'

Judging by the empty jugs on the table, the suits were on a spree. The bloke doing the shouting was in his mid-thirties. His face was flushed with booze and his hair matted by the humidity. The pugnacious look on his face suggested bother.

'If you came here mistakenly then you can have your money back,' JJ said. 'But we don't do requests and we definitely don't play Mean songs.'

The vibey atmosphere in the club had entirely subsided.

'I wanna hear "No Time Like Now"!' the guy demanded for a third time.

'You tell him, Ollie,' another suit said. 'We don't want to listen to this shit any more.' The guy began to bang on the table and chant 'No Time Like Now'. His companions took up the refrain and soon it was echoing around the club.

The bouncer arrived and looked to JJ for guidance. His boss shook his head, removed his guitar and propped it gently against the back of the stage.

Eventually the suits' chanting died down.

'Look, mate, you're not going to hear that song tonight. Not unless you go home and stick it on your stereo. What I suggest you do is collect your entrance money at the bar before I get seriously annoyed with you.'

There was a hard quality to JJ's voice. In my judgement, we weren't very far away from a dust-up. The tension in the bouncer's biceps suggested that we were on the same page. Unfortunately the pissed-up suits weren't even in the same book.

'You were never any fucking good anyway,' one of them commented. 'Cas Greaves had all the talent. All you got was a free ride.'

'Yeah, if it wasn't for him and Chop Montague you'd be sweeping floors for a living,' Ollie added. It proved to be the final straw as far as JJ was concerned.

The suits' table was only yards away from the stage. Ollie hadn't made it to his feet when he took the right hook that floored him. Another suit received a headbutt. His nose broke with a crack that was audible over the screams of the audience.

The other four managed to get their hands on JJ. Tough as he was, I'm not sure that he'd have been able to deal with all of them had it not been for the bouncer's intervention. He wasn't the biggest but he knew what he was about.

One suit was pulled off and had his arm bent behind his back. A quick twist was enough to take him out of the game. JJ locked one of his arms around another guy's throat and they crashed against the table before it collapsed to the floor.

Sober professionals always beat pissed amateurs, and clearly it wasn't the doorman's first rodeo. He stepped inside an attempted roundhouse to put suit number five into a neck pinch that had him whimpering like a ten-year-old girl.

By this time JJ was back on his feet but looking groggy. The last suit standing smashed a glass over a chair. Had someone not chosen that moment to introduce a Lagunitas bottle to the back of his head, then he would probably have put the shattered glass into JJ's face.

'Cheers, mate,' the finest guitarist of his generation said.

'You're welcome,' I replied.

It took a surprisingly short time to restore order. The audience had retreated from the brawl but hardly anyone left the club. Half the punters began taking photos, no doubt eager to tweet that they had just witnessed JJ Freeman in a bust-up.

JJ told the suits that, if they didn't leave immediately, he'd call the police. It was a bit rich considering he'd thrown the first punch, but the battered posse limped out of the club with as much dignity as they could muster.

The band and the bar staff righted the furniture. JJ hoped everyone had enjoyed the floor show and announced that his next bout would be against Tyson Fury. This brought a few laughs and a smattering of applause. Five minutes later, the Chad Williams Band was onstage and it was as though nothing had ever happened.

I stationed myself at the bar with a soothing waga. However righteous it had been, busting someone over the head with a bottle had felt a bit transgressive. My victim didn't seem to have suffered any short-term effects, although he'd probably need more than one aspirin in the morning. JJ spotted me and came over. 'Everything this guy drinks tonight is on the house, Clive,' he said to the barman, and then offered his hand. 'JJ Freeman.'

'Kenny Gabriel. We spoke on the phone this afternoon. You said tonight would be the best time to talk about Emily Ridley . . .'

'Shit, I'd forgotten about that.' JJ sighed. 'Okay, best go upstairs, I suppose.'

We passed through an arch with a distressed tin sign that read WASHROOMS. Any concerns I had that we were about to conduct our discussion in a lavatory cubicle were dispelled when JJ unlocked an unmarked door.

We entered a room that contained a battered roll-top desk and a couple of knackered armchairs. The wallpaper was peeling and there was a damp patch on the ceiling. JJ pulled a cord that snapped shut a set of metal window blinds.

At least twenty cases of Jack Daniel's and almost as many of Smirnoff had been stacked against a wall. I sat in the chair nearest the window while JJ occupied its opposite number. 'You're working for Emily Ridley's mother?' he said.

'That's right.'

'Definitely not the press?'

I held my phone out. 'Give her a call . . .'

JJ shook his head and I swapped my mobile for a notebook.

'Are you in touch with any of the other band members?' was my first question.

'Haven't seen Chop since '95, apart from on that crap TV show.'

'You're not a *Moment in Time!* fan?'

'Is anyone?'

'Over seven million people, apparently.'

'Yeah, well, that tells you all you need to know about the state of music.'

'How did Chop get to be called Chop?' I asked.

'How d'you think?' JJ said.

'Isn't it to do with his guitar style?'

'God, no. Just after Gordon joined the band, we went into a kebab and chicken joint in Lewisham. The guy behind the counter asks what we want and Gordon asks if he could do him a nice lamb chop with some new potatoes. For evermore he was known as Chop.'

'I see. What about Dean Allison? Have you seen him at all?'

'I bumped into him last year after he'd been busted for having the endangered species in his freezer. We didn't have a lot to say to each other, but then we never did have much to say to each other.'

'You didn't get on?'

'Have you met Dean?'

'Not yet.'

'Well, good luck when you do. *If* you do.'

'Why d'you say that?'

'Dean's not exactly Mr Congeniality. And he's a secretive bastard, so don't expect him to spill his guts.'

The pen fell from my hand. For some reason it felt marginally thicker and slightly heavier when I picked it up.

'You all right?' Dean asked.

'What?'

'You're rolling that biro between your fingers like it's a cigar.'

'Everything's fine,' I said. 'From what I've read, Castor had become a little erratic by the time you played the Emporium. Is that how you'd describe it?'

'A fucking nightmare is what he'd become. He couldn't be arsed to write with Chop and he was treating Dean and me like shit. The only time we all met was at rehearsals and Cas was usually an hour or two late for those.'

'Did Castor write anything decent before he met Chop?'

'He didn't write anything at all. Chop brought it out in him. The guy's a pillock but he knows talent when he sees it, I'll give him that.'

'Castor was off drugs when you played the gig?'

'Hard to tell. Regular users get very good at hiding it.'

'What about Emily? Was she on a high?'

'If Cas was happy then Em was happy.'

'She left the Emporium after Dean?'

JJ nodded.

'And about five minutes after she left, Castor said that he needed to visit the toilet. When he didn't come back, Chop went to look for him?'

'Yeah, that's about right. If you're wondering who killed Cas and Em then I can save you a lot of time, mate.'

'How d'you mean?'

'It was a suicide pact. Cas's mum hanged herself when he was ten and they reckon that sort of thing's hereditary.'

'But why would Emily go along with it?'

'Because she was obsessed with Cas.' JJ yawned and sneaked a glimpse at his watch.

'What about the tapes?' I asked.

'Someone mucked around with them.'

'I meant the *Inquisitor* tapes.'

'Fakes,' he said emphatically.

'A lot of experts don't agree.'

'Fuck the experts. It ain't Cas. The *Inquisitor* got an impersonator to sing a couple of songs in his style. They're a bunch of cunts.'

Media commentators had drawn attention to the *Inquisitor's* doubtful journalistic standards. None had expressed themselves as pithily as JJ.

'I know what you mean,' I said. 'But that doesn't mean they get everything wrong. A couple of their stories have turned out—'

JJ was on his feet and looming over me.

'Look, mate, thanks for what you did downstairs, but you're starting to get on my tits. Why Em's mother is paying you to look for her daughter I've no idea, but the truth of it is that she's dead and so is Cas. End . . . of . . . story.'

JJ's final three words were punctuated by a jabbing index finger. What had returned him from post-scrap benevolence to the edge of rage was a mystery.

A knock at the door.

'What?' he barked.

'The police are here,' Clive the barman said. 'They've had reports of an incident and they want a word. Shall I bring them up?'

JJ looked reflexively at the cases of booze.

'No,' he said. 'I'll be right there.'

Clive's feet clattered downstairs. His employer's body language reminded me of the punters in the V when the favourite pulls up at Haydock Park.

'Christ, that's all I need. Look, I'm sorry I got pissy with you but I've been trying to outrun Mean for twenty years. Cas and Em are dead.'

He opened the office door.

'And, quite honestly, I hope they stay that way.'

◆   ◆   ◆

It was only 10.30 when I arrived at the flat, although it had been a long day and my head was buzzing. Hopefully a shot of Monarch of the Glen would draw down the neural shutters. The Monarch doesn't combine a peaty aroma with hints of lowland mists. It tastes as though half a dozen crack addicts distilled it in a vandalised swimming pool. But at £9.99 a litre it gets the job done and that's what counts.

While waiting for the Monarch to weave its magic, I watched a recording of *Moment in Time!* Brief videos were shown featuring the contestants' humdrum lives, after which the show's host would scream it was their 'Moment in time!' and they would bounce on stage to wild applause. Judges judged and the audience voted, after which the tele-visual juggernaut rolled on to the next week minus a tearful wannabe.

Moment's panel comprised three C-list celebs and Chop Montague, who looked as comfortable as a guppy in a tank of piranhas. After Billy from Devizes butchered 'The Way We Were' in memory of his Nana Rose, I switched off and focused my mind on something that had been unusual on the Emporium's roof. It concerned the heating vents. But, like a magic-eye picture, the more I looked, the less it seemed inclined to reveal itself. And then, just as I was about to nod off, I realised what it had been.

EIGHT

I woke at 7.30 feeling a lot better than I had in ages. My headache had diminished and I felt properly hungry. After a plate of scrambled eggs, followed by a pint of black coffee and a trio of Marlboros, I reviewed the day's agenda.

First up was a visit to Jake Villiers's office. Then I intended to head out west, where I could hopefully touch base with Dean Allison, and then even further west where I would interview Pam Ridley and pick up her new client form.

I called the Emporium, to be informed that Kristos wouldn't be in for another hour at least. I left my name and number along with a request for him to call me back. The drizzle of the last two days had lifted and I opted to walk to Charlotte Street.

Half an hour later, I was standing in front of a two-storey Georgian townhouse. The only indication that it had been converted to office use was the brass plaque next to the door that had *Jake Villiers Holdings* engraved upon it. I pressed a brass button. Thirty seconds later the door was opened by a young woman in a business suit.

'Can I help you?' was her first question.

'I have a nine o'clock meeting with Jake,' I said.

'Kenny Gabriel?'

'That's right.'

'Okay, well, you'd better come in, then.'

I followed the woman down a passage and into a room in which eighteenth-century decor collided with twenty-first-century technology. Recessed wall panels had been painted magnolia and wooden shutters were drawn back to reveal casement windows.

Beneath an exquisite chandelier was a glass table attended by half a dozen skeletal executive chairs. At the end of the room a large screen had been attached to the wall.

'Jake's just finishing up a meeting,' the woman said. 'He'll be with you in a few minutes. Can I get you anything to drink, Kenny?'

'I'm good, thanks,' I said, and she left me to it.

After checking my emails, I was wondering whether I had time to call Dr Arbuthnot and cancel the MRI scan that I clearly no longer required, when Jake walked in. He didn't look like a man who had been tossing and turning all night. But he didn't seem entirely relaxed either.

'Sorry to keep you waiting, Kenny.'

'No problem.'

'There's a bakery round the corner. I can ask Imogen to pop out for a couple of coffees and a few pastries if you're hungry . . .'

'I've already had breakfast,' I said. 'Perhaps we could get down to it.'

'Of course,' Jake said. 'I'm sure you're busy.'

The exec chairs were a lot more comfortable than they looked. I eased back in mine, Jake hunched forward in his.

'You want to know what I was doing in Flummery's with Pauline?' he said.

'Only because of your relationship with Stephie. It's really none of my business what you get up to in hotel rooms.'

'I quite understand,' Jake said. 'And I know that you and Steph used to be . . . close.' He ran a hand over his face. 'The fact is that Pauline and I went to her room because we needed somewhere private to talk.'

'About what?'

Jake took a deep breath. 'Kenny, if I told you that I broke the law a few years ago . . . well, twenty years ago . . . would you be obliged to report it to the police?'

'Not necessarily.'

Jake's gaze strayed to a speakerphone perched in the middle of the table, as though it might advise him on the right course of action.

'Okay, then,' he said. 'I have no other option except to trust you.'

I leant forward in order to hear his story better.

'In the late eighties, my father lent me the money to buy a run-down pub in Luton. I borrowed from the bank to develop it into a restaurant. Six years later I had five more. It was around that time that I met Pauline Oakley. Pauline was an accountant with a background in hospitality. I needed to let go of the day-to-day and focus more on the branding and marketing side of things.'

'You were business partners?'

Jake shook his head. 'Pauline was an employee. I was still the owner and sole director and therefore responsible for the running of the business.'

'Okay, got that.'

'After eighteen months, I noticed some serious irregularities in the books. To cut a long story short, Pauline had been submitting fraudulent VAT returns and diverting money into her personal account.'

'Did you report it to the police?'

Jake treated me to a rueful smile. 'It wasn't quite so easy,' he said. 'I'd had my first major flop and it nearly wiped me out. There wasn't enough money in the business to pay the VAT I owed.'

'Couldn't you get the money back from Pauline?'

'She'd cleared her debts and spent the rest. The best I could do was fire her, cut my losses and hope the Inland Revenue didn't uncover the fraud.'

'Which I'm guessing it didn't?'

'Thankfully not. I was able to get the business back on track and things went from strength to strength. And then, last week, I received a call from Pauline out of the blue. She had made copies of the returns – all with my name attached – and was threatening to send them to the authorities if I didn't pay her half a million quid.'

'She was blackmailing you?'

'*Is* blackmailing me,' Jake said. 'There's no statute of limitations on tax fraud. The Revenue would immediately turn the matter over to the police.'

'Can't you say that that she was behind it?'

'Not without evidence. And if I report her for blackmail then I'd still go down for the VAT crime, which would effectively mean my company going under.'

The classic dilemma. Call the blackmailer's bluff and you both end up in the clarts. Depending on whether they go through with it.

'Pay and she'll be back for more,' I said. 'You do know that?'

Jake stretched out his palms. 'What other option is there?'

'Get some evidence she's blackmailing you. At least you'd have extra collateral. Courts hate blackmail. She'd definitely do time.'

'Pauline isn't stupid,' Jake said. 'She took my phone yesterday and searched me. If I said that she committed the crime, then it's my word against hers.'

The only thing filling the ensuing silence was the ticking of a carriage clock resting on the marble mantelpiece.

'Look, Kenny, I'm not asking you to solve my problems,' Jake said. 'All I want to know is that you won't tell Stephie about yesterday.'

'Of course not,' I said, and meant it.

Assuming he was telling the truth, that was.

◆ ◆ ◆

There were two voicemail messages waiting for me after I left Jake's office. The first was from Dr Arbuthnot to say that he had secured me an appointment to have an MRI scan. The second was from Kristos returning my call. I rang Arbuthnot and got his assistant. She said that my scan was scheduled to take place at St Michael's at ten thirty the following day. As Arbuthnot had probably gone to some difficulty in arranging the gig at short notice, I opted not to say that I'd changed my mind.

Kristos answered my second call almost immediately. 'Hey, Kenny, how's it hanging, my friend?' he said. 'You feeling better now?'

'Loads better, Kris,' I said. 'Sorry if I gave you a shock.'

'You got vertigo or what?'

'Something like that. Thanks for showing me round yesterday.'

'No problem, mate.'

'I was wondering whether I could come back again today.'

A brief silence.

'What for?'

'I'd like to take another look at the roof. Specifically the vents.'

'Okay, but you'll have to come right now. I got the afternoon off.'

'Be with you in half an hour,' I said.

In the cab, I ran over Jake's story about being blackmailed by Pauline Oakley. It had sounded plausible, but then Jake knew how to sound plausible. He would, no doubt, expect me to check the verifiable details and I intended to do exactly that.

'Bit of a late start, isn't it?' Odeerie said when I called.

'I didn't get home until late.'

'You should be looking after yourself, Kenny. You're not getting any younger.'

Given that it would need Dyno-Rod to clear Odeerie's arteries, his piety was tough to swallow.

'I was interviewing JJ Freeman at his club,' I reminded him.

'Oh, yeah. How did that go?'

'I'll tell you about it later. Meanwhile, there's a favour I wanted to ask.'

'Go on,' Odeerie said cautiously, what with 'favour' being one of his least favourite words in the English language, third only to 'cholesterol' and 'diet'.

'Would you be able to trace whether someone worked for a company or not?'

'How long ago?'

'Twenty years.'

'It's going to be a long shot. Were they a director?'

'No.'

'Even longer, then.'

'You can't do it?'

'I didn't say that. Who's the person and what's the company?'

'Pauline Oakley. And it's Jake Villiers Holdings.'

'Isn't he the guy going out with Stephie?'

I confirmed this was the case at the same time as the cab pulled up in front of the Emporium club. 'For Christ's sake, Kenny,' Odeerie said. 'The train's left the station. Why can't you accept that?'

'Will you do it or not?'

'Okay,' he sighed. 'I'll see what I can turn up.'

There were issues with the Emporium's fuse box. Kristos was trying to light a fire under an electrician's arse so he could still take the afternoon off. He unclipped the roof key, handed it over, and muttered something about being careful. I took the stairs at a sedate pace, pausing on each landing to catch my breath. The key refused to turn and I thought Kris had handed me the wrong one.

Then I felt the tumblers reluctantly rotate.

A flock of pigeons bustled into the sky. The last time I'd been on the roof it had been blowing a gale. Now it was perfectly still. Traffic sounds carried up from the streets of Soho, as did the clang of builders erecting scaffolding a couple of blocks away. Stone chippings crunched underfoot as I approached the particular heating duct that had lodged in my memory.

The other four were the dull grey that galvanised metal adopts when exposed to the elements. This one was streaked brown and green. Where the cap met the top of the box, the joint was black. I took out my Swiss Army knife and tapped the duct. I did the same to its neighbours. The discoloured vent emitted a duller sound.

I applied the screwdriver to the first screw. It was an effort to shift but eventually I had it out. Within ten minutes all the screws holding the front panel in place were nestled in the back pocket of my jeans. I inserted the tips of my numb fingers into the tiny gap and attempted to pull the panel free. Bastard thing wouldn't budge.

I tried with the knife and met with the same result. Only after the blade had snapped did I notice a small catch on either side of the unit. I unhooked each before repeating my efforts. The panel screeched and fell away from its housing.

The body had been bent over and jammed in the unit. Fronds of blonde hair were clinging to its skull. Mummified skin looked like grey parchment drawn so tightly around the bones that it had given way in places. White teeth were bared in a rictal snarl and the eye sockets had been voided by decomposition.

Footsteps sounded behind me. 'Hey, Kenny,' Kristos said. 'I've got to get going, mate, so if you could—' Kris looked over my shoulder. 'Fucking hell,' he said before crossing himself and muttering something in Greek.

'Call the police,' I told him.

NINE

DCI Tony Shaheen tapped something into his phone and laid it carefully in the space he'd created amongst the mess of envelopes, flyers and invoices in Kristos's office. His suit was dark blue, the shirt dove grey, and a green tie was knotted tight against the collar. He retuned his attention to my statement. 'You know it seems odd that after twenty-four hours on a cold case that's defeated the Met and God knows how many journalists for over two decades, you get a result,' he said.

I shrugged and said, 'Beginner's luck.'

'Or maybe you knew where the body was.'

'How would I know that?'

Shaheen screwed the cap back on his fountain pen and placed it next to his phone.

'Someone told you.'

'Who?'

'Maybe the person who put it there.'

'And that would be?'

'Jean-Jacques Freeman?'

'So you're suggesting that I went to see JJ at his club and after half an hour he tells a total stranger where he stashed Castor Greaves's body?'

Shaheen's head bobbed back.

'Or possibly Emily Ridley's,' I added.

'What makes you believe it's either?'

I gave the DCI a stare. His hand went to his tie and tightened a knot that didn't require tightening. 'We have DNA samples on file, so we should be able to determine whether it's Castor Greaves or Emily Ridley.'

'How long will that take?'

Shaheen looked at his watch. 'The lab's fast-tracked it.'

'Does Emily's mother know we've discovered something?'

'Not yet. We're keeping a lid on things until we know for sure what we have.' Shaheen turned a page over. 'Essentially what you're telling me is that you noticed that the vent with the remains in it had oxidised in a different way to the others.'

'That's right.'

'And you thought that might be because there were human remains inside.'

'I thought it was worth examining.'

'Why not when you first saw the vent?'

'It only occurred to me afterwards. Actually, I'm surprised they weren't opened up at the time. Although the Met wasn't too invested in the case, from all accounts.'

Shaheen's mouth tightened. 'So, you asked Mr Barberis if you could take another look and then removed the front panel?' he asked.

'That's right,' I said. 'How is Kristos?'

'He's been taken to hospital as a precautionary measure.'

Shortly after calling the police, Kris had become very wheezy. I'd helped him back into the building. The medics had beat the cops to the scene by two minutes. They'd taken Kris down on a gurney and passed the officers on the stairs.

A constable had recorded my details before installing me in Kris's office, where Shaheen introduced himself half an hour later. Forty-five minutes after that, he had begun to interview me. It had been two hours since I'd taken the panel off the vent.

'When you said "keeping a lid on things",' I said, 'does that mean you haven't announced that a body's been discovered?'

'Correct,' Shaheen said. 'If at all possible, we prefer to inform the next of kin before releasing information to the public. And obviously there will be heightened press interest in this case for a number of reasons.'

Too right there would be. If the remains turned out to be those of either Castor Greaves or Emily Ridley, the media would go into meltdown. Short of the Second Coming, or the Beckhams divorcing, I couldn't imagine a bigger story.

'On that subject,' he continued, 'I would appreciate you not revealing anything until such time as we release a statement.'

'When's that likely to happen?'

'Later today, hopefully.'

'Can I ask something in return?'

'What?'

'Would you keep my name out of things?'

'I'll do my best.' Shaheen pushed my statement over the table. 'Read carefully and see that everything's in order, Mr Gabriel. Then, if you're happy it's an accurate reflection of your statement, sign and date the document.'

I took a quick squinny through five pages of Shaheen's immaculate writing. It appeared to be in order. 'Can I borrow a pen?' I asked.

Shaheen passed me his fountain pen as though handing a surgeon a scalpel. I'd just removed the cap when his phone began vibrating.

'Tony Shaheen . . . Yes, that's right . . . And that's definite, is it? . . . Okay, thanks for letting me know, Jackie . . . I'll be there as soon as possible.'

He cut the call and glanced at my autographed statement in cursory fashion. 'I'm needed at a case briefing. The results are back from the DNA test.'

'What did they say?'

'Afraid I can't tell you that.'

'But you want me to keep schtum about finding something on the roof? Come on, Tony. Only fair that I know what I'm keeping quiet about.'

Shaheen slipped my statement into a plastic folder and put the pen into his jacket pocket. He stood up. 'Thanks for your cooperation, Kenny. If we need to speak to you again then we'll be in touch. You're free to leave whenever you like.'

Visiting Pam Ridley was no longer an option. Whether the remains were Emily's or Castor's, she would be doorstepped by the press. Ex-members of Mean would receive the same treatment, so Dean Allison would have to wait too.

I opted to deliver Odeerie's update in person. After twenty years dealing with human licentiousness and venality, little surprises the fat man. That I'd found Emily Ridley had a stupefying effect. Half a Battenberg cake remained suspended between plate and lips when I made the announcement in his office.

'Holy shit. When?'

'About three hours ago.'

'There's been nothing on the news.'

'They won't release anything until Pam's been told.'

I spent fifteen minutes answering Odeerie's questions, during which time his excitement mounted. And then came the final piece of the jigsaw.

'I asked the DCI to keep my name out of things.'

'You did *what?*'

'He promised to do his best.'

'Kenny, you've just found someone who's been missing for twenty-two years. We'll be drowning in clients.'

'Yeah, and who needs that?'

'We do!' Odeerie took up where he'd left off with the Battenberg. 'Yeah, well, it doesn't really matter,' he said through a mouthful of sponge and marzipan. 'Because, mark my words, it will definitely get out.'

'You're going to call the papers?'

'Won't have to. Even if your DCI doesn't go back on his word then some hard-up cop is gonna sell the information on the side.'

While I came to terms with this possibility, Nostradamus finished his cake, licked his chubby fingers and reached into his desk drawer.

'I had a look at Jake Villiers,' he said, removing a reporter's pad.

'And?'

'And it's bloody hard to get this kind of information twenty years after the fact. If you were a client you'd owe me five hundred quid.'

'You found something?'

'Yeah, I did. Pauline Oakley was the financial director at Jake Villiers Holdings between 1994 and November 1996, when she left the company.'

I experienced the sensation you get when a lift descends a sight more rapidly than you'd anticipated. 'Jake was telling the truth, then?'

'As far as Oakley leaving he was, but didn't he also tell you that the company was going through a bad patch around that time?'

'Isn't that right?'

'It is and it isn't.' Odeerie consulted the pad. 'The company showed an operating loss, although it had invested in a large site in the Midlands for development. Factor that into the bottom line and they were doing just fine.'

'So why did he lie to me?'

'The same reason anyone lies to anyone,' Odeerie said. 'Because he doesn't want you to find out about something else.'

He spent another half-hour gloating about how the business could treble its profits. I made token noises while wondering why Jake Villiers had misled me about his company's true financial status. Certainly it strengthened his story about Pauline Oakley having left the company for finagling its tax returns. And if that wasn't the reason, there had to be another.

The only way to find out for sure would be to confront Pauline herself.

◆　◆　◆

Early evening and business in the Vesuvius wasn't at its height. Nick was alone behind the bar, watching the TV with three guys perched on high stools. I ordered a waga and was about to head off to one of the tables when the evening news came on. First up was the Emporium story.

Almost immediately we went live to a press conference with the Met and Emily's mother. Pam Ridley was sat behind a trestle table. To her left was DCI Shaheen; to her right the deputy commissioner, in full uniform. Pam looked deathly white, but then I guess that was understandable. The DC was first to speak.

'Thank you for coming along to this evening's briefing,' he said to the assembled reporters. 'Before we get going, I'd like to introduce DCI Tony Shaheen, who is in charge of this investigation and will be able to answer some of your questions. Also taking part will be Mrs Pamela Ridley.'

Pam's name was the trigger for multiple camera motor drives to go into action. She stared ahead with a blank expression. The DC continued.

'First of all, I can confirm that remains discovered in the Emporium on Archer Street this afternoon are those of Ms Emily Ridley.'

Hubbub in the room. Competing questions were thrown out by journalists, to the senior officer's undisguised irritation.

'Please can we have some order?' he barked. 'There will be time for questions at the end of the briefing.'

The noise gradually abated.

'After an extensive search of the premises, no further remains have been found. We are currently conducting a post-mortem that will hopefully reveal the cause of Emily's death in what is being treated as a murder inquiry.'

The deputy commissioner fixed the room with a gimlet eye, presumably to quell any journalists unable to restrain themselves at the mention of the M-word.

'Mrs Ridley has asked to make a brief statement,' he said, 'after which DCI Shaheen will be able to update you on the inquiry.'

Pam thanked the DC and leaned into her microphone.

'Twenty-two years ago, someone killed my beautiful daughter,' she said. 'Afterwards, they dumped her body like it was garbage. And if it hadn't been for the work of a private investigator, Emily might have been there another twenty years.'

Pam paused and looked directly into the camera lens.

'Kenny Gabriel, if you're watching, then I want to thank you for what you did. The other thing I want to say is that the job isn't finished. Now that you've found Em, I want to find the bastard who killed her and bring him to justice. That's it.'

Nothing the DC could do to stop the room from erupting this time . . . Several journalists shouted out versions of the same question: *Who's Kenny Gabriel?*

TEN

The intercom in the flat started buzzing at first light. I took the batteries out but the reporters began shouting up from the street. All they wanted was a few words. The few words I'd like to have given them were 'piss off' and 'leave me alone'. Unable to get back to sleep, I went online to see what the reaction had been to yesterday's events.

The Emily Ridley story was front page for most papers and news sites. The information was accurate regarding the discovery, and most had worked out who I was and what I did. The *Huffington Post* described me as a 'budget private eye', the *Guardian* as a 'skip-tracer operating in the twilight world of insurance fraud'.

A few mentioned the two other high-profile cases I'd been involved in, and pointed out that they had ended badly for virtually all involved. Thank you, the *Telegraph* and *BuzzFeed*. The *Mail* had pretty much the same information, and I was about to exit its site when a paragraph towards the bottom of the piece caught my attention.

The owner of the Emporium, Jake Villiers, commented that the club would be closed until further notice while police conduct their inquiries. Ticket holders for forthcoming events should consult the venue's website for more information.

◆ ◆ ◆

Odeerie answered the phone almost before it had started to ring.

'Have you seen the papers?' I asked.

'Yeah,' he said. 'Told you we wouldn't be able to keep a lid on it. Are you calling to say you've changed your mind about going public? You're probably right. Better we control the situation than the other way round.'

'No, I'm not calling about that.'

'What, then?' Odeerie asked, disappointment creeping into his voice.

'Jake Villiers owns the Emporium.'

'I know. He bought a controlling interest in 2002.'

'And you didn't think to tell me . . .'

'You didn't ask.'

The fat man's mind does have a literal cast to it. All the same . . .

'It's the case we're working on, for Christ's sake!'

'What does it matter who owns the Emporium, Kenny? And Jake had nothing to do with the place when Emily and Castor went missing.'

'It matters because . . . because . . .'

'You're obsessed with the guy.'

'That's not true.'

'Okay, then why's it so important?'

'Isn't it unusual that a man who usually buys up properties and guts them decides to buy a venue in the West End and not do anything at all with it?'

'Not really. The Emporium makes a tidy profit.'

'He's a property developer, not a club owner. It's out of character.'

Odeerie took a deep breath. 'If Jake Villiers bought an aquarium or a sausage factory, that might be unusual,' he said. 'All he's done is see a place that's going cheap and looks like a decent investment. It's what entrepreneurs do, Kenny.'

'I'm telling you there's something dodgy going on.'

'What is it, then?'

'I don't know, but you need to take another look at it.'

◆ ◆ ◆

I spent the next ten minutes trying to answer Odeerie's question. At least, it felt like ten minutes. When I looked at the clock, almost an hour had passed. The fat man was right: 'property investor invests in property' wasn't hugely suspicious. And yet . . . Eventually I gave up the effort and called Pam Ridley.

'Hello,' she said in a tired voice.

'Mrs Ridley, it's Kenny Gabriel. I'm sorry not to have called yesterday but the police wouldn't tell me whose the remains were.'

'I told you she was dead,' Pam said. 'All I wanted was to have her back. At least, that's all I wanted then . . .'

'Yes, I saw your press conference,' I said. 'I'm sure the police will put serious resources into finding Emily's murderer.'

The exhaustion in Pam's voice was replaced by the steeliness I'd heard on TV. 'They won't find who did it,' she said. 'My swami said you're the one to do that.'

If the bloody swami was so good at predicting who would find Emily's killer, why didn't he save everyone a lot of bother and just say who did it? On the other hand, I did need something to do in order to stop fretting about my health . . .

Odeerie had been all for calling a press conference of his own. Instead we'd agreed that I would continue with the case for a limited time if that was what Pam Ridley still wanted. 'You're positive about that, Mrs Ridley?' I asked.

'Yes, I am,' she said. 'And you can call me Pam.'

'Okay, Pam. I'll need to touch base with you to ask more questions about Emily. Are you around later today, around two p.m.?'

'I should be, but there's reporters outside the house.'

'You never know, they may have gone by then,' I said.
Flying pigs might carry them away.

◆　◆　◆

There were two journos outside my own place. Both were in their twenties and looked as though doorstepping 'a semi-professional skip-tracer on the brink of retirement' (the *Mirror*) was not what they'd had in mind when taking on fifty grand's worth of debt to sign up for Applied Media Studies. I told them that Mr Gabriel was on his way down and would be happy to issue a statement. It flummoxed them long enough for me to make my way towards Piccadilly Circus station untroubled by questions. I was busy congratulating myself on my ingenuity when a hand fell on my shoulder.

'Nice one, Kenny,' its owner said. 'You gave that pair of amateurs the runaround good and proper. It'd be funny if it weren't so fucking pathetic.'

The guy was in his early fifties. His green leather jacket had seen better days and his moustache looked like a strip of grey AstroTurf. His eyes were heavily recessed, although I suspected they didn't miss much.

'Do I know you?' I asked.

'Danny Abbott,' he said, releasing his grip on my shoulder and brushing it down. 'I work for the *Post*. All I wanted was a few words on this Emporium business. Turn-up for the books, ain't it? You reckon Cas is still alive or what?'

'No comment.'

Danny exhaled heavily. 'Look, Kenny, I don't blame you for being suspicious, but I'm a proper reporter, not like Pinky and Perky round the corner. Play straight with me and I'll play straight with you.'

'Meaning?'

'Answer a few questions and I'll write exactly what you say.'

'Otherwise . . .'

Danny shrugged. 'Otherwise I'll have to make the whole bleeding thing up. And I don't want to be that guy, Kenny, I really don't.'

I recalled what Odeerie had said about it being better to control the situation. And while Danny's demeanour and outfit didn't scream *my word is my bond*, at least he'd been honest as to what would happen if I didn't cooperate.

'You get three questions,' I said.

'Cheers, Kenny.' Danny produced an iPhone and pressed Start on the Record app. 'First up, what made you think Emily's body was in the Emporium?'

'There was something strange-looking about one of the heating ducts.'

'Which is where you found her?'

I nodded.

'Pam Ridley said that she wanted you to carry on looking for the person who killed her daughter. That what you're gonna do?'

'Hasn't been decided yet.'

'Obviously Cas Greaves did it.'

'Did he?'

'You don't think so?'

'I've absolutely no idea.'

Danny nodded. 'Course not. You think Cas is still alive, though?'

'There's no reason to think he isn't.' I looked at my watch. 'That's your lot.'

'Just one more question. D'you think there's any truth in the Golden Road theory?'

'The golden what?'

'You've never heard of it?'

'Don't think so.'

'You aren't ruling it out, then?'

'How can I when I don't know what it is?'

'No problem,' Danny said. 'Okay, thanks for that, Kenny, I really appreciate it.' He tucked a card in the breast pocket of my jacket. 'I'll let you get on, but if you feel the need for a chat any time, give me a call.'

'What was that golden road thing again?'

'Oh, nothing important,' Danny said, shaking my hand. Oddly enough, he seemed much keener to finish the interview than he had been to start it.

The journey to Euston took twenty minutes, the walk to St Michael's Hospital a further fifteen. The scanning suite was in the Yakamoto Building, opened by HRH Diana, Princess of Wales in 1993, according to the plaque by the lifts. I gave my name to the receptionist, who handed me a twenty-question form to fill in. She admitted me to an antechamber and instructed that I place all metal items in one of the lockers.

The operator emphasised that keeping perfectly still while in the belly of the beast was essential. He placed a pair of ear defenders on me and retreated to the booth.

A minute later my torso rolled into the machine and the thing kicked into action. According to the operator, claustrophobia troubled some patients. I wasn't one of them, although after fifteen minutes of grinding and clicking, I began to suspect that the machine wasn't simply assaying my brain's structure but sifting its essence.

If there were a nugget of doom in there, would my presence on earth have been worthwhile? *I wasted time, and now doth time waste me.* It had applied to Richard II, and it applied to Kenny Gabriel. I was bearing down on my seventh decade, and all I had to show for it was a twenty-a-day Marlboro habit and a beleaguered liver.

Emily Ridley's bent and corroded body came into my mind. How long before my own would be consumed by worms or fire? Her mother had said that someone had discarded her like a piece of garbage. Pam Ridley wanted me to find who that person was. I had no idea how I was going to do that, but I knew I was going to try.

◆ ◆ ◆

Retrieving my phone from the locker, I found an email from Saskia Reeves-Montgomery in response to the one I'd sent a couple of days ago. No doubt the author of *Play Like You Mean It* had been inspired by recent events to click the Reply button. She would be very happy to meet. I suggested early evening. My phone pinged with a response confirming 6.30 p.m. before I'd made it to Euston station.

There was still nothing from Chop Montague. As the most famous ex-Mean member still living, and the one-time songwriting partner of Castor Greaves, he was probably under siege from the press. I rang his agency again and asked if my message had been passed on. Apparently Chop might take a while to respond, as he was very busy. No shit. I left my details and stressed the urgency of the matter.

The call I made before entering the station was to Still Life. The phone at Dean Allison's taxidermy shop was engaged. At least someone was there. Whether it was Dean and whether he would agree to talk to me was a different matter.

Two questions preoccupied me most as I travelled south on the Tube. The first was how to approach Pauline Oakley. *Did you nick a shitload of cash from Jake Villiers, and are you blackmailing him?* Perhaps not the strategy most likely to succeed. The second question was why Jake had really bought the Emporium. By the time my train rolled into Tooting Bec station, I had no answer to either.

◆ ◆ ◆

In common with the other council houses on Burnham Drive, number 35 had been constructed from red brick with a roof tiled in grey slate. Each door had been painted midnight blue and there was small patch of front garden. A gate led from the path to the road and there was a portico in which wheelie bins were sheltered.

Pam Ridley's house had a dozen reporters and paparazzi outside. A bored-looking copper in uniform was supervising them. Entering by the front gate would have probably created a stir, if not pandemonium. Just as well I didn't have to.

Each eight-block row was served by a track to its rear. Pam's lawn had been recently mown and there was a well-maintained ornamental pond in its centre. I walked up the crazy-paving path and tapped on her door.

'Hello, Kenny,' she said, and ushered me into the kitchen. 'Did anyone see you?'

'I don't think so. How are you bearing up?'

Pam was wearing the same cardigan she had worn at the press conference. Her lank hair was greasy and there was a faint mustiness about her. Pounds to peanuts she'd spent the night in a chair. 'I'm okay,' she said, scratching the back of her neck. 'D'you want a tea or a coffee?'

'No thanks,' I said. For some reason we were talking in whispers.

'We can go up to Em's room, if you want to see it . . .'

I followed Pam into a passage. Flowered wallpaper had faded and the stair carpet was worn smooth in the centre. Four doors led off from the landing. One had a rainbow attached to it, under which Emily's Room had been posted in multicoloured letters. Pam opened the door gently, as though her daughter might be sleeping.

In one corner was a single bed covered with a pink duvet. By the window stood a utility dressing table. Lipsticks were corralled behind a cheap vinyl jewellery box and yellowing ticket stubs had been inserted where the mirror met its frame. 'Geoff wanted a clear-out after Em went missing,' Pam said. 'He reckoned we needed to move on.' She shrugged. 'S'pose it can all go now.'

'There's no rush, is there?' I said, forcing myself to speak at normal volume. 'You can keep it like this indefinitely if it makes you feel better.'

'No,' she replied. 'Now Em's been found, I can get rid of her stuff.'

A couple of photograph albums lay on a shelf with a large Humpty Dumpty toy perched on top. 'Would it be okay if took a look at those?' I asked.

'Course you can,' she said.

I sat on the bed and opened the smaller album. The first few pages contained photographs of Emily taken when she was about eight. Two featured a girl in school uniform smiling self-consciously at the camera. Subsequent pages marked the graduation from preteen to adolescence. I flipped to a series taken at a party. *Fifteenth Birthday* had been written neatly at the top of the page in round letters.

The birthday girl had shaken off the gawky cloak of adolescence. Wearing a black dress, she posed for the camera individually and with guests. I turned another page to see Pam and her husband standing on either side of their daughter. All three were contemplating a candled birthday cake.

'Did Emily always live at home?' I asked. Pam nodded.

'Yeah, although she was away quite often on shoots, especially in the year before she died. And she'd stay at Castor Greaves's place sometimes. Em brought him home once. Me and Geoff weren't keen.'

'Why not?'

'Emily was too young to be in a serious relationship. And even though Castor was polite enough, he didn't seem as though he was all there.'

'Drugs?'

'Not so much that as he was just going through the motions when he was talking to you. He treated Em well, though. At least, she said he did.'

'How did they meet?' I asked.

'They were booked for a shoot with the same photographer. Mean were her favourite band. There's pictures of them in the other album . . .'

Indeed there were. Those in the first pages had been taken from the audience. Halfway through the book there were a few of Emily with assorted members of Mean at what appeared to be parties. In another she was sat beside Castor at a mixing desk, and then one in which he had his arm around her waist outside a London Fashion Week event. There were intermittent gaps in the pages. I drew Pam's attention to this.

'You know what girls are like when it comes to photographs. If they don't like them . . .' She mimed a tearing motion with her hands.

'Then why put them in the album at all?' I asked.

'Dunno. Maybe she went off 'em later.'

In subsequent pages there were fewer gaps. Castor and Emily were in swimming gear on a beach, outside Radio City Music Hall in New York, and gooning around with animals at London Zoo. The last picture was of her and JJ Freeman sitting next to each other on a flight of stone steps. They were smiling, but not convincingly.

'Have you any idea when this was taken?' I asked.

Pam bent over to take a closer look. Particles of dandruff descended on to the image of her daughter and JJ. 'She bought that top a week before she went missing.'

'When was the last time you spoke to Emily?' I asked.

'The day of the concert.'

'What time did she leave the house?'

'About six. She was seeing Davina first.'

'Davina?'

'Her best friend since they were at school.'

Pam took the album from me and flicked through a few pages. 'That's her.'

The girls were sitting on bar stools holding up cocktail glasses. Davina was a couple of inches taller, with dark hair and delicate features.

'Did Davina go to the Emporium?' I asked.

'No. She had the flu. At least, that's what she said. Her and Emily hadn't been getting on that well. I think she was jealous about her modelling.'

'Did the police speak to her after Emily went missing?'

'Must have done,' Pam said. 'They interviewed everyone.'

'Where did she live?'

'Dunsinane Road, but she moved out after she went to university and her mum and dad left more than ten years ago.'

'I don't suppose you remember her surname.'

Pam stared at the ceiling for a few moments. 'Jacobs,' she said eventually. 'Although she probably got married, so it could be something different now.'

'Would you mind if I borrowed the photo?' I asked.

'If you think it'll help,' Pam said.

While I was easing the photograph out of the protective cellophane, the front doorbell went.

'I'd better see who that is,' Pam said, and left the room.

Moments later, I heard her in conversation but couldn't make out specifics. After transferring the photo of Emily and Davina carefully to my jacket pocket, I returned the albums to the shelf and put Humpty back in his place.

When I opened the jewellery box, a pink ballerina pirouetted into action accompanied by a tinkling version of 'The Nutcracker'. After a few bars, both she and the music ground to a halt. I opened and closed the box twice to no avail.

Pam came back into the room. 'Just a new bobby coming on shift,' she said. 'They keep asking whether I want a family liaison officer but I can't see the point. I wish those reporters would bugger off, though.

He said most of 'em will be gone by tomorrow. You got any more questions, Kenny?'

'Not right now.'

'This is the thing your boss wanted me to sign.'

'You're absolutely sure about this?' I asked. 'Because the police will reopen the case and do everything they can to find out what happened.'

'Positive,' she said, and handed me the new client form.

ELEVEN

I slipped out of the back passage unnoticed by the jackals of the fourth estate. Then I made my way to Tooting Bec station and began the journey to Notting Hill. En route, I read the first edition of the *Evening Standard*.

The splash photo, presumably taken from a drone, showed the Emporium's roof covered by a large white tent. Also visible were a couple of figures in contamination suits with masks over their mouths, and DCI Shaheen staring skywards with undisguised annoyance. SEARCHING FOR CASTOR was the headline.

Pages two and three carried articles that featured the facts about the discovery – I was mentioned by name but without biographical detail – and 'sightings' that had been reported over the years. In light of recent events these were obviously complete bollocks, but even facts can't always kill off a good conspiracy theory.

Experts on the case – including Saskia Reeves-Montgomery – had been polled as to possible scenarios. Favourite was that Castor had killed Emily in a drug-fuelled row and then committed suicide in an as yet undiscovered location.

If the theory were true then I was on a fool's errand. On the other hand, one 'expert' had pointed out that Castor could be being sheltered by a former friend or associate. That the said friend or associate would turn out to be Dean Allison seemed unlikely. He and Castor hadn't got on well from all accounts, and I couldn't see any reason why Dean would put himself to the inconvenience of harbouring a murderer for twenty-two years, not to mention the lengthy sentence discovery would entail.

Much more likely that someone with a strong emotional bond built up since childhood would be liable to take that kind of risk.

Someone like JJ Freeman.

◆　◆　◆

Sixty years ago, Notting Hill was one of the biggest slum areas in London. Things have changed. You have to be a tech entrepreneur or an oligarch to buy a townhouse in Ladbroke Grove now. Stucco buildings replete with balustraded balconies and bulletproof windows remain uninhabited for long periods while international owners kick their heels in Moscow suburbs or Palo Alto. But when the fat cats do turn up, they spend their lucre. And the boutiques around Portobello Road afford ample opportunity.

Still Life was situated between a shop selling icons and one offering vintage cinema posters. Outside stood two people who probably weren't in the market for either. A thirty-something woman was wearing a long green parka and combat trousers tucked into black boots. Her companion was a skinny guy at least a decade older, sporting a tweed coat several sizes too large for him over a fisherman's sweater and jeans. Hanging from his shoulder was a canvas bag.

'You going in there?' Skinny asked.

'What's it got to do with you?' I asked him back.

'You know what that place is?' was the woman's contribution.

Behind a metal grille, the window display featured a heron perched on the bleached skull of a bison. In its bill was clamped a dead tarantula.

'Is it a newsagent's?'

Skinny snorted, produced a leaflet from his bag and thrust it into my hands. It had been printed on behalf of an outfit called JFA – Justice for Animals – and featured a police picture of a turtle stretched out on a bench flanked by two dead monkeys. A red-lettered headline read: SLAUGHTERED IN THE NAME OF ART.

It wasn't pretty, but then it wasn't meant to be.

'They found those in his freezer,' the woman said.

'I'm not here to buy anything,' I said, returning the leaflet. 'I'm here to interview Dean Allison for professional reasons.'

A secondary door constructed from the same mesh that covered the window protected the entrance to the shop. I pressed a buzzer located under a tiny camera. Twenty seconds later a voice came out of the box.

'Who are you?'

'Kenny Gabriel. I'd like to talk to Dean Allison.'

No response.

'You're wasting your time, mate,' the woman said. 'Reporters have been trying all morning. He told them to piss off.'

I was beginning to think she was right when the intercom crackled again.

'Show me some ID.'

I held my driving licence up to the camera.

'Okay, I'm going to open the security door. Come inside and close it behind you.'

An electronic buzzer sounded and I followed instructions. The security door clanged closed. After a few moments, Dean Allison opened up.

'Fucking scumbag!' the woman screamed.

'Rot in hell, you murdering shit!' from Skinny.

'Barbarians,' Dean muttered, closing the door behind me. The whip-thin proprietor of Still Life was about six-one. He was wearing a charcoal-coloured jacket over a black shirt matched with designer jeans and burgundy brogues. His hair was swept back in a Byronic tangle of brown and grey.

'So, you're the investigator who found Emily Ridley?' he said.
'That's right.'
'Why should I speak to you?'
'Because it might help find who killed her.'
Dean pursed his lips as though mulling this over.
'Very well,' he decided. 'Enter the gallery . . .'

A chandelier on starvation voltage lit the room. The walls had been draped in black material and the floor covered in cork. The only sound was the gentle hum of a humidifier. A white horse's head stood on a plinth, its mouth slightly open to reveal ivory teeth. A six-foot alligator regarded me balefully from the corner of the room. A marmoset monkey holding a set of reins was busy riding a giant tortoise across the floor. In the bleached branches of a small tree were arranged a dozen parakeets.

What caught my attention most was a raven perched on a cactus, the bird's beak slightly open as though cawing abuse at the alligator, daring it to make a lunge.

'Do take a seat,' Dean said. There were three distressed-leather club chairs to choose from. I opted for the one under the parakeet tree.

'May I offer you a drink?' he asked.

'A whisky would be good.'

On a mahogany side table stood a tantalus and half a dozen glasses. Dean removed the cabinet's bracket, selected the appropriate decanter and poured out a pair of generous Scotches. 'I'll join you,' he said. 'It's been a long morning.'

'Are those two outside all the time?' I asked.

He shook his head. 'The JFA work a shift system, each as charming as the last. I can fetch some ice from the kitchen if you'd like . . .'

'Neat is fine,' I said.

Dean passed me a glass with a hand as pallid and hairless as an oyster. He sat in the chair nearest my own and crossed his legs. Framed by the horse's head, he could have been a gent of a certain age posing for an esoteric style magazine.

'Cheers,' he said.

I responded in kind and we sipped our drinks. The superlative Scotch made the Monarch taste like turps by comparison.

'Is the light dim to preserve the animals?' I asked, to get us started.

'No,' Dean replied, 'purely to lend a little theatre. The humidifier keeps the pieces in decent shape. There's a danger of mange without it.'

'How did you get into . . . all this?'

'My grandfather was a taxidermist. When he died, Norman left me his workshop and tools, presumably in the hope that I might take it up. Mean had disbanded and I needed another career.' Dean used the hand not holding the glass to gesture around the gallery. 'It's important to do something one's passionate about,' he said. 'Even if your work isn't universally admired.'

'You're referring to the prosecution?'

Dean's features pinched, as though the sip of Scotch he'd just taken was formaldehyde. 'That was just absurd,' he said, and then appeared to reconsider. 'Actually, "hypocritical" would be the more appropriate term. Society has carte blanche to treat certain animals in any way it wishes. Keep them in cages they can't turn round in, pump them full of noxious chemicals and slaughter them before they're out of infancy. But woe betide anyone who picks on the wrong species . . .'

'One that's endangered?'

'"Doomed" is the better word. You think rhino will be running around Kenya in twenty years? Leatherback turtles dragging themselves up beaches to lay their eggs? No, my friend. The only place that future generations will see these animals are in videos, zoos and museums, which is what makes my work so important.'

'Which *museums* were the animals in your freezer bound for?' I asked.

'Touché, Kenny.' Dean raised his glass in mock salute. 'Although I'm guessing the reason you wanted to see me wasn't to discuss the morality of taxidermy.'

'I wanted to talk about Castor and Emily.'

'Specifically, what would you like to know?'

We'd been pissing around quite a bit and I was beginning to feel creeped out by Dean and his immortal menagerie. Time to get down to it. I sank the rest of my Scotch and asked, 'What happened to them?'

'I'd have thought in Emily's case that was obvious.'

'I was thinking more how it happened.'

'Oh, I see. Well, that's rather an easy one . . .'

The answer took me by surprise. 'You know?'

'Indeed. I know who murdered Emily and why he did it. The question is: why would I be prepared to tell you, and what can you supply in return?'

It had already crossed my mind that Dean had an ulterior motive for allowing me into the gallery. Usually when people offer you information it's for cash on the nail. I had the feeling this wasn't the case in this instance.

'What d'you want?'

Dean uncrossed his legs and leant forward. 'I read that you were the person who actually found Emily and that her body was mummified.'

'That's right.'

'Describe her.'

'What?'

'You heard.'

'Why d'you want a description?'

'Let's say I have a professional interest.'

I've done a few unsavoury things over the years to get at the truth. Conjuring a dead woman for a man who stuffed rare species and sold them to his Eurotrash clients would be top of the list. But if I wanted to know who had murdered Emily . . .

'She'd been bent double. There were strips of her of hair clinging to her scalp. What was left of her skin was shiny like wax paper.'

'And the smell?'

'Damp. Like old books left in a cellar.'

Dean eased back in his seat. 'What did the eyes look like?' he asked.

'One had gone completely. The other looked as though someone had pushed a wad of almond marzipan into the socket.'

'Did you touch?' he asked.

'No, I fucking didn't touch. Who killed her?'

Dean ran a hand through his hair and his eyelids descended lazily.

'What was left of Emily's exquisite lips?'

'Nothing.'

'Don't lie, Kenny.'

'They were black, like liquorice strips. The top one had shrivelled back against her teeth. The bottom was still quite . . . plump.'

'Were her hands visible?'

'Only one.'

'And?'

'The skin had mostly gone but the tendons were still attached to the bones. Her fingers had folded in on themselves as though she was forming a fist.'

'To defend herself with, perhaps?'

Dean answered his own question by nodding gently as though imagining Emily struggling desperately to preserve her life. The humidifier's volume seemed to increase. A brackish taste invaded my mouth.

'Who killed Emily?' I asked.

'Castor Greaves, in a fit of jealous rage.'

'How do you know?'

'Emily and I had a thing. It was long over, although I'm assuming she told him. Emily was a stickler for the truth.'

'Why didn't you tell the police?' I asked.

'I did,' Dean replied. 'They requested that I didn't reveal the information.'

'Why not?'

'Who knows?'

'When did you begin the relationship?'

'About a year or so before Emily met the rock god.'

'Why did no one know about it?'

Dean picked something microscopic off his jeans using his thumb and index finger and allowed it to float to the floor. 'Emily asked me to keep it secret. Her agency frowned on celebrity boyfriends.'

'Then why did—'

'Castor was a different proposition. By this time he was seen as an asset to her career as opposed to someone who could potentially derail it.'

All of which made sense. Mean had gone from relative obscurity to major players in the space of a single summer.

Judging by Dean's body language, our interview was at an end. I tried another question. 'How did Castor get the body on to the roof?'

'Emily was petite. Or perhaps that's where he killed her.' Dean stifled a yawn. 'Are we done, Kenny? It's been lovely talking to you but there are a few things I need to be getting on with . . .' He rose from his seat.

'What do you think happened to Castor?' I asked.

Dean shrugged. 'My money would be on abroad. Castor was far too vain to kill himself, and I can't see anyone taking him in at such short notice.'

'His passport was still at home.'

'If you have enough cash there are ways and means of leaving the country without one. And once you're in mainland Europe, it's reasonably easy to reach Africa as long as you don't mind primitive transport or it taking a while.'

Dean looked at his watch. There had only been one reason he'd allowed me into the gallery. Now he was keen for me to leave. He led me to the door.

'Thanks for your time,' I said.

'On the contrary,' he replied. 'Thank you for yours.'

'Just one other thing – who were you meeting after you left the Emporium?'

I didn't have much hope that an ambush question would get the truth out of Dean, although it brought a response of sorts. 'A friend's wife,' he said. 'The police know who she is, although, for obvious reasons, I've never gone public with her name. Now, I really will have to insist you leave . . .'

My exit caught Skinny and colleague off guard. He was checking his phone. She was rolling a cigarette. Dean had the door closed before any abuse could be hurled.

'Did you get what you wanted?' the woman asked.

'I think so,' I said. 'How does your organisation fund itself?'

'Charitable donations. Wanna make one?'

There were three tenners in my wallet. I pulled one out and then, after a moment's hesitation, extracted its companions.

'Thanks a lot,' she said after I'd handed them over. 'Dean must have really pissed you off.'

'Yeah,' I said. 'He did a bit.'

TWELVE

Dean Allison may have been lying to me. It's easy to say that you had a clandestine affair with a woman who's been dead for more than twenty years when there's no one around to corroborate the story. And yet his claim had the ring of truth. After years spent listening to people bullshit me from arsehole to breakfast, I'd learned to tell the difference between fact and fiction. At least I liked to think I had. But the person who might be able to verify his story lived at Pegler's Wharf in Southwark.

Nowhere in London does the past merge with the present quite as seamlessly as it does on the river. One minute I was walking down a busy thoroughfare of former dock buildings converted into pizza parlours and souvenir shops; the next I was clattering down a gangway supported by stilts rising from alluvial mud.

Dusk helped sharpen the sense of concurrent rather than linear time. Out on the swirling water, the ghosts of nineteenth-century bargees jostled for position, the bones of suicides were being ground remorselessly on the riverbed and the timbers of ancient landing stages rotted into oblivion.

The gangway led on to a series of wooden pontoons lashed together with steel cables. Moored to them were twenty or so houseboats in varying states of repair. A couple had gleaming brass portholes and well-tended deck gardens. The paintwork on others was peeling in places, and one barge was little more than a hulk.

Saskia Reeves-Montgomery's boat was named the *Anna Marie* and was moored at the end of the final pontoon. I'd agreed to call on her at 6.30 p.m. and was ten minutes late. There was no buzzer or bell, so I rapped on a varnished wooden door. No answer, and I rapped again. My third attempt produced a response. 'Whoever you are, for fuck's sake would you stop banging on my bloody door,' said a gravelly voice.

Moments later I was looking at its owner. Saskia Reeves-Montgomery's hair was a bob of tight grey curls that might have been cut with a rusty penknife. Her cheeks featured a series of broken veins that made them look like scarlet road maps. A lit fag was clenched between lips with as much collagen in them as a stone.

'Who are you?' she asked after removing it.

'Kenny Gabriel. We had an appointment . . .'

Saskia threw her fag into the water, where it extinguished with a brief sizzle. She drew back the inelastic sleeve of an ancient cardigan to consult a battered Timex. She frowned, shook the watch and held it to her ear.

'It's fucked,' was the verdict. 'Welcome aboard.'

The sitting room of the *Anna Marie* doubled up as a workspace. At one end were a sofa and a seaside deckchair. A TV of similar vintage to my own was perched on a huge spool that had once contained industrial electrical cable. The rattan rug was heavily stained and a pub ashtray needed emptying. At the bow end was a large desk on which was an open Apple PowerBook. To its left were three dirty coffee cups.

Saskia booted open the galley doors and entered bearing a tray. I rose from the sofa but was waved down. 'Yours is on the left.' I took the red mug; Saskia removed the other. She dumped the tray on the floor and occupied the deckchair.

'Sorry, I forgot you were coming. I've got a deadline for the latest piece of crap – sorry . . . masterpiece – I'm penning. If I don't submit a final draft by next Tuesday, the publisher won't pay. Not that the bastards are paying much anyway.'

Saskia reached beside her chair and produced a half-bottle of Teacher's. She unscrewed the top, poured a shot into her coffee and offered it to me. I nodded, and a similarly sized belt of Scotch went into my mug.

'But that's not what you're here to talk about,' she said, replacing the cap. 'You want to discuss the mysterious disappearance of Castor and Emily.'

'If you don't mind.'

'Why not, darling? I've been speaking to newspapers and radio stations about it all day. You've stirred up quite the hornets' nest.'

Saskia took a sip of coffee and wrapped her hands around the mug. I followed suit. It wasn't the warmest on the *Anna Marie*.

'I read your book,' I said.

'Good for you.'

'And I had a few questions.'

'What do I think happened on the fateful night?'

'That would be one of them.'

'Until you made your grisly discovery, I'd always been in the double-suicide camp. Now I suppose all eyes turn to Castor Greaves.'

'Including yours?'

Saskia shrugged her considerable shoulders.

'You don't seem a hundred per cent sure,' I said.

'It's just that I can't see why he would do it. I saw them together when I was writing the book. She adored him and he seemed to adore her.'

'I can maybe shed some light on that . . .'

While I recounted my meeting with Dean Allison, Saskia pulled a fresh pack of Camels out of her cardie. She split the seal and offered me one. I broke off my story to spark it up. By the time I'd finished, each of us was nearing the filter.

'You're sure he was telling the truth?' Saskia asked.

'Why wouldn't he?'

'How about because he's an unpleasant little bastard?'

'Maybe, but what he said sounded plausible. And he was very good-looking.'

Saskia ground out her cigarette with extreme prejudice. 'Didn't he know it. Must have stung like hell when Castor took over as the pin-up boy.'

'You think Castor would have been capable of murdering Emily?'

'Hard to say. His drug use and his ego had started to get out of control, by all accounts. Who knows what he could have done in the heat of the moment?'

'If he was off his tits would he have had the presence of mind to dump Emily's body in the air vent and find a way to beat two security cameras? In fact, I don't see how he could have managed that in twenty minutes even if he'd been stone-cold sober.'

A horn sounded on the river while Saskia considered the question.

'Put like that, it does sound a bit far-fetched, darling,' she said. 'But who else was likely to do the dirty deed?'

'Chop Montague?'

Saskia dissolved into a coughing fit that took her thirty seconds to bring under control. 'If Castor didn't have the time, then neither did Chop.'

'I suppose not. You wrote in the book that his and Castor's process was to listen to each other's ideas on tape and then decide which ones to develop.'

'That's what they told me,' Saskia said.

'Who was the most talented?'

'I'd say Chop, in light of subsequent events.'

Saskia reintroduced the bottle of Teacher's. She sloshed some into her empty cup and emptied the rest into mine.

'Up your bum, darling,' was the toast.

'Cheers,' was my response.

We each took a hit and Saskia continued the conversation.

'It was Castor who had problems producing. Trust me, you can't take a shit from one day to the next on smack, never mind write a decent tune.'

I suspected Saskia was speaking from personal experience, although it would have been impolite to ask. 'Did you know JJ well?' was my next question.

'Now, that boy did have a temper,' was her reply. 'If he didn't have a rock-solid alibi then I'd have a big question mark over him.'

'He doesn't seem to bear a grudge.'

'Nor should he. JJ made his fair share out of Mean.'

'And he was close to Castor,' I said. 'According to him they were like brothers. What if you're right about him killing Emily, and JJ got him out of the country?'

This theory brought forth a big sigh from Saskia.

'Maybe when Lord Lucan did a bunk, you could hole up in some foreign field that will always be England, but the world's changed, darling. The only place Castor would be safe from an iPhone camera these days is on the dark side of the moon. Unless he took the Golden Road, of course . . .'

'The what?'

'You've never heard of the Road?'

'Actually, someone mentioned it this morning,' I said, recalling my 'interview' with Danny Abbott. 'I've no idea what it is, though.'

'Music industry legend. When an artist is addicted to booze and drugs, or their popularity is waning, the Golden Road organisation makes them an offer.'

'What kind of offer?'

'In return for signing over all future royalties, said artist has his or her death faked and is taken to a private island paradise in some far-flung part of the world. They live there in luxury under the protection of the organisation.'

'What happens when the royalties dry up?'

'The artists write songs for other artists and theme music for ads and TV, which brings in more revenue for the Road. When they die for real, they're buried at sea.'

'Who's meant to have taken the Golden Road?' I asked.

Saskia yawned and peered despondently into her empty mug. 'Depending on who you listen to . . . Hank Williams, Elvis Presley, Janis Joplin, Jimi Hendrix, John Lennon, Bob Marley, Kurt Cobain, Amy Winehouse . . . and Castor Greaves.'

'No one believes that, do they?'

'You'd be surprised.'

'How about you?'

'On the one hand, it's clearly a ridiculous conspiracy theory . . .'

'But on the other?'

'The more you dig into the music industry, the weirder and nastier things become, especially where money's involved.'

As if to endorse this downbeat assessment, there was a mournful blast of a boat horn from the river. Saskia struggled out of her deckchair.

'It's been a delight, darling, but the grindstone calls . . .'

'Thanks,' I said. 'You've been very helpful.'

'Well, if there's anything else you want to run past me then you know where I am. And do be careful, Kenny. Golden Road or no Golden Road, when you start poking around in the past, a whole ava-lanche of shit can rain down on your head.'

'I'll bear that in mind,' I said.

The mist had cleared when I clambered out of the *Anna Marie*. The City was lit up against the night sky, with the Gherkin and the Shard showing to particularly good effect. Unfettered capitalism might not suit everyone's moral compass, but there was no denying it made for a decent chunk of horizon candy.

The tide was coming in fast and the water slapped against the wooden stanchions supporting the pontoon. After my chat with Saskia, I was back to square one. Could there be anything in the Golden Road theory? I was pondering the question when I heard footsteps behind me. What felt like a fist hit me hard between my shoulder blades.

My surprised cry allowed freezing-cold water to rush into my mouth when I hit the river. I surfaced after a few seconds and spat it out. I took a huge gasp of cold night air and heard someone walk briskly away along the pontoon.

I tried to reach the deck. No chance. Even had I been able to get my hands on to the slippery wood, the weight of my sodden clothes would have prevented me from hauling myself on to it. I clung to one of the mossy stanchions and shouted for help. Help didn't arrive. The marina's residents had settled in for the night.

Swimming to the shore wasn't an option. The current would carry me away after a few seconds. Already its incessant tug was attempting to ease me free from the stanchion. I shouted a few more times. My cries were lost on the breeze.

The cold numbed my hands to the degree that I could barely feel them. I kicked off my shoes. It did little to ease the downward pull of the inky water.

Father Thames was claiming me. What was the point in struggling? My exhausted body already felt as though it belonged to him. All I had to do was open my arms and embrace oblivion. I had made my decision when I heard footsteps again.

'What the fuck are you doing down there, darling?' Saskia asked.

THIRTEEN

It took the efforts of Saskia and three others to rescue me, using a hook ladder and two boating gaffs. In the struggle, my trousers were dragged free and borne downstream by a spiteful river. Saskia wrapped a blanket round me and led me back to the *Anna Marie*. A second bottle of Teacher's was opened and administered, after which she dumped me in a hot shower for ten minutes. The Scotch and the hot water returned warmth to my bones, and a strategic chunder liberated a pint of the Thames from my stomach.

Understandably, Saskia wanted to know what had happened. I concocted a story about tripping and taking a header. I decided against telling her that someone had shoved me into the water. All I wanted to do was get back home.

Saskia borrowed jeans, a sweater and a pair of trainers from one of her neighbours. She bunged what was left of my clothes into a dryer, which left them damp and covered in silt, and crammed them into a Tesco bag.

She had come on to the pontoon as I'd left my phone behind. Carelessness had saved my bacon, and now it enabled me to summon an Uber. After saying goodbye to Saskia and promising to return the borrowed garb at the soonest opportunity, I made my way warily to the bank, where Ahmed and his Land Cruiser awaited.

My driver showed no surprise at meeting a man wearing a reindeer jumper in March and a pair of scarlet trousers three inches too short for him. During the journey, I pondered who had pushed me and why. Unless it was someone who enjoyed arbitrarily depositing people into the river, my attacker had a motive.

The only one I could think of was that he or she wanted me to quit looking for Emily Ridley's murderer. It meant two things: firstly, someone thought I might be close to finding an answer, and that someone might be part of the Golden Road.

Secondly, they were prepared to kill me.

◆ ◆ ◆

It had just gone ten thirty when the call came through. I'd shovelled down a late supper of sausage and chips – surprising how peckish a near-death encounter can make you – when my phone's screen lit up with a withheld number. I was tempted to let it go to voicemail as the land of nod beckoned. Professionalism and curiosity overrode my exhaustion. Just as well, bearing in mind who it was.

'Is that Mr Gabriel?' an adenoidal voice enquired.

'That's right,' I said. 'Who's this?'

'Chop Montague. You left a message with my agent a couple of days ago. Apologies for not calling sooner, but things have been incredibly hectic.'

'No problem,' I said. 'You're probably aware why I was calling.'

'Maggie said it was in connection with Emily Ridley and Castor Greaves. I believe you're the person who found Emily's body.'

'That's right.'

'Must have been quite a shock for you.'

'And for you.'

'Naturally. Do you still want to speak to me?'

'I'd love to,' I said, reaching for pen and paper.

'I'm afraid I'm at the TV studio at the moment. However, I've got the day off tomorrow, thank God. Could you come to my house?'

'Where do you live?' I asked.

'Mickleton Lodge in Epping. Hope that's not too out of your way.'

'No problem,' I said. 'What time?'

'About nine o'clock? I'll text you the details.'

A minute after we ended our call, a message came through with Chop's address. I immediately entered the postcode into Google and half a dozen images came up. They featured a nineteenth-century house in several acres of grounds. Nice enough, but nothing like the pile that someone with Chop's cash could have bought.

The conversation had left me feeling wide awake and I decided to call Odeerie. The fat man rarely sleeps more than four hours and never retires before two in the morning.

He answered immediately. 'You've been bloody quiet, Kenny.'

'Weren't you meant to be calling me about Davina Jacobs?'

'Tracking her down's proving a bit trickier than I expected. You sure that's definitely the right name and address?'

'So Pam Ridley told me.'

'And she definitely lived on Dunsinane Road?'

'According to Pam. Look, I don't think it's going to be any biggie if you draw a blank, Odeerie. Davina was Emily's best mate, so the police must have interviewed her. And if it was no use to them . . .'

'I'll keep trying,' he said. 'How did today go?'

It took fifteen minutes to cover off my various encounters.

'You should get checked out by a doctor,' Odeerie said. 'A lot of boat owners pump their raw sewage straight into the water.'

'Thanks for that.'

'Just looking out for you, Kenny. Who d'you think gave you a shove?'

'Presumably someone who doesn't want me looking into Emily's death.'

'How would they know you were at Saskia's boat?'

Few things in life are more irritating than having doubt cast on your reported murder attempt. 'I'm telling you it was deliberate, Odeerie,' I said.

'Then why not report it to the police?'

'Because they'd probably give me the same bullshit you are.'

The fat man redirected the conversation. 'So, in all probability Castor killed Emily in a fit of jealous rage after she told him that she'd been in a relationship with Dean?' he asked.

'I can't see any other likely scenario,' I said.

'But why do that if she knew what he was like?'

'Maybe they got into an argument and she wanted to wound him. Having said that, Saskia mentioned something about an organisation called the Golden Road. You heard of them?'

'Yeah, I think they're mentioned in the *Inquisitor* piece. Shady organisation that disappears music stars and makes money on their estate.'

'That's them.'

'And Saskia reckons that's what happened to Castor?'

'No, she doesn't, but it got me thinking about where his royalties go. And who benefitted in his will. Assuming he made a will, that is.'

'Good point,' Odeerie said. 'I'll check out whether Castor's been declared dead first thing tomorrow. It's been over seven years, but that doesn't mean it's automatic. Someone has to apply and the coroner's office has to agree. On a different subject, have you had any reporters at your door?'

'A couple this morning but it looks like they've given up. You?'

'They've been pressing my intercom all day and asking for a comment.'

'Have you given them one?'

'Course not.'

'What about Jake Villiers buying the Emporium?'

'Totally legit. The lease came up for sale and Jake bought it. Simple as that. On the subject of giving comments, though,' Odeerie continued quickly, 'it would be great publicity for the business if we did, Kenny. You sure you don't want to do a little press conference? I've got this contact at LBC radio who'd love to—'

'Night, Odeerie,' I said, and ended the call.

FOURTEEN

The alarm woke me at six. My left eye seemed to have some kind of film over it that resisted my efforts to remove it. I wondered if my dunking in the river might be responsible. Half a pint of stewed coffee teamed with a pair of smokes did the trick and gradually the vision sharpened.

There hadn't been any concrete developments in the Emily Ridley story, although there was no shortage of features about her and Mean. The *Guardian* had an insightful piece about the incendiary pressures of fame. The *Express* claimed that a stripper-turned-psychic had been retained by the Met to trace Castor's whereabouts. Mystic Mandy was pictured hanging horizontally off a pole and then gazing into a crystal ball. Maybe I should give it a go. The ball, that was, not the pole.

And then I checked out the *Post's* website.

The headline read CAS GREAVES TAKES THE GOLDEN ROAD. Beneath it was a photograph of me lifted from Odeerie's website, and below that the interview that I'd allegedly given exclusively to the *Post's* Danny Abbott. According to Danny I was convinced Castor Greaves was alive, equally certain that he had murdered Emily Ridley, and thought it highly likely that he had taken the Golden Road (the existence of which I felt there was irrefutable evidence for).

What had I expected? Trust a man in a green leather jacket to faithfully represent the truth and you get everything you deserve. The only silver lining was that the *Post's* reputation was only half a notch above that of the *People's Inquisitor*. Once Odeerie had calmed down, I'd get him to issue a statement denying that I'd ever met Danny Abbott and was considering suing the *Post* for substantial damages.

Over a couple of rounds of toast, I contemplated my day. The morning would be spent talking to Chop Montague. Unless he had anything sensational to reveal, or Odeerie located Davina Jacobs, I wasn't sure what I'd be doing in the afternoon. Perhaps it would be an opportune time to touch base with Pauline Oakley.

Exactly how I was going to do that was another matter. Jake had been fibbing about the downturn in his company's fortunes when Pauline had worked for him, but she had definitely worked for him. Ms Oakley could well be blackmailing him over something other than VAT fraud that he was too embarrassed to admit to.

And if I did find out that Jake had a skeleton in his cupboard, how would I break it to Stephie? Anonymously seemed the best option. If Pauline reported our conversation to Jake then I'd end up looking like a jealous former boyfriend who had grassed up his rival in a bid to get back in his ex-girlfriend's good books.

Which, of course, was a million miles away from being my true motive.

◆　◆　◆

It took nearly an hour to reach Epping on the Central Line. I spent half the journey clutching the passenger rail. A woman with a 'Baby on Board' badge was offered a seat at Chancery Lane. Hopefully, London Underground would introduce an 'Old & Knackered' version to prompt those who couldn't spot the telltale signs.

Numbers thinned out considerably after Stratford. During the final leg of the journey, I was alone in the carriage. I'd pondered the Pauline Oakley situation and come to the conclusion that I didn't have much to lose. We were above ground by this time, so I accessed Flummery's website and gave them a ring.

'How may I help you?' asked a sprightly female voice.

'You have a guest called Pauline Oakley,' I said. 'Would you mind putting me through to her room?'

'Hold the line, please . . .'

Fleetwood Mac assured me that I could go my own way for ten seconds until interrupted by a ringing phone. It was answered promptly.

'Pauline Oakley?' I asked.

'Who's this?' came the reply.

'My name's Kenny Gabriel, Pauline,' I said. 'I'm a friend of Jake Villiers. I wondered if we could meet for a quick chat.'

'About what?' Pauline asked. Her voice had gone from vaguely suspicious to positively hostile in the space of a single sentence.

'Might be better if I explain that when I see you,' I said.

Silence on the line.

'Come to Flummery's hotel around twelve thirty,' Pauline said. 'Make sure you're alone.'

'Okay,' I said to the dial tone.

◆　◆　◆

Shortly before we pulled into Epping, Saskia Reeves-Montgomery called. Her voice boomed through the tiny speaker to the degree that I had to hold it an inch away from my ear. 'I take it you made it home without further mishap, darling?' she asked.

I confirmed that was the case.

'Where are you now?' was the follow-up question.

'On my way to an appointment with Chop Montague.'

'Well, well,' she said. 'How interesting.'

'If you're calling about the clothes, I'll return them as soon as possible.'

'Forget the clothes. What are you doing around mid-morning? There's something I'd like to discuss.'

'Can't you tell me on the phone?'

'I'd rather do it face to face. D'you know Assassins on Greek Street?'

Assassins was a private club that drew its members from the creative industries. Two years ago, I'd attended a charity auction there during the search for the killer of my ex-employer's daughter.

'I'm having brunch there with someone,' Saskia continued. 'Pitch up around eleven, we should be through by then.'

I commissioned a taxi from the rank outside Epping station. We drove through roads that had a variety of housing stock, including converted labourers' cottages, mock-Tudor mansions behind wrought-iron railings, and 'executive' estates put up in the last couple of decades to serve the growing army of commuters.

The houses became less frequent, and the roads bordered by ploughed fields. Eventually the driver pulled up in front of a gate set in a dry-stone wall. There wasn't much to see, as mature oaks obscured the view. The sign at the side of the gate read *Mickleton Lodge*. It was 9 a.m. on the nose.

The house was at the end of a couple of hundred yards of gravel drive that bisected beautifully maintained lawns and flowerbeds. The letters *H&D* were picked out above the door, along with the date *1853*. The building was constructed from red brick and had a pair of chimneys emerging from a slate roof. Ivy festooned the walls. I pressed the bell and, a few seconds later, was greeted by Chop Montague in person. 'You found the place, then, Kenny?' he said, extending a hand.

'The taxi driver did,' I said, and we shook. 'You have a lovely house.'

'Thank you. It's been in the family four generations. I have an apartment in town but I rather like the peace and quiet out here. Do come in . . .'

On the left of the entrance hall was a grandfather clock with an insistent tick. A walnut side table supported a large porcelain bowl decorated with tiny blue flowers. Above it hung an antique mirror on which the silvering had begun to corrode.

'Do let me take your coat,' Chop said. While he transferred my overcoat to a wardrobe, I examined the clock. A Latin inscription on the dial read *ultima latet ut observentur omnes*, along with the details *Henry Sawston, Bath, 1813.*

'It translates as "our last hour is hidden from us, so that we watch them all",' Chop said, returning from the wardrobe. 'Clock mottoes are usually a bit more cheerful. Henry must have been in a sombre mood that year.'

My host was wearing a pair of corduroy trousers and a denim shirt, over which was a grey woollen tank top. His hair had receded until there was just a smattering of grey around the rim of his scalp. He sported a pair of thick-framed black glasses.

Not Liam Gallagher exactly.

'Have you had any breakfast, Kenny? Happy to rustle something up if not.'

'A coffee would be nice,' I said.

Chop led me down a panelled passage that smelled of beeswax and cinnamon. He pushed open a door. We entered a room that was part kitchen, part conservatory. It extended twenty yards into the back garden. To my left was an old-fashioned Aga range. Under the glass roof stood a large pine table with six chairs.

'How do you take it?' Chop asked.

'Milk with a couple of sugars,' I replied.

Chop dropped a capsule into a gleaming machine that stood on a polished granite work surface. The contraption gurgled, and thirty seconds later a stream of molten liquid descended into the mug he'd positioned under a spout.

'Your back garden's as impressive as the front,' I said.

'Unfortunately I can't take the credit for that,' Chop said. 'My gardener does all the real work. I just deadhead a few roses now and then. Have a seat . . .'

Chop placed the steaming mug before me and sat on the opposite side of the table. An advantage of premature hair loss is that you look the same as you get older. Give or take a few lines, he could have just stepped off the Emporium stage in 1995.

'How's *Moment in Time!* going?' I asked, to make conversation.

Chop winced. 'It's the most abysmal experience.'

'Why did you do it?'

'I've a compilation album out in a couple of months. My agent thought judging a talent show would be an effective way to get me current with the Snapchat generation. God knows why I listened to her.'

Chop stared morosely at the surface of the table. I took a sip of coffee and asked, 'Have you had much fallout from the press about Emily's body being found?'

'A few paparazzi and reporters doorstepped my flat in London. Once they'd got their pound of flesh that was it, though. How about you?'

'Same,' I said. 'Although I think Emily's mum's having a tougher time.'

'Yes, I saw her press conference. It must be like going through the whole thing again. At least she knows the worst now. That must be a comfort of sorts.'

'Pam wants to find out who was responsible,' I said. 'The popular theory is that Castor was the one who killed Emily and hid her body.'

'Is that what the police think?'

'I'd be amazed if they didn't. It fits the facts perfectly, apart from one detail . . .'

'Why did he do it?' Chop suggested.

I nodded. 'According to Dean Allison it was in a fit of jealous rage because he discovered Emily had once been in a relationship with him.'

'Emily and *Dean*!'

'So he said yesterday.'

'I'd be amazed if that was the case.'

'Why?'

Chop looked at his watch. 'Would you mind if we went to the studio?' he asked. 'There's a program running I need to check on . . .'

◆ ◆ ◆

At one corner of the cellar was a computer stack that fed into a large monitor. There were half a dozen speakers of differing sizes and a pair of keyboards arranged one above the other. A rack held three acoustic guitars, and a vintage Les Paul leant nonchalantly against a Marshall speaker. The light from the ceiling spotlights caused the guitar's burnish to glow, and glinted off the chrome work on a large drum kit.

A Grammy and three Brit statuettes stood on a shelf above a sofa. Something was flickering on the monitor. Chop sat behind the keyboard and pressed a few buttons. The screen dissolved to black.

'Have a seat, Kenny.'

The sofa was a bit low-slung for a man whose knees were as flexible as lumps of lignite. I fell into it like a scuba diver off the stern of a boat.

'What were we talking about?' Chop asked.

'You thought it unlikely Dean and Emily were having an affair . . .'

He removed his glasses and began polishing them on his sweater. 'I can certainly imagine Dean making a play for Emily. I just can't see her falling for it.'

'He's a handsome man.'

'And a total creep.'

No disagreeing with Chop on that one. He finished with his specs and replaced them on top of his head.

'Can I ask a few questions about what happened in the Emporium the night Cas and Em went missing?' I asked.

'If you must,' he said without enthusiasm.

'Cas had been gone twenty minutes when you checked on him? Is that right?'

Chop nodded.

'What were you worried about?'

'To be honest, I didn't buy that Cas had cleaned up without any help. I was concerned he might have passed out in one of the stalls.'

'But they were clear?'

'Yes.'

'What did you do after checking them?'

'Took the stairs down to the auditorium. When I couldn't find him there, I quickly went through the rest of the building before coming back to tell the others.'

'How long were you away?'

'Fifteen minutes. Twenty at most.'

'Did anyone go on to the roof?'

'Not that I'm aware of.'

'When you couldn't find him, everyone assumed that he'd gone home and followed suit?'

'That's right. Without Cas the party was effectively over. The guy who ran the place locked up and that was that.'

'You personally saw everyone leave the building?'

Chop looked up at the low ceiling. His head bobbed several times as though he was retrospectively counting out Kristos, JJ and Sweat Dog.

'Yes,' he said. 'They definitely left.'

All of which had been faithfully reported in dozens of articles and books over the years. I decided to ask something less well known.

'What made the pair of you such a good writing team? JJ said that Castor had never shown any talent in that direction.'

'Only because he didn't know the basic principles. Once I'd introduced him to a few techniques, Cas took to it like a duck to water.'

'Must have been frustrating for you when he stopped writing.'

Chop grimaced. 'I thought it was the end of my career. Cas brought out in me what I brought out in him. We were a team.'

'But you found that you could carry on alone?'

'Yes, although I wouldn't be where I am today if I hadn't met Cas. Sometimes I feel guilty about how it turned out for him and how it turned out for me.'

'What do you think happened that night?' I asked.

'Assuming he isn't lying then Dean's theory sounds plausible. Cas killed Emily because he'd found out she'd been seeing Dean. He couldn't live with the guilt and subsequently took his own life.'

'Why would Cas kill Emily and not Dean?'

Chop pursed his lips and considered the question.

'Perhaps their affair had nothing to do with it. Em could have said something and he snapped. I know she'd been nagging him about the drugs. I'd said a few things myself and it didn't go down well, to say the least.'

Chop's phone began to ring. He made an apologetic sign and accepted the call.

'Chop Montague . . . Hi, Charlotte . . . No way! We did all that yesterday . . . You're joking . . . Okay, well, if there's no other option then I suppose so. Can you send a car? . . . Three o'clock, and I need to be back by six at the absolute latest.'

He cut the call and swore under his breath.

'Bad news?' I asked.

'There's been some sort of continuity problem on the show. I have to go in and record some fills this afternoon.' He checked his watch.

'Would you mind if we left things there, Kenny? I hope it's been useful in some way.'

'Of course,' I said, despite having learned nothing much I didn't know already. 'Can I ask what prompted you to return my call? To be honest, I wasn't expecting it.'

Chop stood up and arched a crick out of his back. I got out of the sofa as though I'd slipped a disc. 'As I said, I saw the interview with Emily's mother and I'd like to do anything I can to help find out what happened to Emily.'

'Even if it helps prove that Castor murdered her?'

Chop thought about this for a few seconds.

'Yes, even that,' he said.

FIFTEEN

During the cab ride to Epping station, I took stock of my interview with Chop Montague. If it's true that opposites attract, then it was never more so than with Chop and Castor. Discount the basement studio, and Mickleton Lodge could have been the home of a retired civil servant. Had he not met Castor, Chop would probably have ended up as a music teacher in a private school. Life comes down to a couple of chance encounters and a dollop of good or bad fortune in the final analysis.

That Emily had been in a clandestine relationship with Dean didn't surprise me as much as it had him. Looks trump all other things when you're a teenager. More interesting was that she had kept it from her parents as well as her agency. Perhaps it was an indication as to what they would have made of Dean Allison.

And would the news that his girlfriend had once been in a relationship with a bandmate before she met him really have sparked Castor into such a murderous fury? Particularly when he was allegedly sober at the time Emily died. Even if it had been the case, how did he manage to disappear into thin air afterwards?

Assuming that Castor wasn't dead, the person most likely to lend him logistical and financial support was JJ Freeman. Exactly how I was going to pursue that line of enquiry was another matter, particularly given JJ's penchant for throwing punches first and asking questions second. By the time I was on the Tube heading back into Central London, I had no strategy in mind.

Joshua Reynolds and Dr Johnson founded the first Soho club in 1764 above the Turk's Head pub on Gerrard Street. Nine members, including Edmund Burke and Oliver Goldsmith, met to discuss literary and scientific matters. These days, private members' clubs comprise D-list celebs who meet to talk bollocks, take selfies and snort coke off lavatory cisterns. Josh and Dr J must be spinning in their graves.

That said, Assassins wasn't the worst example. Applicants needed more than the ability to set up a standing order to make it past the committee. CVs from those in the film and TV professions were regarded with a favourable eye; those from bankers and media executives consigned to the bin. It had just turned 11.15 when I pressed the entrance button and announced that I was scheduled to meet Saskia Reeves-Montgomery. The electronic lock buzzed and I entered the building.

Reception was womanned by a pair of blondes in their thirties. One was on the phone, the other reading a copy of *Vogue*. She laid the magazine aside and informed me that Saskia was in the small drawing room and how to get there.

The small drawing room turned out to be the size of a tennis court. Decorated in faux country-house style, it had heavily varnished oil paintings hanging from the walls and a central chandelier with fake candles adorning it. I was trying to locate Saskia when a booming voice saved me the bother. 'Hey, water baby, over here!'

Saskia was sitting alone at a table underneath a portrait of a gent in a frock coat and a periwig who peered out of a gilded frame as though he'd always known this was how the world would end. She was wearing a green cable-knit sweater that more or less camouflaged her ample bosom, and clutching a gigantic glass of white wine.

'You're late, darling,' she said as I joined her.

'Sorry, couldn't be helped.'

'Chop Montague spilling his guts, was he?'

'Not exactly.'

'Right, well, you can tell me all about that in a bit. First things first . . .' Saskia signalled to an aproned waiter who approached our table. 'I'll have another one of these, Terrence,' she said. 'And my friend here would like a . . .'

'Jameson and ginger ale, please.'

'A large one,' Saskia answered before Terrence could pose the question. 'I suppose you'll want something to eat,' she asked, as though my need for food was an unfortunate weakness.

'Could I have a chicken club sandwich and fries?'

Saskia drained her glass in a single gulp and handed it to Terrence, who left to fulfil our order. 'How were the fleshpots of Knightsbridge?' she asked.

'I haven't been to Knightsbridge.'

'Then where did you see Chop?'

'At his place in Epping.'

Saskia whistled, and her bushy eyebrows rose a millimetre or two.

'Wow, you are truly honoured.'

'What makes you say that?'

'Not many people make it up to . . . what's it called?'

'Mickleton Lodge.'

'My oasis of tranquillity. The place that I can shut the door, put the cares of the world behind me and be who I truly am in life.' Saskia's voice dropped a couple of octaves to its usual register. 'That's how Chop described it in the *Observer* last year,' she explained. 'What's it really like, Kenny? Murals of naked girls on the walls? Albino tiger in the back garden? Sex dungeon . . . ?'

'He's got a pretty decent coffee machine.'

Saskia slumped in her chair. 'Right, well, we may not include that sensational revelation in the book,' she said.

'What book?' I asked.

'We'll get to that,' Saskia said.

Terrence arrived and laid our drinks on the table. He said that my club sandwich would be turning up soon and left us to it. Saskia resumed the conversation.

'Did Chop tell you anything juicy about Castor and Em?'

'Why do I get the feeling you're pumping me for info?' I asked.

'Because I am, darling,' she said.

'He thinks Cas may have killed Em because he knew about her and Dean. Or that she'd been badgering him to stop using smack so much that he lost it and tried to hide the consequences. After which he couldn't take the guilt and topped himself.'

Saskia nodded and said, 'It's good either way.'

'For what?' I asked.

'After you left last night, I got a call from the publisher of *Play Like You Mean It*. To cut a long story short, they're interested in reissuing the book. When I mentioned that I'd been having a chat with you, they became very interested.'

She took another sip of wine and fiddled with the paper doily.

'Basically, they'd like us to collaborate on a version that includes you finding Emily's body and your subsequent search for her killer.'

'I don't know, Saskia . . .'

'They'd pay an advance.'

'You see, the problem is that—'

'A hundred thousand.'

My turn to take a drink. A long one.

'What if I don't find the killer?'

Saskia shrugged. 'Obviously they'd prefer it if you did, but it won't make a hell of a lot of difference if you don't. Not to the advance, anyway.'

'I'd need to talk it through with my business partner.'

'It would be amazing publicity.'

True enough, and fifty grand was more than I'd earned in the last two years. Also, it wouldn't involve six hours hunkering down in a freezing Fiat Punto while trying to photograph a dodgy ticket collector in action.

'They need to know quickly,' Saskia added. 'Otherwise the deal's off the table.'

'I'll do it,' I said.

She beamed. 'Wonderful. I'll give the publishers a call. They'll probably want a few details up front to salt the mine. Just so you're aware of that.'

My eye caught the portrait of the periwigged gent. When I'd arrived, he'd been gazing out of the frame at an imaginary horizon. Now he was staring directly down at me with a look of distinct disapproval on his cracked lips. I closed my eyes and took a couple of deep breaths. Next time I checked him out, the guy had reverted to his expression of general irritation. All the same . . .

'I can't reveal anything about the investigation until it's over,' I said. 'It's completely confidential. I'd be thrown out of the SIA.'

'Isn't there *anything* you can tell me, darling? Feed the buggers a bit of intrigue and my agent might be able to get us each an extra ten grand.'

'What kind of intrigue?'

'Sex and violence usually works . . .'

'Someone tried to kill me yesterday.'

Saskia's glass froze in mid-air.

'I didn't fall into the river. Whoever it was pushed me in the back and walked away. If you hadn't come along when you did . . .'

'Have you gone to the police?'

'No point. All they'll do is write it up and forget about it.'

'Probably, but at least we'd have some kind of evidence it happened. Do you think it was connected to the investigation?'

'Why else would someone attempt to drown me?'

Saskia produced a vape machine the size of a luger and clamped its barrel between her teeth. A steam cloud enveloped her head.

'If someone was following you then they probably intended to do something,' she said, impervious to the irritation of an American film director at an adjacent table. 'If they hadn't shoved you into the river then they could have nudged you on to a Tube track, or pushed you under a bus, or knifed you down an alley, or—'

'Yeah, I get the picture, Saskia,' I said. 'What you're saying is I was lucky.'

'Very lucky, darling. They'll absolutely lap it up in Grub Street, particularly with the Golden Road connection.'

'We're back to that again.'

'You have to admit it's a hell of a coincidence, Kenny. You find Em's body and the next day you damn near wind up in the morgue.'

'D'you think I should be worried?' I asked.

'I'd certainly keep your eyes open, put it that way.'

'How about telling the police?'

'That the Golden Road tried to kill you?'

'That *someone* tried to kill me.'

'Can't you tell that nice man in charge of the investigation? Might be a good opportunity to see how things are going . . .'

I was about to tell Saskia that the DCI Shaheen wasn't likely to update me on a case in progress simply because I informed him that a person, or persons, unknown had shoved me into the Thames, when the movie director touched her arm.

'Wanna put that thing out, honey?' he said. 'Some of us like to lead healthy lives.'

Saskia blew a column of steam into the air and gave him a radiant smile.

'Fuck off, cuntie,' she said. 'There's a love.'

◆　◆　◆

Saskia was requested to extinguish her vape by Terrence when he arrived with my sandwich. Charm succeeded where command had failed. She shrugged and stuck the contraption in her bag. By this time a mushroom cloud hung above our table that looked as though we'd successfully detonated a tiny nuclear device.

While I consumed my lunch, Saskia talked me through her plan. She would update the book as much as possible, accenting it towards the mysterious disappearance and the discovery of Emily's body, and incorporate new material as she went with my assistance. I still had my misgivings, but fifty thousand quid papers over an awful lot of ethical cracks. Pretty much all of them, in fact.

Saskia and I said our goodbyes and I headed for the stairs. On the landing, Stephie was in earnest conversation with a tall dark-haired woman in her late fifties. It was a surprise to see Stephie in Assassins at all – she was generally scathing about any private members' club that wasn't subterranean or founded after 1970 – but it was particularly so as she was with Toni Barclay, who owned the place.

'Anything else I can show you, Steph?' Toni asked.

'I don't think so,' Stephie replied. 'It's exactly what we're looking for.'

'Okay, well, if you talk it over with Jake and let me know by the end of the week, that should be fine. We can work out the details later.'

'No need,' Stephie said. 'Jake just wanted me to come along to make sure that I was absolutely happy with the place.'

'And are you?'

'Of course! It's every bit as gorgeous as he said it was.'

Just as strange as Stephie being in Assassins was her gushing demeanour. She noticed me for the first time and gave an acknowledging wave.

'It's a yes, then?' Toni asked.

'Absolutely,' Stephie said.

The pair embraced. Toni said that she'd be in touch and gave me the briefest of appraising looks before clacking downstairs on three-inch heels.

'Hey, Kenny,' Stephie said. 'What are you doing in here?'

'Work,' I said. 'What's your excuse?'

Stephie looked at the floor. It was the first time I'd seen her blush. Maybe the first time anyone had seen her blush. 'Can you keep a secret?' she asked.

'Of course,' I said.

'Jake and I are getting married.'

SIXTEEN

Assassins' library featured first editions by the world's great authors. Unfortunately they existed only as images on the wallpaper. At least it eliminated the need for tedious activities like dusting and reading. Mobiles and laptops were banned, which probably accounted for the place being virtually empty.

'Congratulations,' I said after Stephie and I sat down. 'When's the happy day?'

'Twenty-seventh of May,' she said. 'Jake proposed last month but we wanted to keep it under wraps until the preparations had been made. You'll get an invitation in the next couple of weeks now we've sorted a venue.'

'You didn't want to use the Vesuvius?'

'Are you serious? Anyway, Toni's a mate of Jake's, so she was able to fit us in here. Could he help your nephew, by the way?'

'I'm sorry?'

'You said you were trying to get him a job in hospitality . . .'

'Oh, yeah,' I said, recalling the pretext I'd used to get Jake's phone number. 'He said that he'd ask around to see if anything was going.'

'That's Jake for you. Always eager to help.'

Stephie sat back and stretched her long legs out. Her camisole top fitted in all the right places and her cheekbones stood out in delicate relief. She had told me in Pizza Express that she was on a diet. Now I knew the reason why.

'Oh, and congratulations to you too, Kenny,' she said.

'For what?'

'Finding Emily Ridley. I nearly fell over when I heard the news. You must have felt like a dog with two dicks.'

'Not sure that's how I'd describe finding the mummified remains of a brutally murdered woman,' I said.

Stephie's expression changed abruptly. 'Sorry, Kenny. All I meant was that it must have been, you know . . . professionally rewarding to get a result so quickly.'

'Yeah,' I said. 'That bit was okay.'

A waitress arrived and asked if we'd like anything to drink. Stephie ordered a chamomile tea. I opted for a double espresso.

'How long have you been with Jake?' I asked after she left.

'Only nine months,' she said. 'But it feels like a lifetime.'

'Course it does. Although I guess it's only when you get to know people better that they really show their true colours.'

Stephie's shoulders tensed.

'What the fuck is that supposed to mean?'

'All I'm saying is that Jake may well be everything you think he is, but what's the harm delaying the ceremony a few more months? You never know what might come out of the woodwork . . .'

Not the best choice of words, all things considered. Stephie's forehead creased and her nostrils flared. I prepared myself for a torrent of something toxic.

And then she smiled.

'Is that what you'd do, Kenny?'

'Definitely.'

'How long? Six months? A year?' The smile turned into a grimace. 'No, that would be way too quick. Kenny Gabriel would need to leave it at least ten years before he did anything as rash as taking a chance on someone he loved.'

Stephie got to her feet.

'Jake and I are getting married in two months' time, so you'd better get used to the idea,' she said. 'Hopefully we'll spend the rest of our lives together, but even if we split up at least we gave it a try, and at least we'll know what it was like.' Her face was a few inches from mine. 'We're going to Bermuda for the honeymoon,' she said. 'I'll be sure to send you a postcard.'

◆ ◆ ◆

It had just gone noon when I left Assassins. Anaemic sunshine was trying to make itself felt and the wind wasn't quite as ball-freezingly cold. Tourists were making the most of the light to photograph the glories of Greek Street, an idling rickshaw driver was exchanging views with a traffic warden, and a guy outside Maison Bertaux was shouting that we were all fast-tracked for damnation if we didn't mend our ways.

In a month, the flowerbeds of Soho Square would be in bloom and muscle queens would be tripping down Old Compton Street in Lycra shorts. Customers in Bar Italia could sip their al fresco coffees without the need for fingerless mittens, and the windows would be thrown open at the French House. Autumn would bring down summer with a flying tackle sometime in mid-September, after which the Christmas bunting would go up in Liberty's and we would all stagger towards 2018 like zombies on Mogadon.

Stephie was right. In twelve months I would probably be standing in the same spot listening to the same nutter tell me that I was about to be cast into the same lake of burning fire and brimstone if I didn't turn my face to the Lord.

I needed drastic change, and drastic change needed money. My options were selling a body part or accepting the advance on Saskia's book. And that assumed I'd have the time to spend it.

I dug out DCI Shaheen's card and called his mobile. He answered on the eighth ring.

'You said to call if anything important came up.'

'Has it?' the DCI asked.

'Someone tried to murder me yesterday.'

A few moments' silence.

'How?' Shaheen asked.

'They pushed me into the water at a marina in Southwark.'

It was hardly as dramatic as a shooting in Tottenham or a knifing in Hackney. Shaheen's tone reflected this. 'Who pushed you?' he asked.

'I've no idea,' I said. 'It was dark and they walked away.'

'Were there any witnesses?'

'No.'

'How d'you know it wasn't an accident?'

'Call it a hunch,' I said, using what was probably Shaheen's least favourite term. 'I think it had something to do with the Emily Ridley case.'

'Yes, I wanted to have a word with you about that,' Shaheen said. 'Pam Ridley was in an emotional state at her press conference. The best people to find her daughter's killer are the police, and this is an active investigation.'

'Meaning?'

'Meaning that if you fail to disclose any information that could prove useful in apprehending a suspect, that would be considered a criminal offence.'

'Isn't that what I'm doing now?'

Shaheen sighed. 'It sounds to me as though you haven't got any real evidence that whatever happened was connected to the Emily Ridley case.'

'You're not going to do anything about it, then?'

'If you feel a genuine attempt was made to harm you, then report it to the local station. Now, if there's nothing else, I need to get back to work.'

'How *is* the case going?' I asked.

'Read the papers,' Shaheen said, and hung up.

It took a few seconds to check that our conversation had recorded successfully on my phone. Saskia would be pleased I had evidence an attempt had been made on my life, even more so that a senior officer had shown scant interest in pursuing it.

'Be sober-minded; be watchful. Your adversary the devil prowls around like a roaring lion, seeking someone to devour,' the crazy preacher yelled.

Was there a reason he was looking in my direction? One attempt had been made on my life. Who was to say there wouldn't be more?

Odeerie called me in the cab on my way to meet Pauline Oakley at Flummery's. 'I've just seen today's *Post*,' he said. 'What the hell were you thinking, Kenny?'

'Actually, I was meaning to talk to you about that.'

'That's nice of you.'

'Everything Danny Abbott wrote was cobblers. The only reason I spoke to him was that I felt a bit sorry for the bloke.'

'So you don't think the Golden Road exists?'

I avoided Odeerie's question by asking one of my own. 'What's the word on Davina Jacobs?'

'Her name wasn't Davina Jacobs,' he said. 'It was Davina Jackson.'

'Please don't tell me she lives in Honolulu now . . .'

'Stamford Hill. She married a dentist and has two kids. Works as a Pilates instructor at a place called City Stretch in Crouch End.'

'Have you been in touch?'

'Thought that was your department.'

'Okay, send me her details,' I said. 'Anything else to report?'

'I have, as a matter of fact,' he said. 'It's about Castor Greaves's cash.'

'Where did it go?'

'A month before he went missing, Castor set up an account at a bank in Zurich. As far as I can make out, all his assets went into it post-disappearance.'

'Including his Mean royalties?'

'That's right.'

'Who inherits?'

'I don't know. Like I said, you can't see a will before probate and you can only apply to have someone declared dead after they've been missing seven years. Any doubt – and there's quite a bit in Castor's case – the application can be denied almost indefinitely.'

'So the money just stays in the account?'

'Or someone might be drawing on it.'

'It's odd that he set it up, isn't it? Why not leave it in the Nationwide?'

'Any number of reasons. Tax avoidance would be top of the list, and the Swiss have a very stable currency. Castor might have been concerned there was going to be an economic dip and wanted to find a financial safe haven.'

'He was a heroin-addicted rock 'n' roll singer, Odeerie, not Warren Buffett. There's only one theory that makes any sense . . .'

'I know. He took the Golden Road.'

A chunk of Shakespeare surfaced in my brain: *There are more things in heaven and earth, Horatio, than are dreamt of in your philosophy.* Did the Golden Road really exist? More importantly, were they intent on nailing yours truly? If so, then the *Post* interview wouldn't have helped matters much. Ordinarily I'd have thought about going to ground for a couple of days until things died down. What with time not being on my side in more ways than one, that wasn't really an option.

'Let's say someone spoke to Castor and suggested he channel all his cash into an anonymous account. Then he could go missing and draw on it from anywhere in the world. That would work, wouldn't it?'

'In theory,' Odeerie said.

'Then, before he's due to go AWOL, Castor finds out that Emily hadn't told him about her relationship with Dean Allison. He thinks it was still going on while they were seeing each other and decides to get his revenge. What if the whole thing at the Emporium was a carefully executed plan and not just some horrible accident that forced Castor to go into hiding or top himself?'

'Why would he want to go missing?'

'By all accounts, Cas saw himself as some kind of mystic. Maybe he fancied sitting in a rainforest and communing with nature for the rest of his life.'

'While occasionally nipping off to an ATM?'

'Take the piss all you like, Odeerie, but I know what I think . . .'

'What's that?'

'The bastard's still alive.'

◆ ◆ ◆

My phone rang again as the taxi rounded the corner into Wimpole Street. 'Is that Mr Kenneth Gabriel?' a woman with a plummy accent asked.

'Speaking,' I said.

'Gaynor Levine here. I'm Dr Arbuthnot's PA. The doctor would like to schedule a follow-up appointment. I was wondering when you could make it in.'

'I'm super-busy, Gaynor. Can't you just give the all-clear over the phone?'

'Dr Arbuthnot likes to see all patients in person after an MRI scan. He's suggested tomorrow morning between eight and ten thirty . . .'

As the cab had just passed the building Gaynor was calling from, the obvious solution suggested itself. 'I've a meeting at Flummery's Hotel at twelve thirty,' I said. 'Any chance the doc could see me after that?'

'Hold the line a moment.' The cab had pulled up outside Flummery's before Gaynor came on the line again. 'Two o'clock would work,' she said.

No doubt Arbuthnot was being flexible in case I gave my brother a duff report and he retained another quack to minister to his stressed execs. I confirmed that I'd present myself in an hour and a half and mounted the steps to Flummery's entrance.

'You again,' my favourite doorman said.

'Me again,' I replied.

'Found any more wallets?'

'Not that you're getting hold of.'

He opened the door by eighteen inches, obliging me to squeeze through it like a burglar insinuating himself through a gap in a chain-link fence.

'Aren't you the man from City Strolls?' the receptionist asked when I approached her desk.

'That's right,' I said. 'I'm here to see Pauline Oakley.'

'Haunted Holborn again?'

I shook my head. 'Seedy Soho.'

She dialled a number and had a brief conversation before disconnecting. 'Ms Oakley says you're to go her room. It's number 34 on the third floor.'

SEVENTEEN

The corridor was richly carpeted and dimly lit. Chamber music played at low volume from concealed speakers. There was a faint citrus aroma in the air. Pauline Oakley answered the door with the security chain on. Green eyes peered through the gap.

'Alone,' I said. 'As agreed.'

The bolt was slipped from its bracket and the door properly opened. Pauline was getting on for six feet in height. She had thick auburn hair that fell to her shoulders and a complexion that appeared make-up free but probably wasn't. She was wearing black jeans tucked into knee-length brown boots and a cream sweater.

A bed large enough to play five-aside on stood on a low wooden platform. The walls had been decorated in a blue silk, fleur-de-lis pattern. A circular glass table bore a closed MacBook and had several documents strewn across it. Velvet drapes had been drawn against the dusk.

'You've got ten minutes,' she said, hands on hips. 'So say whatever Jake wants you to say and then piss off.'

'Jake doesn't know I'm here,' I said.

'Thought he was a mate of yours . . .'

'More an acquaintance.'

Pauline's appraisal began with my piebald Hush Puppies and finished at my six-quid haircut. 'You certainly don't look like one of his inner circle,' she said.

'He's marrying a friend of mine. I'd like to check a few things out about him.'

'You're a private investigator.'

'How d'you know that?'

'You're all over the web for finding Emily Ridley. Jake didn't kill her, did he?'

'Not that I'm aware of.'

Extortionists usually aren't too fond of their victims. Pauline Oakley seemed to have an almost visceral dislike for Jake Villiers. She crossed the room and occupied one of the four seats surrounding the glass table. I wasn't invited to join her.

'Jake told you all about me, I'm guessing,' she said.

'He mentioned you were blackmailing him.'

If this came as a surprise to Pauline, it didn't register on her face. She unclipped a pair of opal earrings and laid them on the table. 'Did he tell you why?'

'You committed VAT fraud twenty years ago without his knowledge. Now you're threatening to inform the authorities and he'll take the fall. Unless he coughs up half a million quid, that is . . .'

Pauline laughed as though I'd cracked the punchline to a sick joke.

'Not true?' I asked.

'Let's say he's been very selective,' she said.

'What don't I know?'

'Why should I tell you that, Kenny?'

'Because my friend's one of the kindest people I've ever met. If she's about to make a colossal mistake then she deserves to know about it.'

'Jake's really in love with her, is he?'

'I think so.'

'And if she broke it off then he'd be devastated?'

'Presumably.'

Pauline ran a hand through her hair and chewed her bottom lip. Then she used the heel of her left boot to slide out one of the chairs from the table.

'Take a pew,' she said.

◆　◆　◆

Pauline made me relate everything Jake had told me about their relationship. She shook her head a few times and actually snorted when I went into specifics about the tax fraud. After I'd finished, she leant forward and planted her elbows on the table.

'I'd just turned thirty and I was working for a pub chain and Jake was looking for someone to oversee the financial side of his business. He offered to match my salary along with five per cent equity. His lawyer drew the agreement up and I went to work.

'Within three years the company was thriving and Jake and I were living together. Around that time, we put in a bid for a disused Victorian textile mill in Birmingham. It was a huge project that would take the business to the next level. At least, it was going to until Arnie Atkinson entered the picture.'

The name was a vaguely familiar. Pauline had continued with her story before I could work out why.

'Arnie was a local property developer. He wanted to turn the mill into luxury flats and he put in several counter-bids. Jake should have walked away but he tabled a final offer, and, unexpectedly, Arnie threw the towel in.'

'So Jake got the place?'

Pauline nodded. 'Although he'd paid over the odds, which meant that it needed to be open and bringing cash in within a year to pay back the interest on the loans he'd taken out. And that was when things started to go pear-shaped.

'The contractors quit the job a week before they were due to start. Jake struggled to get a local firm to replace them. In the end, he had to bring in an outfit from down south. By the time they got going, we'd lost a couple of months. Even then Jake would probably have got away with it if things hadn't gone wrong on-site.'

'What kind of things?'

'Machinery was vandalised and a fire broke out. It didn't damage the building's superstructure but the contractors had to redo a lot of work.'

'Which took more time?'

Pauline nodded. 'We increased security, but the final straw was when one of the builders fell off the rigging. The guy broke both legs and the council closed us down for a month while they conducted a safety assessment.'

'That was unlucky.'

'Not really. He was pushed.'

'By whom?'

'God knows. Anyone wearing a hi-vis jacket and a hard hat could have got on-site. By then we were hiring dozens of casuals to make up for lost time.'

I began to sense the direction Pauline's story might be travelling in.

'Did Arnie Atkinson have a hand in this?'

'Let's say it turned out to be a convenient series of events as far as he was concerned. Arnie offered to take the mill off Jake's hands. Not for the amount he'd paid for it, obviously, but something was better than nothing.'

'Had that been his intention all along?'

'Probably. Arnie had been around the block a few more times than Jake and saw an opportunity to work things to his advantage. It was a clever enough plan, and, to be fair, there was no way he could have foreseen how it would go wrong.'

'How did it go wrong?' I asked.

Pauline stared at me levelly.

'Jake said that if we were to avoid losing everything then we needed to generate some extra short-term cash in order to buy time to put things right.'

'Which involved you cooking the books?'

'Exactly.'

'And you agreed?'

'Not initially. I said that if we sold off the other bars and restaurants then we could just about avoid bankruptcy. We had each other and that was enough.'

'Jake disagreed?' I asked.

'That's one way of putting it. We had a row, after which I ended up in A&E with a broken arm and a fractured skull. Hard to imagine, isn't it?' Pauline said, reacting to my expression. 'Jake Villiers beating his girlfriend up to the point that she's in hospital for a week. Not that there hadn't been warning signs.'

'Such as?' I asked.

'Jake slapped me once when I suggested he cut back on his gambling. Of course I forgave him in the same way I forgave him when he punched me in the stomach after I laughed too hard at some guy's joke at a dinner party. He had an entire florist's worth of flowers delivered and promised it would never happen again.'

'And did it?'

'Not until the business with Arnie Atkinson,' Pauline said. 'When I was discharged from hospital, I told Jake it was over. He threatened to put me in the morgue if I didn't file a false return, or if I even thought about leaving him.'

'How did you get away?'

'It was quite simple in the end. I perpetrated the fraud and took copies of all the documents. I said that I'd left instructions with my solicitor that if anything untoward ever happened to me, then the papers should be forwarded to the police.'

'Jake didn't see that one coming?'

Pauline leant back in her chair. 'You know, I don't think he did,' she said. 'Like most narcissists, Jake Villiers has his blind side. He can't imagine any woman resisting his charms, no matter how badly he treats them. And, of course, Jake can be *very* charming when he chooses to be . . .'

I was about to ask what happened with the mill when a couple of synapses teamed up with half a dozen neurons to haul a news item out of my memory swamp.

'Arnie Atkinson went missing, didn't he?'

'That's right,' Pauline said. 'Although I'm sure Jake had the perfect alibi and there were quite a few people Arnie had screwed over in his time, so there couldn't have been any shortage of other suspects for the police to investigate.'

'So there's no actual proof Jake was behind his disappearance?'

Pauline's arched eyebrows provided her answer.

'What did you do afterwards?' I asked.

'Led a fairly rackety life,' she said. 'It was almost as though being associated with Jake had cursed me in some way. I ran through my savings in a couple of years and ended up doing a series of jobs that were mundane at best and borderline illegal at worst. I went bust at forty-two and was jailed for fraud three years later, which I suppose would all be deeply ironic if it weren't so fucking pathetic.'

'Still time to turn things round,' I said.

'No, there isn't. I'm in my fifties, I've got a criminal record and I haven't held down a proper job in fifteen years. I'm booked in here on a maxed-out credit card. If Jake weren't stumping up the cash, I'd have to do a runner.'

The double-knock gave the pair of us a galvanic start. Pauline crossed the floor and said, 'Who is it?' through the closed door.

'Ivan, miss. Your dry cleaning's back.'

A guy in hotel uniform was holding a dress swathed in polythene. Pauline produced a banknote from the pocket of her jeans. The guy grinned and left. Pauline laid the black gown on the bed. We continued our conversation.

'D'you really think Jake's going to hand over half a million quid and let you walk away with evidence that could put him away for years?' I said. 'If you carry on like this, you'll eventually need more cash and you'll know where to get it.'

'That's all behind me,' Pauline said.

'Maybe it is and maybe it isn't. The point is that Jake's not going to know for sure and he won't take any risks.'

'I need the money, Kenny.'

'Not that much, you don't.'

A conversational hiatus gave me time to think. Two hours ago I'd been keen to stop Stephie marrying Jake. Now I was positively desperate.

'Could you tell my friend all this?' I said.

'You seriously think that's going to happen? You can tell her if you like, but there's no way I'm doing it. And if you go to the police, I'll deny all knowledge. They'll think you're off your head.'

'My friend's not going to believe me.'

'That's her problem.'

'Think about it, Pauline. Even if Jake gives you the money then he can still come after you. That means you'll never feel truly safe, no matter where you go.'

It occurred to me that Pauline's situation wasn't a million miles away from Castor's. Even if he were under the protection of the Golden Road, he'd always be looking over his shoulder to a degree.

'I'll take my chances,' she said.

Perhaps Castor had too.

EIGHTEEN

After my meeting with Pauline, I had a drink in Flummery's bar to digest everything she'd told me and kill time before my appointment with Dr Arbuthnot. The walk to his surgery barely registered. In fact, my preoccupation with discouraging Stephie from marrying a stone-cold killer almost sent me under the wheels of a Harrods van on the corner of Queen Anne Street. The driver communicated his opinion visually and we went our separate ways.

I was on the steps of Fleming House when my phone rang. 'What are you doing tomorrow morning?' Saskia asked before I'd had a chance to say hello.

'Not sure yet,' I said. 'By the way, I called Shaheen and told him that someone—'

'Don't worry about Shaheen. There's something I found in my files I need to show you.'

'What is it?'

'I'm not a hundred per cent sure, but if it's what I think it might be then we can add another nought to the book advance.'

'What is it?' I repeated.

'You need to see for yourself, Kenny.'

'So take a photo and email it over.'

'No way am I doing that,' Saskia said, as though I'd suggested she run down Oxford Street naked. 'What's the earliest you can get here tomorrow?'

'Nine o'clock?'

'Great. See you then.'

◆ ◆ ◆

Every measure in the good doctor's waiting room had been taken to lend it a soothing ambience. A shoal of angelfish patrolled a large aquarium and the walls had been painted clover green. There were black-and-white photographs of sunrises and the branches of winter trees laden with snow. The coffee table was strewn with current editions of *Country Life*, *Horse & Hound* and the *Financial Times*.

The only other occupant was a man in his sixties. He had a patch over one eye and was attempting to focus on an iPhone by holding it at arm's length. I was distractedly reading an article on the merits of building a therapeutic swimming pool for thoroughbreds, and wondering what Saskia had found that had excited her so much, when Gaynor announced that Dr Arbuthnot was ready for me.

Arbuthnot was wearing a charcoal-grey suit and a muted smile. He rose from his desk and we shook hands. 'Thanks for coming in at short notice, Kenny,' he said. 'I'm on holiday in a couple of days and I wanted to see you personally.'

For some reason I felt as though I was in the headmaster's office. Probably it was down to Arbuthnot's air of natural authority and my abiding sense of juvenile guilt.

He removed a few papers from a cardboard slip file.

'The blood tests have arrived, as have the MRI results.'

'What's the verdict?'

'I'm sorry to say that it's not what we were hoping for. You have a tumour in the left hemisphere that requires immediate attention.'

The room became two-dimensional. Almost as though I could scrunch it up into a ball and throw it away. 'The positive news is that it's probably benign,' Arbuthnot continued, 'although I'm afraid the mass is significant, which is why the consultant feels the need to act as soon as possible.'

'Surgery?' I asked.

He nodded. 'Usually the first step would be to take a biopsy and then decide on a course of treatment, although the headaches you've been experiencing and the fainting episode are due to the increased pressure in your skull.'

'I've been feeling better recently.'

'Sometimes the brain compensates in the short term. I'm afraid that probably won't be the case for much longer. If things are allowed to proceed untreated, then those symptoms will reappear along with a range of others.'

'Including my vision being affected?'

'Has that happened?' Arbuthnot asked.

I wondered whether I should reveal the full extent of my issues in that department and decided against it. He might call an ambulance on the spot.

'Things were a bit hazy in my left eye when I woke up this morning. It went away after half an hour and I didn't think anything of it.'

'Probably a result of pressure on the optic nerve. The longer we leave it, the more difficult the procedure could turn out to be.'

'But it's going to be tricky anyway?'

'The consultant will be able to give you a steer on that. You can arrange a telephone consultation with Mrs McDonald. I have her details here. . . .' Arbuthnot wrote something on a pad, tore off the sheet and passed it to me.

'Do you know the risks?' I asked.

'Not in your specific case. It really would be a lot more advisable if you spoke to Mrs McDonald in person . . .'

'And I'll do that,' I said. 'But what are the possible outcomes?'

Arbuthnot interlaced his fingers. 'There's a fifty per cent chance you'll come out of the surgery with relatively minor effects, and forty per cent that there will be some form of cognitive or physical impairment.'

'Such as?'

'It could affect your speech, your eyesight or general mobility. It's very hard to say, which is why I strongly recommend that you speak to—'

'That's only ninety per cent,' I said.

'There is a small chance the procedure could prove fatal,' Arbuthnot admitted, 'although I have to emphasise those are the *global* statistics. Your operation will be conducted in one of the finest hospitals in the world and you'll be in the hands of an incredibly skilled surgical team. There's every reason to be optimistic.'

'But there's still a fifty per cent chance of brain damage or death?'

'Those are the figures,' Arbuthnot said. 'Assuming you want to go ahead with the operation, Kenny, it would be good to decide as soon as possible . . .'

'When can they get me in?' I asked.

'Ten days' time,' Arbuthnot replied. 'Earlier if possible. I'm going to prescribe you something that should limit the possibility of a stroke.'

'There's a chance of that?'

'Your risk is elevated by the tumour, although your blood pressure is surprisingly okay, so it's a precautionary measure. However, you do need to start taking it immediately.'

I nodded and Arbuthnot began typing.

'Along with something else I'll prescribe, this should decrease the headaches and vision issues – always assuming you get lots of sleep and avoid exertion, that is.' Arbuthnot looked up from the keyboard. 'That's not a problem, is it?'

'No,' I said. 'No problem at all.'

◆　◆　◆

I walked out of Arbuthnot's surgery into a world of beauty and magic. A pigeon flashed through the air and alighted perfectly on a stone balustrade. A kid carrying a balloon looked as though he had stepped straight out of a Botticelli painting. Traffic lights shone like emeralds and rubies. Idling engines formed an urban symphony. The world is never more precious than when you may be scheduled to leave it.

I had my script made up and wandered back to Brewer Street like a man in a trance. I put John Coltrane on the turntable and stretched out on the sofa. My phone rang a couple of times and was ignored. In my dream I was a child picking up stones on a deserted beach. My dad asked if he could look in my bucket. The pebbles had turned into tiny yellow fish that we released into the shallows and watched swim away.

I woke at 9.30 p.m., my heart beating like a jackhammer. I concentrated on my breathing until it began to slow down. I had five missed calls. Four were from Odeerie. I pressed Redial and the fat man picked up immediately.

'You know I wish you'd answer your bloody phone, Kenny,' he grumbled. 'It would be nice to know what's going on from time to time.'

'Sorry, Odeerie, it's been a difficult afternoon.'

'Cork snap in the bottle, did it?'

'I haven't been drinking.'

'What, then?'

I took Odeerie through my appointment with Arbuthnot, including diagnosis, prognosis and relevant statistics. There were a few seconds of silence before he spoke.

'Christ, Kenny, I'm really sorry. How are you feeling now?'

'Still getting my head around it.'

'Yeah, well, that's only to be expected. Jump in a cab. I'll cook us something and you can sleep on the sofa bed.'

'No offence, Odeerie, but I'd prefer to be on my own.'

'Does your brother know?'

'I'm about to call him.'

'Okay, I'll ring Pam Ridley and say that you can't continue with the case.'

'Would you mind if I did that? I'm the one who should let her know.'

'No problem,' Odeerie said. 'Look, if you change your mind about coming round then all you have to do is pitch up. You know that, don't you?'

'Yeah, Odeerie,' I said. 'I know.'

◆ ◆ ◆

It was early morning in Hong Kong when I rang my brother. The call went to voicemail. I asked him to call me back when he got the chance. My tone must have indicated something was wrong as his name lit up the screen minutes later.

Malcolm became a copywriter after leaving school. Ten years later he co-founded his own ad agency. Now he's the major shareholder in one of the country's largest marketing consultancies. He got where he is through imagination, hard work and pragmatism. Once he'd absorbed my news, the latter quality took over.

He intended to contact Arbuthnot and make sure that my care was the best it could be. If that meant me travelling to the States then that was what would happen. I told him it probably made sense to stay where I was. He rang off, telling me not to worry more than I had to and that he'd call again the following day.

At 10.15, I rang Pam Ridley. I wanted to break the news as soon as possible that I couldn't carry on looking for her daughter's killer. She answered sounding groggy, but perked up when she heard my name.

'You got my message, then?'

'What message, Pam?'

'On your phone. About the photographs?'

'Photographs?'

'You know . . . the ones Em took out of the album.'

I recalled the spaces in Emily Ridley's photo album. It felt as though I'd seen it in a different lifetime instead of yesterday morning.

'Where were they?' I asked.

'Stuck in an envelope at the back of her chest of drawers. I found it when I was cleaning all her stuff out for the charity shop.'

'Are they interesting?'

'Yeah, they are, as a matter of fact. I reckon you need to come round and take a look at 'em, Kenny.'

'Actually, that's why I was calling, Pam. I'm afraid I'm not going to be able to come round because . . .'

Because what? Because I had to spend the next week in bed thinking about having my skull sliced open? At least working on the case would take my mind off of everything. And I wouldn't be doing anything stressful or overly exerting myself . . .

'You still there, Kenny?'

'Yes, Pam,' I said, 'Still here.'

'You were saying you couldn't come round . . . ?'

'I'll be with you at nine.'

'You sure about that?' she asked.

'Positive,' I replied.

After speaking to Pam I fell into a fitful doze. Had the phone not started buzzing then I may well have spent the rest of the night in the chair. The number was unidentified. Thinking it might be my brother calling back, I answered.

'Kenny Gabriel?' a man asked in a digitally synthesised voice.

'Who's this?'

'Castor Greaves.'

I sat bolt upright.

'I can't talk long, Kenny, so I'll get right down to it. You need to end your investigation and you need to stop talking to the press.'

'Who are you really?' I asked.

'Who I say I am.'

'Where are you calling from?'

'Nowhere you're going to find me.'

It flashed through my mind that Danny Abbott might be playing some kind of gotcha prank. Nevertheless, I carried on with the conversation.

'Did you kill Emily Ridley?'

Castor sighed. 'That doesn't matter, Kenny. If you don't stop what you're doing then the Road will make another move, and trust me, they won't fuck up twice.'

'You took the Golden Road?'

'What do you think?'

'I've no idea. You could be anyone.'

'That's true. And I guess it's up to you whether you believe me. All I can tell you is that they'll come for you, Kenny, and there won't be a thing I can do to help. And you'd better tell the fat guy to watch his step. He's on the list too.'

After which advice, 'Castor' terminated the call.

NINETEEN

Despite the pills, the fuzziness returned to my left eye during the night. While shaving, a shudder of nausea passed through me and I retched a dribble of acidic yellow liquid into the lavatory bowl. The idea of anything solid passing my lips in the opposite direction wasn't appealing. All this and not a drop of Monarch taken.

I wondered whether my late-night caller really had been Castor Greaves. That he hadn't tried to convince me of his bona fides suggested it might be, as did my gut reaction at the time. If anything, the caller had seemed keen to get the conversation over with rather than spin me a comprehensive yarn. Set against this was the fact that anyone with my number could have been on the end of the line.

Immediately on waking, I'd checked my phone to see if the conversation had happened at all. Sure enough, a two-minute call at 3.07 a.m. was showing in my Recents. Could I really be sure of its nature, though? I'd had my fair share of mental malfunctions recently.

Under normal circumstances I would have acted on Castor's advice and quit the case. But these were not normal circumstances. In a few days I might either be dead or wishing I were. If the Golden Road took me out a few days early then perhaps they'd be doing me a favour. And, of course, I'd promised Pam Ridley that I'd continue to search for her daughter's murderer.

Recent events had caused me to forget that I'd agreed to meet Saskia first thing. Her phone rang for a minute before going to voicemail. I left a message saying that something had come up and that I wouldn't be able to get to her until later in the day. If she called, then we could arrange a time. The fact that she wasn't picking up made me wonder if she was busy sleeping off an enthusiastic afternoon's drinking.

Riding the rail with the nine-to-fivers was out of the question. I eschewed the Northern Line in favour of a cab. Halfway over London Bridge, my vision normalised. Rain coursed down the windows. The Thames looked like a murky python slithering through the city, the buildings like brooding sentinels.

What I needed was an unshakeable belief in a benevolent deity, or the stoic's acceptance that life was to be endured rather than enjoyed. What I had was a hairball of anxiety and dread in my guts. So much for the everyday wonder of the world.

The weather conditions, or the lure of another story, had entirely dispersed the reporters from outside Pam Ridley's house. The short walk from the taxi to the front door left me damp and dishevelled. When Pam opened up, her eyes widened slightly.

'You all right, Kenny?'

'Fine,' I said. 'And you, Pam?'

'Yeah, I'm okay. Get inside, for God's sake.'

The gas fire was on full blast and the front room bakery-warm. The TV was tuned to a shopping channel on which a breathy presenter was extolling the benefits of a treadmill. Lying on a worn armchair was *The Jumbo Book of Crosswords*.

Pam entered the room with two steaming mugs. Also on the tray were a plate of chocolate biscuits and an A5 envelope. She laid the tray on a coffee table in front of the leather sofa. We sat down and she handed me a mug of strong tea.

'How's it going, then?' she asked.

'Slowly, I'm afraid.'

'What about all that stuff in the *Post* about the Golden whatsit having kidnapped Castor and him definitely being the one that murdered Em?'

'I'm afraid they made that up, Pam.'

'Yeah, I thought as much,' she said.

'On the plus side, Odeerie tracked down Emily's friend Davina. I'll be in touch with her today. Have the police told you anything?'

'Not a lot. I can't have Em's body for at least a week 'cos they've got to do more tests. I've started cleaning out her room for the charity shop, though. When that's done, I'm going to stay with my sister in Plymouth for a few days.'

'Are those the photographs?' I said, nodding at the envelope.

'Yeah,' Pam replied. 'I should probably take them to Shaheen, but I wanted to see what you thought first . . .'

I extracted around twenty photos from the envelope. In the first shot, Dean Allison's face had been obliterated by a flurry of ballpoint scars that in places penetrated the paper. Were it not for his distinctive haircut, it wouldn't have been possible to recognise him at all. In the next photo he was sat beside Emily at a table covered with plates of party food. BASTARD had been scrawled across his features.

Not a single photo was unscathed. In a couple, Dean's face had been removed entirely, and in one his eyes had been burned out by what had probably been the tip of a cigarette.

'Were any of him left in the albums?' I asked.

'They'd all been taken out,' Pam replied.

'Did Emily ever say that she was involved with Dean?'

'Nope. She never mentioned him. Must have been something going on, though. Why would she do that otherwise?'

'Dean said they were seeing each other before she took up with Cas.'

'Why didn't Em tell us?'

'Perhaps she didn't perceive the relationship as being significant. And we've only got Dean's word that she was going out with him at all. He could be making the whole thing up.'

'Then why did she do this to the photos?' Pam asked.

It was a question to which I had no ready answer. Instead I asked one of my own.

'Had they accidentally fallen behind the drawers?'

'No, they were stuck on a ledge at the side,' Pam said. 'You had to take the whole drawer out to get them. The police must have overlooked 'em when they searched Em's room after she went missing.' She leant forward. 'Did he kill her, Kenny?'

'I don't see how,' I said. 'Dean left the building while Emily was still inside, and he couldn't have returned without someone letting him in. Plus there's no way he could have avoided being caught re-entering on the CCTV footage.'

'Maybe he was in league with someone else.'

'Possibly,' I said. 'But God knows who.'

I gathered the pictures together and replaced them in the envelope, minus the shot in which Dean's eyes had been scorched out. 'Can you hang on to these for a couple of days before taking them to the police? I'd like to keep this one if I could.'

'Course you can,' Pam said. 'What you going to do with it?'

'Stick it under Dean Allison's nose.'

She nodded and took a sip of tea. 'Are we still all right for money? If you need more, I'll need to get it out of the bank before I go to Plymouth.'

'I'll have a word with Odeerie,' I said. 'Although we should be good for a few more days yet, and he can bill you retrospectively. You can pay with a cheque.'

Suddenly assailed with hunger, I wondered whether I'd be able to keep a chocolate digestive down. It's bad enough having to admit to a client that their case is progressing sluggishly without chundering all over the floor two minutes later.

'What's the matter?' Pam asked. 'You haven't touched your tea and you're staring at those biscuits like they're gonna jump off the plate and bite you.'

'I'm not feeling too hot. It's just a twenty-four-hour bug.'

Pam assessed my face like a referee deciding whether a punchy boxer is sufficiently compos mentis to continue. 'No, it ain't,' was her decision. 'You don't have to tell me what it is, but you've got more than a touch of Delhi belly.'

'How d'you know?'

'See it in your eyes.'

Like all expert interviewers, Pam Ridley knew when to shut up and let silence do the work.

'I've had a health scare,' I said. 'It means a big operation. It might go okay, but then again it might not.'

'Does that mean you could peg it?' Pam wasn't the type of woman to draw inferences from significant looks and pregnant pauses.

'There's a chance,' I said.

'When's it happening?'

'In a few days' time.'

'What about the case?'

'It'll help keep my mind off things.'

The wind had really blown up and rain was battering the window. The guy on the shopping channel had left the treadmill and was doing his best on a mini-trampoline. Pam picked up the remote control and put him out of his misery.

'Can I give you a bit of advice, Kenny?'

'Of course.'

'When Em died it was like the earth had swallowed me up. What stopped it being even worse was that everything was okay between us when it happened.'

'So, what's the advice, Pam?' I asked.

'If there's anything you haven't said or done then sort it out. Just in case.'

◆ ◆ ◆

Before calling an Uber, I nipped into Kat's Café on the parade. Three blokes in paint-spattered overalls were discussing something in what may have been Bulgarian. A guy sporting a goatee beard was tapping away at a laptop. He looked vaguely uneasy, like a migratory bird blown off course by freak weather conditions.

My stomach was gurgling like a drain. I ordered a bacon bap and a mug of coffee before settling down at a table strategically close to the gents.

My first call was to Odeerie. Usually the fat man responds with a mordant comment about what a pleasure it is to receive the occasional update. This time his attitude was a model of employerly concern. 'How are you feeling, Kenny?'

'Hopefully a lot better when Kat fetches my bacon sarnie.'

'Has your brother arranged a live-in nurse?'

'Not exactly. I'm in a greasy spoon round the corner from Pam Ridley's house. I've decided to continue working the case until I go into hospital.'

'What made you change your mind?'

'Couple of things. Firstly it'll give me something to think about other than you-know-what; secondly I had a call from Castor Greaves last night.'

'What?'

'Or at least someone pretending to be him. He said that if I didn't stop poking around and talking to the press then the Golden Road would come after me again, and that this time they wouldn't make a mistake.'

'Did it sound like Castor?'

'He disguised his voice.'

'Have you told the police?'

'What's the point?'

'Someone's made a threat against your life, Kenny.'

'Actually, it wasn't only my life. He mentioned you as well.'

A long pause in the conversation.

'By name?' Odeerie asked in a higher register.

'Not exactly. He said that the . . . He said you should watch your step.'

'That's it, then. We're off the job.'

'You're overreacting, Odeerie. You never set foot outside and you've got more locks on the front door than the Bank of England. How will they get to you?'

'They're the Golden Road, Kenny!'

'Or some chancer trying to scare us off.'

'Either way, you ought to let Shaheen know.'

'He won't take it seriously.'

'Then we should stop. It's not worth the risk.'

'What risk? I've not exactly got the best chances of making it to Christmas as it is. And if it really was Castor Greaves telling me to lay off then it means that we're getting close to something. And the other thing . . .'

'What, Kenny?'

'The other thing is that this could be the last chance I get to do something meaningful with my life. I'm not passing on it just because some tosser decides to yank my chain at three in the morning pretending to be Cas Greaves.'

There were a few moments of dead air and for a moment I thought Odeerie was going to pursue the matter. He went in a different direction.

'Why did you visit Pam?'

I told him about the defaced photographs of Dean Allison. 'Emily didn't sound like the kind of girl to burn the eyes out of her boyfriend's photograph because he didn't notice she'd had her hair done. In addition to which, her parents weren't aware she went out with him.'

'Maybe she didn't,' Odeerie said.

'Who knows? Anyway, the order of the day is that I'm going to visit Sweat Dog and see what he has to say. Then I'm going to see Dean.

If there's any time left over and I feel up to it, I'll use it to see Emily's friend Davina Jackson. Oh, and I need to put in an appearance with Saskia. She thinks that she's dug out something interesting from her old files.'

'Who the hell's Sweat Dog?' Odeerie asked.

'The roadie who was in the dressing room after the Emporium gig. He's running a tattoo parlour in Muswell Hill these days.'

'What will happen to the photographs?'

'Pam thinks she should take them to the police. I've asked her to hang on for a bit until I've had a chance to hear what Dean has to say.'

'Excellent idea,' Odeerie said. 'You should make as much progress as possible before handing it over to the cops. That way we get maximum publicity for the business. I don't suppose you've had any other thoughts on that, Kenny . . . ?'

I'd been wondering when the time was right to tell Odeerie that I'd agreed to write a book with Saskia. As a bacon bap and a cup of steaming coffee had just been plonked in front of me, I opted to postpone what might be a tricky conversation.

'Sorry, mate, the signal's breaking up. I'll speak to you later . . .'

The bap tasted sensational. More importantly, it stayed down. After wiping grease and tomato sauce from my lips I called the landline number for Davina Jackson. It went to voicemail. Next up was Still Life. The person who had answered my earlier call did so again.

'Can I speak to Dean Allison?'

'I'm afraid that won't be possible.'

'Is he in the workshop?' I asked.

'St Bart's Hospital, actually.'

◆ ◆ ◆

Dean had been attacked outside his house just before midnight. He'd suffered a fractured jaw and multiple contusions but was scheduled for discharge later that day. I clucked sympathetically and said that I was a long-standing customer. Robbie supplied his boss's home address in order that I could send flowers. I terminated the call when he asked which particular pieces I'd bought from the gallery.

It was a toss-up as to whether Justice for Animals had given Dean a pasting or whether it was a common-or-garden mugging. During the cab ride to Muswell Hill, I googled whether it's possible to speak with a wired jaw. Apparently Dean's lips might move but his face probably wouldn't. Something to look forward to.

The rest of the journey was spent pondering Pam's advice. There weren't many people I needed to square things away with. One benefit of a life unencumbered by commitment is that you don't have to worry about your emotional legacy.

Stephie was the exception. Somehow I needed to prevent her from marrying Jake Villiers. Was there any way I could persuade Pauline Oakley to give Stephie the lowdown on her fiancé? It was the only option that had any chance of working. As the cab passed the entrance to Ally Pally, I called Flummery's and asked to be put through to Pauline's room. Fleetwood Mac insisted that I made lovin' fun until interrupted by a ringing phone. I disconnected after a minute and redialled to ask if Pauline was in the hotel, claiming to be her cousin calling about a family emergency.

The receptionist promised to locate Pauline and have her ring me back. I thanked her and disconnected. The driver pulled up in front of a building sandwiched between a wine bar and a delicatessen. Its window had been blacked out. Above it was a sign in Germanic script: *Howl at the Moon – Tattoos and Piercings.*

Time to say hello to Sweat Dog.

TWENTY

The wall to my right had been decorated with framed pictures of tattoo designs including flowers, parrots, snakes, roadsters and – for the more traditionally minded – semi-naked women. The left wall had a full-length mirror complemented by a gallery of album covers including *On The Spot* by Mean.

The buzzing noise came from the implement held by a forty-something guy in a Motörhead T-shirt. Muscular arms were sleeve-tattooed and a Victorian patriarch would have envied his beard. The young woman in his chair had her right palm face down on a table as Beardy decorated her shoulder. 'Help you, mate?' he asked.

'I'm looking for Sweat Dog,' I said.

'You got an appointment?' I shook my head. Beardy switched off his ink gun and knocked on a door, above which hung an autographed picture of Slash.

'Someone to see you, Dog.' No answer. 'For fuck's sake,' Beardy muttered. He opened the door and shouted, 'Dog, there's someone here to see you . . .'

'Be right there,' came a transatlantic reply.

Sweat Dog was at least six foot six, and maybe an inch above that. Grey hair had been tied into a ponytail. He had a goatee beard and untamed eyebrows, and was wearing black jeans, scuffed motorcycle boots, and a leather waistcoat over a collarless shirt. Pale-pink hearing aids protruded from both ears.

'Kenny Gabriel,' I said, and offered my hand.

'Dog,' said Dog. 'How can I help you?'

'I have a few questions about Emily Ridley and Castor Greaves.'

'Great. Stick 'em in your ass and fuck off.'

Hardly the cooperative start I'd been hoping for. 'I'm not from the media, if that's what you think,' I said. 'I'm trying to find out who murdered Emily.'

Dog's watery blue eyes narrowed. He looked down at a forty-five-degree angle and examined my face. 'You're the guy who found her body, right?' he said.

'That's right. Now I'm trying to find out who killed her.'

'You think it was me?'

Dog may have been approaching pension age but he wasn't the kind of guy you accused of anything face to face. Not that we were face to face, exactly.

'All I'm looking for is any information that might help,' I said.

'If I knew anything useful I'd have said it by now.'

'I'm sure that's the case. But what's inconsequential to you could be significant when connected to something else.'

Dog fingered his straggly beard while Beardy's tool hummed like a demented wasp battling a windowpane. 'You got any ink?' Dog asked. As there was a steel rack containing bottles of the stuff only six feet away, it was a puzzling question.

'You're out of ink?' I said.

'No,' Dog said. 'I'm asking if you *have* any ink.' He pulled his shirtsleeve back to reveal an electric guitar on his forearm with a plethora of musical notes.

'Oh, you mean am I tattooed? No, I'm not,' I said, adding, 'I've got a thing about needles', in case Dog thought I was passing some kind of aesthetic judgement.

'Know what Harvey reckons?' Dog pointed at Beardy. 'Never trust anyone who don't have ink, which kinda leaves you with two options here, Lenny.'

'What are they?' I asked.

'Get some ink or take a hike,' Dog said.

'Can't we just have a chat? I'll happily pay for your time.'

Dog lowered his head. I repeated myself into what was presumably the better ear.

'That ain't the deal,' he said. 'And here's the rider, Lenny. Squeal and it's game over. Trust me, the best way around this needles issue is to take it like a man.'

'It's Kenny.'

'Say again . . .'

'It's Kenny. My name is *Kenny*.'

Dog removed a hearing aid that looked as though the NHS had made it in 1973. Holding it under the light, he adjusted something and pushed it back into place.

Beardy shook his head. 'You need new aids, Dog,' he said. 'You might as well shove a pair of walnuts in your ears.'

'Bullshit,' was his boss's opinion. 'We got a deal?' he said to me.

'How big does the tattoo have to be?' I asked.

'Small,' he said. 'I got someone in half an hour.'

'Where's the least painful place to have it?'

'Butt cheek,' was Dog's verdict.

'Seriously?'

'Seriously.'

'Okay,' I said. 'We have a deal.'

Dog handed me a folder. After flicking through half a dozen laminated pages, I pointed out a simple design that had three concentric circles. I tried not to watch while Dog loaded his gun with ink. Instead, I attempted to blot out the mental image of a needle flashing in and out of my lilywhite arse.

'Okay, Kenny,' he said. 'Assume the position.'

The dentist's chair turned out to be more like a massage table that hinged in the middle. A scalloped section afforded space for my head to hang. At least I wouldn't have to witness the desecration happening. I lowered my jeans and pants a discreet distance, only to have Dog fully expose the target zone.

'First I'll run a razor over you, then you'll feel the antiseptic wipe,' he said. 'You want to go left or right?'

'Surprise me.'

Something scraped across my left buttock, followed by a chilly sensation.

'I'm gonna start,' Dog said. 'Remember I don't hear too good, so speak up. Whine and you get to walk home with half a tattoo on your ass.'

I signified my understanding and the gun fired up.

Imagine someone dragging a broken plastic fork over your sunburned buttock while you're trying to hold an intelligible Q&A session with them. Then imagine not being able to make any sound of discomfort and having to bellow your questions. That gives you an inkling of what talking to Sweat Dog was like.

'When did you start working for Mean?' was my opener.

'When they toured to support *Charlie Rides Again*,' he replied over the electronic hum of the gun. 'So that would have been fall of '93.'

'What were they like?'

'JJ was a shit-hot guitar player, Cas was a decent vocalist, Chop could play pretty much any instrument under the sun, and Dean Allison was a sonofabitch.'

'Were they getting on well?'

'Dean played the gig and then did his own thing. JJ and Cas had known each other since they were kids and they had their own take on shit that left Chop out of the loop. Then Cas and Chop would piss off to write and it would be JJ left holding his dick.'

'Did he resent that?'

'He wasn't thrilled, put it that way.'

The needle found a tender spot, forcing me to stifle a cry of pain.

'Were there many arguments?' I asked.

'Would have been more, apart from Chop was really good at smoothing things down. If the guy hadn't been a musician, he could have joined the UN.'

'How did he manage it?'

'Whenever they wrote a song, Chop would invite JJ to input. Usually it would just be a couple of ideas about a guitar phrase or something. Not enough to get JJ a credit but enough to stop him feeling completely sidelined.' Dog switched off the gun. 'We ain't done,' he said. 'Just gotta make a few adjustments.'

I made use of the silence to ask a question at normal volume. 'What did you make of Emily?'

'Sweet kid. *On The Spot* had just been released when she first came on the scene. She was a looker, that's for sure. There were a lot of groupies around by then, and most of 'em wanted to fuck Cas's brains out. Em made him do the running.'

The gun resumed its buzz.

'I spoke to Dean Allison,' I said. 'He claimed that he was seeing Emily before she met Castor.'

The gun clicked out.

'He said what?' Sweat Dog asked.

I repeated myself, adding, 'His take on things is that she told Castor about the relationship and he killed her in a fit of rage. Does that sound at all likely, Dog?'

'Cas was the jealous type and he was fuckin' unpredictable.'

'Due to the drugs?'

'Not just that. He was turning into Jim Morrison. Quoting Rimbaud and Nietzsche all the time. Thinking he was some kind of guru communing with the universe. It was getting to the point that Em couldn't have a regular conversation with him.'

Dog switched the gun on. Immediately it bit into my arse again.

'Ever heard of the Golden Road?' I asked through gritted teeth.

'Sure.'

'You think there's anything in it?'

'Who knows?'

'A month before he disappeared,' I continued, 'Castor amalgamated all his assets and put them into a numbered account. There's no way I can find out what's going on with it. Maybe he took the Golden Road.'

'Or it could have been a tax dodge,' Dog said. 'Cas didn't like to throw his cash around. When I went back to the States, he stayed at my place to save on rent. Place looked like a squat when I got back. All kinds of crap lying around.'

'Such as?'

'Mostly books and compilation tapes. I had a clear-out a few years ago and gave 'em to JJ. He was the nearest thing Cas had to family.'

'Did the arguments ever turn physical?' I asked.

'Only once that I saw. They were in the green room after a gig. Outta the blue, JJ coldcocks Cas, after which JJ goes AWOL for a week and it looks like it's the end of the band. Then he shows up again and things are back to normal.'

'Any idea what sparked it off?'

'Nope. JJ's a hothead but that was outta character even for him.'

Was it? I thought back to the Junction club, when JJ had done much the same thing to the suits. He'd been provoked, but all the same . . .

'What do you think happened the night Em and Cas went missing?' I asked.

'If what Dean says is true, that's your answer right there. Cas killed Em and then offed himself in some outta-the-way spot. Jumped into a river or something.' The gun stopped buzzing. 'Only thing I know for sure is that you've got a minor masterpiece on your ass. Wanna check it out?'

I got off the chair and pulled my jeans to thigh height. Shuffling across the parlour floor like a convict in a chain gang, I examined my backside in the mirror.

'It's a bit fuzzy.'

'It'll sharpen when it heals,' Dog said.

There was a knock at the door. Beardy took the latch off and a guy wearing a camouflage jacket and trailing a Yorkshire terrier walked in. Dog selected a plaster and a tube of ointment from the shelf. He signalled for me to turn and lean against the chair.

'What was Chop's take on Castor's bust-up with JJ?' I asked while antiseptic balm was applied to my outraged buttock.

'The guy was really cut up. Chop's actually a couple of years younger than JJ and Cas, but it was like he was the only adult in the room.'

Dog eased the plaster into place.

'Okay, you're done, fella,' he said. 'Leave the dressing on for twenty-four hours. After that, moisturise it every day for a week. If it starts lookin' ugly, see a doctor.' He removed his latex gloves and dropped them into a swing bin. Then he put the ointment back on the shelf. 'Any of that help?' he asked.

'Maybe,' I said. 'I'll let you know.'

'Cool. Ninety-five pounds.'

'You're charging me?' I asked.

'Everyone pays,' Dog replied.

◆ ◆ ◆

I bargained Dog down by pointing out that the cost of my tattoo would be billed to Pam Ridley. This, combined with the fact that his next client was keen to get going, secured me a twenty per cent discount for cash. The demented Yorkie snapped at my ankles as I left the parlour. On the pavement, I checked my phone to find a message from Sebastian Regis at Flummery's asking me to call as soon as possible.

'Seb speaking,' he said, breezily.

'Kenny Gabriel,' I said. 'You left a message for me . . .'

'Yes, of course.' His tone became more downbeat. 'I believe that you're related to Ms Pauline Oakley, one of our guests. Is that the case?'

'Absolutely,' I said. 'Pauline's my cousin. I'm keen to get in touch with her, as our aunt's been taken gravely ill. Is it possible to put me through?'

'Unfortunately not. I'm afraid I have bad news, Mr Gabriel.'

'What is it?' I asked.

'Pauline was found dead this morning.'

TWENTY-ONE

Having delivered the information about Pauline Oakley's death, Sebastian was keen that I contact the police. They were the last people I wanted to speak to. After his condolences for my loss and my quite genuine expression of shock, I set to extracting as much information as possible. 'Who found her?' was my first question.

'I believe an early-morning jogger,' he replied, 'Pauline was discovered on Hampstead Heath. It appears she may have committed suicide.'

'You're sure it's her?'

'She was carrying ID, according to the police.'

'How did she do it?' I asked.

'It would be so much easier if you spoke to the officer in charge of the case,' Sebastian said, clearly uncomfortable with the conversation. 'I have the name and number if you could just bear with me . . .'

'Seb, all I want to know is how my cousin died. I think that's reasonable, don't you?'

'Of course,' he replied, and cleared his throat. 'Pauline hanged herself.'

'Did she leave a note?'

'Not that I'm aware of.'

'Was her room disturbed?'

'As a matter of fact, yes. We had a burglary last night. An intruder went through a couple of suites.'

'Had anything been taken? From Pauline's room specifically, I mean.'

'Difficult to say,' Seb replied. 'Why do you ask?' His suspicion indicated we were nearing the end of the conversation. I answered his question with one of my own.

'Was her laptop missing?'

'I'm afraid I can't discuss this matter any further.'

Seb terminated the call.

◆ ◆ ◆

What were the chances Pauline Oakley had decided to end it all on Hampstead Heath at the same time an intruder broke her room? Probably about the same as the CCTV cameras in Flummery's getting a decent shot of the intruder's face or her laptop still being around.

There was no longer any way to bring Jake to book for murdering Arnie Atkinson, or prevent him marrying Stephie, at least not one that I could think of. But then what had I expected? The ruthless and the rich get away with pretty much anything they want to in life, unless they're careless or unlucky, that is. Jake Villiers was neither.

I lit up a Marlboro and gazed at the citizenry of Muswell Hill. Some were ferrying shopping bags to cars, others staring into estate agent windows. A little girl tripped along holding her mother's hand and trailing a pink scooter. It was the everyday world of those who had set a steady course early in life and were reaping its rewards.

Could I have been the gent in the tweed jacket supervising a couple of workmen loading a walnut escritoire into a van? In a parallel universe maybe the kid with the scooter was visiting Grampie Kenny and the guy with a tattooed arse didn't exist. Pauline Oakley hadn't died mysteriously and Stephie was in the kitchen icing a birthday cake. And Jake Villiers was slopping out in Wormwood Scrubs.

◆ ◆ ◆

During the cab ride to visit Dean Allison, I called Saskia. Voicemail again. Presumably the exciting 'discovery' had been no such thing and she was either too embarrassed to speak to me or too hungover to be able to. I left another message to the effect that I'd be unable to visit until that evening and then called the Junction club. JJ answered immediately.

'Hi JJ, it's Kenny.'

'For fuck's sake, you're over an hour late!'

'Am I?'

A pause, during which the only thing I could hear on the line was the faint sound of Buddy Guy singing 'Stone Crazy'. 'You're not the bloke delivering the mixers?' JJ asked.

'No,' I said. 'I came to see you a few days ago. Pam Ridley retained—'

'Yeah, I remember,' he said. 'What d'you want?'

'Another chat. Obviously things have changed in light of recent events . . .'

'Congratulations. You found Em's body. What's it got to do with me?'

'I've just spent some time with an old colleague of yours . . .'

'Who's that?'

'Sweat Dog.'

Buddy Guy went into a guitar solo that JJ didn't talk over for a good five seconds. 'What did Dog have to say?' he asked eventually.

'Quite a bit. Some of which I'd like to discuss with you . . .'

'Go on, then.'

'Face to face.'

'When and where?' JJ asked. The aggression had morphed into truculence, but you'd need a tin ear not to detect an undertone of anxiety.

'Two o'clock tomorrow at the Vesuvius Club, Greek Street. That work for you?'

'Whatever,' he grunted.

◆ ◆ ◆

The cab had reached the King's Road when I checked Google for any mention of Pauline Oakley. Her body had been found near the bathing ponds. The police hadn't issued a statement, but it was assumed the dead woman had committed suicide.

The only hope I had was that the break-in at Flummery's might seem too much of a coincidence even to an overworked cop. And yet it sounded as though Jake (or more likely an accomplice) had covered his tracks by burgling several rooms rather than just Pauline's. I was wondering if an anonymous call might at least provoke the constabulary to ask a few questions, when the cabbie pulled up.

Number 9 Chartwell Street was one of several two-up two-down cottages built in Chelsea between the wars. Back then they had been modest purchases; now you would need a couple of million to afford one of the pastel-coloured buildings.

Dean Allison's was candyfloss pink with a sky-blue front door. The window box had some hardy shrub varietal growing in it and the black curtains had been drawn. Options on the front door were a brass dolphin-shaped knocker in its centre or a bell attached to the side. I brought the dolphin's tail down firmly, several times.

'Open up, Dean,' I said loudly. 'I've a photo you'll be interested in.'

Dean's left eye had taken a direct hit. At the centre of a swollen red pouch was a slit that he may or may not have been able to see through. The grazing around his temple was extensive and there was a plaster stretched across the bridge of his nose.

'What photo?' he asked, like a rubbish ventriloquist.

The sitting room was small and immaculate. Wallpaper featured a jungle scene from which peeped parrots, monkeys and tigers. A pair of green chesterfield sofas took up a lot of floor space, as did an intricately woven Turkish rug. Above the fireplace hung a large mirror that gave the illusion of depth. The stifling temperature, combined with the exotic wallpaper, made me feel in need of a panama hat and a malaria shot.

'Take a seat,' Dean said. On a side table by one sofa lay a box of co-codamol, a bottle of Glenlivet, an empty glass and an iPad. I chose its opposite number, hoping that the booze and the pills were more likely to make him loquacious than leery.

'Who attacked you?' I asked after Dean had lowered himself down with a degree of discomfort that suggested the blows he'd taken weren't exclusively to the head.

'Take a wild guess,' he said.

'Justice for Animals?'

Dean nodded and immediately wished he hadn't.

'Have the police arrested anyone?' I asked.

'I didn't involve them.'

'Why not?'

'What's the point?'

'Did you get a look at whoever did it?'

'No. They attacked me from behind when I was leaving the shop. One minute I was locking up, the next I was flat-out on the pavement. If someone hadn't interrupted him, then God knows what would have happened.'

The sound of trumpeting elephants and whooping chimpanzees emerged from the walls. Judging by Dean's expression, he wasn't hearing them. I shook them out of my head and continued with the questions.

'What time was this?'

'About ten thirty.'

Wikipedia had been right. Dean's wired jaw allowed his lips to move but his face was immobile, and speaking clearly caused him discomfort. Shame.

'Did the witness who intervened get a look at your attacker?' I asked.

'Too dark.'

Greg Keen

'But it was just one person?'

'Yes.'

'Definitely male?'

He pointed to his jaw. 'You think a woman did this?'

'You've no real proof it was the JFA, then?' I said, ignoring the sexism. 'It could easily have been an opportunist mugger or someone with a grudge.'

'What kind of grudge?'

I slipped my hand into my jacket and produced Emily's photo. 'This kind.'

Dean leant forward in order to get a better look at the picture. 'Where did you get this?' he asked after scrutinising it for a few seconds.

'Emily's mother found it. To be fair that's the only one that's actually had the eyes burned out. The others had "bastard", "arsehole" or "shithead" scrawled across them. You know – the kind of thing besotted young women often write.'

'Just the photographs?' Dean asked, which was a curious question.

'What else were you expecting?'

'Nothing,' he replied. 'Nothing at all.'

Dean laid the photo on the arm of the sofa. He unscrewed the Scotch bottle and poured himself a shot without offering me one. It made me especially delighted that a third of the glass's contents spilled down his shirt when he tried to drink it.

'What d'you think this proves?' he asked, brushing himself down.

'That you and Emily weren't star-crossed lovers.'

Had Dean been able to smile, I think he would have. He appeared more relieved than stressed. Odd bearing in mind what I'd just confronted him with.

'It proves nothing of the sort,' he said.

'Really? Convince me.'

'I don't have to convince you, but if it gets you out of my bloody hair . . .' He took a more careful hit on his drink. 'Emily probably defaced the photos when I finished the relationship. Hell hath no fury like a woman scorned . . .'

'*You* stopped seeing *her*?'

'Didn't I tell you that?'

I shook my head. 'I thought you broke up when she met Castor.'

'God, no. We were well and truly over by then. Emily was physically stunning but mentally vacuous. Eventually I became bored with the tedious conversations and said we should go our different ways.'

'How did she react?'

He handed the photo back.

'Badly, as you can see . . .'

Fifteen minutes ago Dean had been visibly anxious. Now he was as relaxed as a man with a busted jaw probably gets. He looked at his watch.

'Kenny, I'm sorry for what happened to Emily and I hope that you find out who was responsible. But I don't know any more than I've already told you . . .'

'Thanks for your time,' I said. 'I'll see myself out.'

TWENTY-TWO

During my time with Dean it had become properly dark. I felt like ordering a pizza, having a bath and rubbing a tube of Sudocrem into my aching behind. Stereophonic wallpaper was probably a sign that I should down tools for the day, and possibly for good. All that stopped me was that I still hadn't heard from Saskia.

When my third call of the day to her went to her voicemail, I hailed a cab and instructed its driver to take me to Pegler's Wharf. The traffic was flowing like cement so I used the time to phone Davina Jackson. The man who answered sounded as though he had just been woken. He asked me to hang on. A minute later the receiver was picked up. 'Davina speaking.'

'Hello, Davina, my name's Kenny Gabriel. I'm calling in connection with an old friend of yours . . . Emily Ridley.'

'How did you get this number?'

'I'm not from the press,' I said reassuringly. 'I'm working on behalf of Pam Ridley. You're probably aware that her daughter's body was discovered recently . . .'

Given the amount of media coverage, this was tantamount to saying that she was probably aware the sun rose this morning. It made Davina's reaction all the more surprising.

'They found Em?' she asked after a moment's silence.

'Er, yes, it's been in the news a fair bit.'

'I'm just back from a yoga retreat. Where was she?'

'In a heating duct on the roof of the Emporium club.'

'Someone murdered her?' Davina's voice sounded as though it was being transmitted by ancient equipment over a vast distance.

'The police haven't confirmed that yet, although it's hard to draw any other conclusion,' I said. 'I'm a private investigator working for Pam Ridley—'

'I'm not talking to you,' Davina Jackson said. 'I'm not talking to anyone.'

'I fully understand what happened was a long time ago but—'

'Do *not* ring this number again,' she said, and terminated the call.

Not many relish being dragged into a murder inquiry. When it's as high-profile as Emily Ridley's, the number approaches zero. And yet the vehemence of Davina Jackson's refusal was unusual. Was it purely that she didn't want the publicity, or had some other factor caused her to put the phone down?

Ten minutes before we were scheduled to arrive at Pegler's Wharf, I called Odeerie. The fat man answered straight away. 'How are you, Kenny?' he asked.

'Not great,' I said. 'I've just had my arse tattooed.'

Not the answer Odeerie had been expecting. Dead air reflected this. I delivered a digest of my encounter with Sweat Dog followed by a résumé of my interview with Dean Allison, including details of the injuries he'd sustained.

'Dean thinks the JFA beat him up?' the fat man asked.

'Yeah,' I said. 'But there was no positive ID, so it could well have been someone else. If the guy hadn't been interrupted then he would have kept on going.'

'You don't think it might have been the Golden Road?' Odeerie asked.

'Nope. Dean said there was no specific threat and I believe him.'

'A mugging?'

'Muggers don't go to town like that.'

'Probably was the JFA then,' Odeerie said, relief in his voice. 'The animal rights brigade are a right bunch of nutters.'

'Apart from Dean was lying about something. Or he wasn't being entirely truthful, which amounts to the same thing.'

'How d'you know?'

'Eye tracking calibration.'

This brought a sigh from Odeerie. 'I wish I'd never sent you on that NLP course,' he said. 'You can't spot porkies by the way people blink. It's psychobabble bullshit.'

'It worked on you.'

'That was just luck. What was Dean lying about?'

'His relationship with Emily. He said that he was the one to finish things. She went nuts and that's why she defaced his photographs.'

'Mmm, I dunno, Kenny,' Odeerie said. 'None of this adds up to anything concrete, does it? Did this Sweat Dog character give you anything useful at all?'

The fat man's scepticism put the kibosh on me telling him the one thing Dog had mentioned that might prove significant. I'd check it out personally first.

'Not specifically, but I just finished chatting to Davina Jackson.'

'And?'

'She hadn't heard that Emily Ridley's body had been found. When I mentioned it, something spooked her and she told me not to get in touch again.'

'What d'you think that was?'

'No idea, but I'll pay her a visit tomorrow.'.

'Don't hassle her, Kenny. The last thing we want to do is interest the police.'

The prospect of an unscheduled visit from the law was a constant anxiety for Odeerie. It might lead to an examination of his hard drives, on which there would likely be multiple transgressions of the Data Protection Act. I assured him that I'd be discreet.

'What are you doing now?' he asked.

'On my way to see Saskia Reeves-Montgomery at Pegler's Wharf.'

'Okay, well, call me if it's anything I should know about, and go straight home afterwards. You need your sleep, Kenny.'

'Tucked up by ten,' I promised.

I could hear a thumping bassline before I'd walked through the gate at Pegler's Wharf. A party was taking place on a barge decked out in balloons and bunting. The aroma of barbecuing meat caused my stomach to turn. A woman in a pirate's hat gestured at me to come aboard. I shook my head and she responded with an exaggerated shrug of disappointment.

Lights were on in the *Anna Marie*. I rapped on the door and waited for a minute. Then I knocked again. Still nothing. I tapped on a glass porthole and shouted Saskia's name. Silence. Was she on the party boat? I was about to retrace my steps when I detected a smell considerably less appetising than griddled sausages and chicken.

A mental image of Saskia with a lit Camel in one hand and a glass of Teacher's in the other came to mind. It was displaced by one of her passed out while the sofa went up in flames. Several bangs on the toughened-glass porthole brought no response.

The lock splintered on the third kick. I descended into the living quarters. The desk had been overturned and there were documents all over the floor. Half the books and vinyl had been swept from the shelves, one of which hung by a single bracket.

Saskia's face was crimson and lurid. The left eye was blistered over; the other stared sightlessly up at me. Blood and brain matter had congealed around an indentation above her temple. The electric iron had burned through the rug and the rubber underlay. Had the fuse not blown then the entire boat might have gone up in flames. Whoever had killed Saskia had hopefully done so before applying the red-hot element to her face. But what would have been the point in that?

My first instinct was to leg it. Not because the killer might still be on the boat, more that it was the natural reaction to put as much distance between me and something so horrific that it possessed an almost cartoonish quality. I closed my eyes and counted to five before opening them again. Sadly, I wasn't hallucinating.

After withdrawing a carving knife from a block in the galley, I searched the rest of the *Anna Marie*. Having drawn a blank I returned to the cabin, panting as though I'd been on a cross-country run instead of prowling around a deserted boat. Castor Greaves had said that I needed to stop investigating or face the consequences from the Golden Road. Had Saskia received a similar call and chosen to disregard it? If so, what had happened to her might well soon be happening to me. And Odeerie.

After covering Saskia with my jacket, I called the emergency services and explained what I'd found and where I'd found it. I was advised to stay where I was, not to move anything and that help was on its way. I stood by the door and lit a cigarette. The nicotine hit soothed my jangling nerves and allowed me time to take in the chaos more objectively. Saskia's laptop had gone, although her printer remained on a low pedestal. I noticed there was document under its lid at around the same time as the sound of pounding boots first became audible. I folded the piece of yellowing newsprint and transferred it to the back pocket of my jeans.

Seconds later, the first cop barrelled through the door.

TWENTY-THREE

The last time I'd seen DCI Tony Shaheen he had been immaculately turned out in a dark-blue suit, polished Oxfords and a carefully knotted tie. Sartorial standards had slipped. The man facing me over the table looked as though he hadn't slept much in the last four days. His suit jacket had been draped over his chair and there wasn't a tie in sight. The shadows under his eyes looked like they had been stencilled on. If he weren't being such a pain in the arse, I might even have felt sorry for him.

The DCI flicked through my three-page statement. The frown and occasional shake of the head suggested that he didn't much care for its style or content.

'Okay, if you're happy with that then sign and date it,' he said, sliding the document over the table. I did so at the place where it said that I believed the statement I had given to be true, and returned the sheets to him.

'Can I go now?' I asked.

'I've got a few more questions,' Shaheen said.

'I thought I was purely here as a witness. If you want to interview me officially, then shouldn't I be cautioned and assigned a duty solicitor?'

Shaheen stared at the ceiling as though considering the point.

'We could go down that route,' he said. 'Or you could leave and then I decide that, on refection, I'd like to pull you back in to be interviewed as a suspect in a murder investigation.' He looked at his watch. 'Maybe in a couple of hours' time . . .'

'Okay,' I said. 'What d'you want to know?'

'You've found two bodies in less than a week. That doesn't happen, Kenny. Not without there being a reason.' Shaheen held my statement up by its corner as though it had been dusted in anthrax. 'This doesn't come close to giving me the reason.'

He laid the document back on the table and composed himself.

'Tell me about your relationship with Saskia Reeves-Montgomery.'

'*Again?*'

'Again.'

I sighed, to underscore that we'd already been over this three times in the last forty minutes. 'Saskia wanted me to contribute to a book about Castor Greaves and Emily Ridley. She called to say that she'd found something interesting in her files that she'd like me to take a look at. I called back and said that I'd come round as soon as possible. Check the messages on her phone if you haven't already.'

'You've no idea what the something was?'

'None at all. She said that she'd show me when we met.'

Shaheen sniffed several times, as though something malodorous had just come to his attention. 'Let's move on to the fact that someone attempted to murder you on the last occasion you went to Pegler's Wharf,' he said.

'That could have been an accident.'

'Not what you said yesterday.'

'Telling you about that was Saskia's idea. She thought that I should let you know what had happened in order that we had a record for the book.'

'So it wasn't an attempt on your life?'

'Actually, I think it might have been.'

'Then why didn't you follow through, Kenny?'

'What was the point? I didn't see whoever was responsible and there was no one else around. I thought you'd have told me I was imagining things.'

'We could have examined CCTV in the area or asked the residents if anyone suspicious had been hanging around the marina. All of which might have prevented Saskia Reeves-Montgomery's death. And if there's anything else you could be telling me that you're choosing not to, then I strongly suggest you reconsider your position. *Is* there anything else you haven't told me, Kenny?'

'Absolutely nothing,' I said.

Shaheen drummed his fingers on the table. It may have been something they taught him to do in Interrogation 101, or just a habit. Either way, it was bloody irritating. I was glad when there was a knock on the door of the interview room. A uniformed officer poked his head around it. 'Can I have a word, sir?'

'Can't it wait?' Shaheen asked testily.

'Not really, sir.'

While Shaheen was away, the temptation to whip the newspaper article out of my pocket and take a look was almost overwhelming. Thankfully I managed to resist the urge, as the DCI was back in the room less than a minute later.

'Okay, you're free to go,' he said without retaking his seat. 'I'll have a copy of your statement made and arrange a lift home for you.'

'You're not arresting me, then?' I asked.

'Don't tempt me,' Shaheen replied.

◆ ◆ ◆

Odeerie shoved a mug of coffee in front of me and sat down. The clock in the office showed 12.45 a.m. The fat man is a world-class insomniac,

169

probably because the most exercise he gets during the day is walking to the fridge and back.

He'd left several messages asking me to call, as reports were already beginning to circulate on social media that there had been an incident at the Pegler's Wharf marina involving Saskia Reeves-Montgomery. I'd given him an overview as to what had taken place since we last spoke and he had insisted that I come round.

The only reason I'd agreed was laid on a steel table. The page had been taken from the *Essex Courier* in June 2001. The headline was BLAZE AT POP STAR'S HOUSE. The picture accompanying the piece showed two fire engines and an ambulance in attendance at Mickleton Lodge. The article read:

> *Fire broke out at the country retreat of ex-Mean member and Emmy Award-winning writer Chop Montague shortly before dawn on Tuesday morning. Mr Montague's gardener raised the alarm and assisted his employer and a guest to safety. The Epping Fire Brigade were called to the scene at 5.15 AM and were successful in saving the building's superstructure. However, some memorabilia and paintings were thought to have been destroyed. A man in his thirties was treated locally for the effects of smoke inhalation, although not taken to hospital. In a statement released through his management company, Mr Montague thanked the emergency services for their prompt attendance.*

In the photograph, Chop was standing in front of his house wearing a coat over a T-shirt and tracksuit bottoms. A few feet away from him was a woman wrapped in a blanket and a man – presumably the heroic gardener – clutching an oxygen mask while being attended by a paramedic. It was the kind of moderately significant news event that made it into the local press. Nothing to get excited about.

Except that the woman was a dead ringer for Emily Ridley.

'It can't be her, Kenny,' Odeerie said, biting into a doughnut. 'She'd been dead over six years by the time that was taken.'

'Assuming the body in the duct was Emily's.'

'Of course it was. The police might not be geniuses, but they're hardly likely to get something like that wrong.'

Odeerie dispatched the second half of the doughnut and wiped the jam off his lips with a tissue. I took a sip of coffee and positioned the magnifying glass over the photograph again. Emily Ridley's face stared back at me. Except it couldn't be. It was just someone who happened to look very, very like her.

'How d'you know that was what Saskia wanted to show you?' Odeerie asked. 'She might have just been copying stuff and left it on there. I do it all the time.'

'You don't think it's weird that it just happens to be a photograph of Emily Ridley with Chop Montague standing outside a blazing house?'

'For God's sake, Kenny, there's no way it can be—'

'Yeah, yeah, okay. Even if it isn't her then it's still interesting.'

'Why?'

'Because it might indicate that Chop was obsessed with Emily Ridley. That's why he dated someone who looked exactly like her six years after her death.'

Odeerie's brow crinkled. 'And you think that proves he murdered her?'

'He didn't come back for twenty minutes after leaving the Emporium dressing room. That's enough time to kill Emily, hide her body in the heating duct and then go back and say that he couldn't find Castor.'

Odeerie's brow became positively corrugated. 'Why would he do that?'

'Maybe he came on to her and she knocked him back.'

'Chop Montague is a judge on a TV talent show. He's not some cold-eyed killer on the quiet.'

'If working for you has taught me one thing it's that people surprise you.'

Odeerie sat back and placed his hands over his chest.

'Kenny, you've just had a traumatic experience and you aren't in the best shape right now. It's not surprising your mind's running wild on this one. And you might have a point that Saskia thought it was odd that Chop Montague was seeing someone who looked a bit like Emily Ridley—'

'A lot like Emily Ridley.'

'Okay, a lot like her. But from what you've told me, Saskia Reeves-Montgomery was an eccentric with a penchant for the dramatic. People like that often pump things up beyond their usual significance. Makes them feel important.'

'That doesn't alter the facts.'

'Right, so you think Chop Montague found out Saskia had this photograph and decided to torture her with an electric iron and cave her head in?'

'I'm not saying that,' I admitted.

'Thank God. Because what's a lot more likely is that some toerag thought she had money hidden away somewhere. That's why he took the iron to her face and nicked the laptop. You read about this kind of thing in the papers every week. They ought to bring back capital punishment, there's far too many bleeding-heart liberals—'

'Can we look online for any more pictures of the fire?'

'What will that prove?'

'It'll only take a minute . . .'

Odeerie sighed before switching on one of his desktop computers. While it booted up, my mind chewed over something Shaheen had said at West End Central. Would Saskia still be alive had I reported my dunking at Pegler's Wharf? Probably not, but it might have made a difference. Should I be continuing with the investigation at all bearing in mind my condition? These weren't the happiest of thoughts.

Odeerie's pudgy fingers flew over the keyboard like a demon pianist's. Within a few seconds we were looking at the results on the screen.

'Looks like it's the only picture,' he said. 'Hang on . . .'

The same image of the smouldering house enlarged. The mystery woman still looked like Emily Ridley's doppelgänger. More so, if anything. Chop's expression was also better defined.

'Christ,' I said, 'it's like a vampire staring at a crucifix.'

'Or a public figure who hates having his privacy invaded.'

'Okay, but you have to admit that mystery girl looks like Emily.'

More lightning finger work from Odeerie brought a shot of Emily Ridley up on the screen. He alternated between the fire shot and the studio shot several times.

'Yeah,' he said, 'she does a bit.'

'Is the photo credited?'

Odeerie shook his head. 'Probably a freelance pap listening to the police frequencies or a cop making a few quid on the side.'

'What about the reports?'

There was only one other article concerning the fire at Mickleton Lodge, written a week after the event. It didn't say much more than the *Courier* piece, apart from that the fire had probably been started by a faulty kitchen appliance.

'Can you print a decent copy of the photo?' I asked.

'What are you going to do with it?' Odeerie said.

'Show Chop Montague.'

'And what d'you think he's going to say? "You got me bang to rights, Kenny. I killed an anonymous woman and concealed her body in a disused heating duct. Then I imprisoned Emily Ridley and switched the DNA records in the police lab. If only the bastard Moulinex hadn't blown a fuse, I might have got away with it . . ."'

'Of course not.'

'Or maybe he'll break down and say that he murdered Emily in a fit of fury because she objected to him goosing her in the corridor. Then he came back to the dressing room in the Emporium and suggested that everyone start looking for Castor Greaves because that's just the kind of psycho he is.'

'All I want to do is check out his reaction.'

Odeerie buried his face in his hands. 'Which way people's eyes go is cobblers, Kenny. All Chop is likely to do is call the police and tell them that you've been harassing him. It won't get you anywhere.'

'You don't know that for sure.'

The siren of a passing emergency vehicle cut into the silence of the office and then faded away. The fat man chewed his bottom lip while staring at me thoughtfully.

'Let's quit the job, Kenny. Pam Ridley asked you to find her daughter and that's what you've done. We've both had death threats and you're in no shape to continue.'

'What about the money?'

'There'll be other clients. Your health is more important.'

It may have been the softness in Odeerie's voice or the gentle squeeze he gave my arm that caused the energy to depart from me like the air from a ruptured balloon. I was a man in late middle age who needed to face up to his own mortality.

'You're right,' I said. 'Time to call it a day.'

Odeerie urged me to stay the night at his flat. It was tempting, but the walk from Meard Street to Brewer Street would only take ten minutes and I wanted to wake up in my own bed. Assuming I managed to get any sleep, that was. Saskia's mutilated face peered out at me from the dull plate glass of each shop window I passed.

The wind bit and the streets were deserted. *The worst is not so long as we can say 'This is the worst'*, Shakespeare had it. I wasn't convinced that it applied to me.

Saskia Reeves-Montgomery had died at the hand of a sadist who would probably walk away scot-free. A man who had almost certainly killed someone and faked her suicide would soon be marrying the only person I had ever cared about, and maybe the only person who had ever cared about me.

In a few days' time, someone would place a mask over my face and I would descend into oblivion. If I emerged at all then it might be in an altered state that meant having to learn how to wipe my own backside again. Best-case scenario was that, after a few weeks' convalescence, I returned to what I'd been doing for the last six years.

I'd just completed this cheerful life-audit when I saw her hovering a foot off the ground at the corner of Lexington Street. The wind ruffled the feathers of her outstretched wings. A dazzling white dress finished mid-thigh. Fishnet stockings stretched over slim legs into a pair of gold patent-leather Doc Marten 1460s.

In her left hand was a foot-long cigarette holder and in her right was an open bottle of Moët grasped at the neck. Vintage. Her fluorescent smile would have been flawless had an incisor not been missing on the left-hand side.

Her wings flapped a couple of times to correct a wobble. She took a swig from the bottle. Its contents fizzed and cascaded down her front, causing the material of her dress to become translucent. Her nipples stiffened and she looked at her breasts in apparent shock. Then she stuck out her tongue and winked at me.

A car alarm went off and my pissed angel – if that's what she was – disappeared as though she had never been there, which, of course, she hadn't. Either the tumour or exhaustion, or probably both, was causing me to seriously trip out.

Whether I was in any fit state to carry on with the case occupied my mind for the remainder of the journey back to the flat. And it would probably have occupied it for the rest of the night had a more familiar figure not been standing on my doorstep.

TWENTY-FOUR

Stephie crossed her legs and took a drag on the Marlboro. 'Love what you've done to the place, Kenny,' she said. 'You've emptied the ashtray and that old beer can used to be on the coffee table. It's so much more effective on the TV.'

'Different can,' I pointed out.

'Well, you've got to spend a few quid to get things right,' Stephie said. 'Nice that you've left the wallpaper curling by the door, though. Be a shame to destroy original features in a room like this. And the way you've resisted putting a shade on that light bulb is a stroke of genius. Not many have your aesthetic vision.'

'Did you come round to take the piss?' I asked.

'Nope,' Stephie replied. 'But now that I'm here . . .'

During the fifteen minutes we'd been in the flat, I'd poured each of us a large Macallan from the bottle she'd brought and then refreshed our glasses. Stephie gave up smoking years ago, but usually made an exception when I waved a Marlboro packet under her nose.

We had chatted about this and that, although I still wasn't entirely sure as to the reason for her visit.

'Thanks for this,' I said, taking a hit on the whisky. 'It isn't every day I get to drink decent malt.'

'It's certainly better than your usual rubbish.' Stephie held her empty tumbler out. 'Go on, pour me another . . .'

'You sure, Steph? You've had two biggies already.'

'If I can't have a few drinks on my day off, when can I?'

I sloshed more Macallan into her glass and did the same to mine. Candy is dandy but liquor is quicker, as Ogden Nash so aptly put it.

'Cheers,' she said. We clinked glasses and leant back on the sofa.

'Any particular reason you're here?' I asked. 'Not that you need one . . .'

'I wanted to apologise for what I said in Assassins. No one said you had to come to Manchester, and it's stupid that I've been so mardy about it since getting back.'

'It wasn't the right time, Steph. I was feeling like shit and all I wanted to do was hole up in here until I felt better. Then I fully intended to get on the train—'

'Yeah, you said all that,' Stephie interrupted. 'And to be fair, if you had turned up then I probably wouldn't have met Jake.'

'You wouldn't have wanted to meet Jake.'

I fully expected Stephie to disagree with this, potentially with extreme prejudice. Instead she stubbed her cigarette out and took a drink.

'What did you mean when you said that you need to know people well before they show their true colours?' she asked. 'I've been with Jake for nine months. Don't you think that's long enough?'

'Do you?'

'Yes, as a matter of fact. Part of getting married is discovering more about one another as each day passes. That's how it was with me and Don . . .'

Stephie's first husband had died in a car crash. He'd been a kind, intelligent and decent man, as opposed to a psychopathic nutjob.

'You and Don were in a hurry to get married because you were pregnant,' I said, what with all of the above being unverifiable. 'Why the rush with Jake?'

'We're not as young as we used to be and we want to get on with it. And once we're hitched, he plans to get me involved with the business.'

'Did you know Jake owns the Emporium?'

'What?'

'Has done since 2002.'

'What are you suggesting, Kenny? That he had something to do with Emily Ridley's murder? Because if you are—'

'Just wondered if you knew about it, that's all.'

Stephie pulled out a small velvet box from her bag. 'Check that out,' she said.

The engagement ring must have cost a mint. Just as well Jake had saved himself a few hundred thousand by murdering Pauline Oakley.

'Why aren't you wearing it?' I asked.

'Needs resizing.' Stephie snapped the box closed and placed it on the arm of the sofa. 'My point is . . . if Jake didn't love me, then why would he give me a fuck-off rock like that?'

She knocked back the rest of her drink. I followed suit.

'Were we in love, Steph?'

'What kind of question's that?'

'You don't have to answer if you don't want to . . .'

Stephie put her empty glass on the floor and took a deep breath.

'I was gutted when you didn't show up in Manchester,' she said, slurring her words slightly. 'You didn't return my calls and you couldn't even be arsed to email or even text that you weren't coming.'

'I did try to call a—'

'Trying isn't the same as doing, Kenny,' Stephie interrupted, her face flushed with annoyance and booze. 'Christ, you'll stop at virtually nothing when it comes to tracking down someone you've never even met, but not when it's someone you allegedly want to spend the rest of your life with.'

'Is that a yes or a no, then?' I asked.

Suddenly our mouths were together and tongues intertwined. Our hands were roving over each other like a pair of wrestlers trying to find a competitive hold. It felt like old times. At least it did until Stephie pushed me away.

'I can't do this.'

'Why not?'

'Because I'm pissed!' She stood up. 'God knows why I came here. It was a stupid thing to do.'

'No, it wasn't.'

'I'm in love with Jake and we're getting married.'

'You're making a mistake,' I said.

'Not jumping into bed with you? I don't think so, Kenny.'

'That's not what I meant . . .'

Stephie's eyes narrowed. 'What *do* you mean?' she asked.

'There's something you don't know about Jake Villiers.'

'You told me. He owns the Emporium. So what?'

'Not that.'

'What, then?'

'Twenty years ago he was with a woman called Pauline Oakley. He knocked her around a bit and put her into hospital when she refused to commit a tax fraud in order to save the company. She kept the documents and tried to blackmail him last week. I'm pretty sure Jake murdered her and made it look like suicide.'

Stephie broke a short but intense silence.

'Are you out of your fucking mind?' she asked.

'And I think he also had a business competitor called Arnie Atkinson killed as well,' I said, to put her fully in the picture. 'Although I can't prove that.'

'But the rest you can?'

'Not now Pauline's dead.'

Whatever reaction I'd expected from Stephie, it wasn't that she'd burst into laughter. 'You seriously thought I'd believe that crock of shit?'

'It's true, Steph.'

'No, it isn't. Jake's the kindest man I've ever met. And all that other stuff is so ridiculous that I'm not even going to take it seriously.'

Stephie wasn't laughing anymore. Quite the opposite, in fact.

'One thing I always admired about you, Kenny, was your honesty. If something didn't go your way then you took it on the chin. At least, you used to.'

'It's all true, Stephie.'

'Apart from you can't prove it?'

'No,' I admitted.

Stephie grabbed her bag. In doing so, she knocked the Macallan over. The lid was off and the Scotch began to seep into the carpet.

'You're pathetic, Kenny,' she said, making no effort to stop the flow. 'And quite frankly, if I don't see you for the rest of my life, it'll be way too soon.'

'Steph, the only reason I'm telling you this is because—'

A slamming door interrupted me, followed by the sound of feet descending the stairs. In her haste to leave, Stephie had left the ring behind. I removed the glittering chunk of carbon from the box. Nestled in my palm, it felt like a synthesised version of Jake Villiers.

Had there been a hammer handy, I'd have smashed the diamond into dust. Instead I slipped it back into its box and drank what remained of the Macallan.

TWENTY-FIVE

I emerged at 8 a.m. from one of the deepest sleeps I'd known in years. My left eye was unfocused for five minutes, but there was no repeat of the nausea I'd felt the previous day. I took a long shower and examined my tattoo. Perhaps having a target plastered across my arse cheek wasn't the wisest choice I'd ever made. But what was done was done. I rubbed moisturiser into my buttock as Dog had instructed, after which I brewed a pint of coffee and risked a boiled egg. Then I checked my inbox.

> *If you want information as to the fate of Castor Greaves, we can supply this. Choose to take our offer up and we will contact you again at 6.00PM. Respond to this email by sending Accept before 10.00AM GMT. Should you not respond, or respond after this time, we will assume that you have no interest in the matter. Any attempt to trace the source of this message will prove futile.*

It wasn't the first peculiar email I'd had since finding Emily Ridley. There had been at least half a dozen from people who needed to be admitted into full-time psychiatric care or, at the very least, have their meds adjusted. This was different. For one thing it was coherent and for another it didn't accuse me of being in league with Satan or to *stop medling in things that do not koncern u!!!*

And so what if the sender was a fruitcake? All that would happen was that I'd get something at 6 p.m. that confirmed they were batshit crazy. No harm in that. I stubbed out my smoke and sent *Accept* at 8.53 a.m., and waited for a response that might confirm receipt. All that had fallen into my inbox fifteen minutes later was a message from Faith Bellow of the FBI, who was writing to advise that the Secretary General of the United Nations had formally sanctioned $44,000,000 be released into my account. All Faith required were the relevant details . . .

First decent break I'd had in a long while.

The last time I'd called Chop's agency, I'd spoken to a lackey; this time it was the woman herself. Maggie Riggs didn't try to fob me off when I asked for her client's mobile number. Neither did she oblige me. 'I'm afraid we're not authorised to give out personal details,' was the predictable response.

'Can't you make an exception?' I said. 'It's a matter of some urgency.'

'What I can do is give Chop a message and ask him to call you back.'

'When's that likely to be?'

'I'm afraid I don't know. Chop is rather busy at the moment . . .'

'Can you tell him it's regarding Saskia Reeves-Montgomery,' I said. 'She was the woman who was murdered at Pegler's Wharf yesterday.'

If it was a surprise that her client was being associated with a dead woman then Maggie's voice didn't indicate it. 'I'll be sure to mention that to him,' she said.

'Could you also mention there's a photograph I'd like to show him?' I added for good measure.

Curiosity got the better of Maggie this time.

'What kind of photograph?' she asked.

'Just a photograph,' I said, and cut the call.

◆ ◆ ◆

Shortly before leaving the flat, I forwarded the mystery email to Odeerie, along with the information that I'd had second thoughts about quitting the search for Emily's killer. Was there any way he could trace the message? My phone rang with his number while I was on the way to the Tube. Not fancying a tricky confab as to why I'd changed my mind, I allowed it to go to voicemail and descended to platform level.

The commuter herd had left multiple copies of the *Metro* in its wake. I checked one out to see if there was any mention of Saskia or Pauline Oakley. The first featured on page three; the second on page twelve. Homicide was clearly more newsworthy than suicide.

A picture of Pegler's Wharf accompanied the piece about Saskia's death. All that was known at the time of going to print was that she had been assaulted on her houseboat and that the police were investigating. Biographical information listed her age (61) and that she was a freelance author who had recently completed the co-written biography of Marcie Bell, doyen of popular soap opera *Albion Alley*.

The news that a woman had been found hanging on Hampstead Heath only merited three paragraphs. She had been found shortly after dawn by a jogger who had alerted the police. The woman had been identified as Pauline Oakley and her next of kin had been informed. The police were not treating her death as suspicious.

Relatively close to Central London, the Heath was a favoured spot for suicides. Many of its eight hundred acres were covered in trees and undergrowth. If you wanted to bid the cruel world goodbye, you were unlikely to be disturbed so long as you did so during the hours of darkness. It also provided perfect cover for someone to hand over a huge amount of money to someone blackmailing them.

During the journey to Crouch End, I imagined how Jake might have arranged matters. Contacting Pauline to say that he had raised the cash would have been the first step. Meeting on Hampstead Heath after dark would have triggered a few alarm bells in Pauline's mind. Jake had probably countered them by saying that, if she wanted the money, it was the only place he was prepared to hand it over.

Greed and desperation had won out. It was a potent combination that, while I'd been working for Odeerie, I'd seen bring people low. Pauline and Jake would have met where there was no CCTV coverage. Whether he would have been able to subdue and hang her on his own was a moot point. Jake was in good shape, but it would still have been an effort to single-handedly overpower a woman fighting for her life.

Jake wouldn't have chosen an accomplice he couldn't trust implicitly, but ultimately the only person you can really trust is yourself. If I could find out who his assistant had been there was a chance I could persuade them to talk. But as they would be implicating themselves in murder, it was a slim reed to hang my hopes upon.

Per square mile, there were probably more yoga studios in Crouch End than in Santa Barbara. It was the favoured method for mummies to stay yummy and retired professional ladies to remain limber in their later years. Also available on the Broadway was an artisanal butcher, a dental spa, an art-house cinema called the Arthouse cinema, and at least one cafe in which you could order a yak-milk latte.

City Stretch was sandwiched between an estate agency and a florist. Its window featured photos of toned bodies in extended positions. Classes for all levels were available, said the sign on the door. Intermediate Pilates, led by Davina, was scheduled to finish in five minutes, according to the website.

A tubby guy in his forties was folding towels behind reception. The sleeves of his linen shirt had been rolled up to the elbows to reveal a pair of plaited bracelets on one wrist and an Apple Watch on the other. Ginger hair had been dragged back over his skull and was fastened in a nub resembling a docked poodle's tail.

'Can I help you?' he asked with a faint Geordie accent.

'I've an appointment with Davina.'

'And your name is . . . ?'

'Kenny Gabriel.'

The guy put the towel he was folding on to a shelf and consulted an iPad. 'You don't seem to be down here,' he said. 'When did you make the appointment?'

'Yesterday evening. Davina and I know each other socially. She said that I should drop by this morning after she finished her first class.'

'No problem,' the receptionist said. 'Dav should be through quite soon. Could I offer you a tea or coffee?'

I declined both in favour of water from the cooler and took a seat. For the next five minutes I listened to low-volume sitar music and watched Tubby graduate from folding towels to arranging multicoloured foam blocks. Then the double doors to the right of his desk opened and a stream of chattering women emerged.

'You can go into the studio now,' he said.

Four large windows built into a vaulted roof lit the room with the assistance of half a dozen halogen spots. Each white wall had a large fractal print attached to it. At the furthest end of the studio was a platform that stood six inches proud of the wooden floor. A dozen or so foam mats were spread equidistant from each other. A woman was dragging a pair of them towards a pile in the corner of the room.

Davina Jackson was wearing grey leggings and a powder-blue top. She had cropped brown hair and a pair of rimless glasses. An athlete's rangy physique would have been the envy of a woman half her age. She deposited the mats on the pile and registered my presence for the first time.

'Davina Jackson?' I asked.

'That's right.'

I pulled the doors closed.

'My name's Kenny Gabriel, Davina. We spoke on the phone yesterday . . .'

'I specifically told you not to get in touch with me again.'

'You did. The only reason I'm here is because I think you might have information that could prove useful.'

'What makes you think that?' Davina snapped.

'Girlfriends have a tendency to share secrets, particularly in their teens. And to be honest it seemed when we spoke that you knew something.'

'Well, I don't. Get out or I'll have you thrown out.'

She bent down and grabbed the corner of another mat. I took a few steps towards her. 'Davina, however Emily died it wasn't painlessly. For over twenty years Pam's been hoping against hope that her daughter's still alive and now she knows the truth. I can only imagine what that must feel like, but then I haven't got kids.'

Nothing from Davina.

'Have you?' I asked.

She nodded.

'Who knows, maybe Emily would have too. And yet whoever killed her is almost certainly still out there enjoying life. D'you think that's fair?'

'I don't know anything,' Davina said, with slightly less conviction.

There are times to talk and times to shut up. The latter was the right option for me to take as far as Davina Jackson was concerned. She placed the mat in the corner and began to re-space those that remained. Thirty seconds before she looked at me again.

'I just want to live my life in peace.'

'So does Pam Ridley,' I said. 'And if she can find out who killed her daughter then she might have the chance to do that. I promise that anything you tell me will be treated with complete confidentiality.'

The only sound in the studio was the sitar music from reception and the cheeping of a starling perched on the ledge of one of the windows. Davina wrapped her arms around her body as though the temperature had dropped several degrees.

'You swear it stays between you and me?'

'Do you know something that might help?' I asked.

'Yes,' she said. 'I think I might.'

TWENTY-SIX

I chose to sit on a moulded plastic chair, Davina cross-legged on the floor. 'My family moved to London when I was eight,' she began. 'I was a shy child and not that great at mixing with other kids. On my first day at school, Emily marched up to me in the playground and introduced herself, which was pretty much typical of her.'

'And you became best friends?' I asked.

'You could put it that way. Not that we were particularly similar. I was a bit of a swot and Emily wasn't all that bothered with schoolwork. Not after she was signed by the agency, anyway. That was when things began to change.'

'Different agendas?' I said.

'Pretty much. Although we'd still meet up from time to time. Even when things really started to take off for Em and I went to uni.'

The door opened and the receptionist stuck his head round. 'People are starting to arrive for your eleven o'clock, Dav,' he said. 'What shall I do?'

'Can you keep them in reception, Andy? We shouldn't be long.'

Andy nodded, cast a curious glance in my direction and left.

'Where was I?' Davina asked.

'Saying about how you saw less and less of Emily after she signed . . .'

'Oh, yes. Well, I hadn't seen Em for about two months when she called and suggested a drink. By this time she was in magazines and on posters, but she was probably most famous for being Castor Greaves's girlfriend.'

'When was this?' I asked.

'I'd have been in my first year at UEA, so early '95.'

'The year they went missing?'

Davina nodded. 'When we met, Em said that something was bothering her. I asked what it was and she said she was getting unwanted attention.'

'From whom?'

'Dean Allison.'

'You're sure about that?'

'Positive. They'd met a couple of years earlier and started seeing each other. Emily told him they had to keep it secret as the agency was dead against the girls on their books having celebrity boyfriends and it could ruin her career.'

'Was Dean a celebrity then?'

'No, but he probably thought he was.'

'Then why did Emily—'

'She had lied to him about her age. Dean thought she was over sixteen, when actually she was a few months younger.'

'Christ.'

'Without make-up on, Em looked like a schoolgirl. When she dolled herself up, you'd have no problem believing she was twenty.'

'So Dean really had no idea?'

'None at all.'

'Who ended the relationship?' I asked.

'He did, after a few months. Emily might have looked like a sophisticated young woman, but she was only a kid. Dean must have found the conversation tedious and he quickly got sick of them never being seen out together.'

'How did Emily react to being dumped?'

'A bit miffed to begin with, but her career was beginning to take off and there was a lot going on in her life.'

'Plus she met Castor Greaves,' I said.

Davina nodded. 'Cas was doing a shoot with a photographer Emily was booked in for a session with. She arrived early and they got talking in the bar. Em was almost eighteen by then so the age thing didn't matter, and the agency were positively thrilled that she was seeing an up-and-coming rock star.'

'But I'm guessing Dean wasn't quite so happy?' I asked.

'Furious. According to Emily, he and Castor were like chalk and cheese, although the one thing they both had in common was gigantic egos.'

'So he got back in touch with Emily?'

'Yep. He said that if she didn't dump Castor then he'd tell him they'd been sleeping together. Emily said that she'd just deny it and tell Cas that he was trying to wind him up. That was when Dean told her about the video.

'Dean had asked Em whether she'd mind him filming them having sex together and she'd said that she really didn't want that. He'd said okay but recorded it secretly. No way could Emily tell Castor that she hadn't been with Dean when he'd seen the pair of them in action.'

'But wouldn't Cas have thrown Dean out of the band?'

'That was on the cards anyway. Dean was a journeyman drummer at best and there were already discussions about replacing him.'

'Which meant he had nothing to lose.'

'Exactly.'

'If Dean was blackmailing Emily, why didn't she go to the police?'

Davina propped her glasses on her forehead and rubbed her eyes. 'Castor would almost certainly have got to hear about it one way or another.'

'Why did she come to you?'

'Because she trusted me and because she wanted to see if I could help.'

'Could you?'

'Yes. At least, I had an idea that I thought might work.' Davina looked at her watch. 'Would you mind helping me lay some equipment out?'

In one corner of the studio were two wire baskets. One contained a dozen or so partially deflated rubber balls. Davina instructed me to put one at the top of each mat while she did the same with individual swaths of blue elastic.

'What was your idea?' I asked, dropping a ball and toeing it into position.

'I suggested she tell Dean that she didn't believe him and ask for a copy of the video. There was no reason he shouldn't send her one, which is what he did.'

'What purpose did that serve?' I asked.

'Back then, virtually all recordings had the time and date embedded on the tape . . .'

'So what?'

'Think about it . . .'

The penny dropped.

'It would have been proof that Dean was having sex with Emily when she was underage. That meant she could have taken it to the police and brought charges.'

'That's right,' Davina said. 'It was one thing being thrown out of the band a few months early; another thing entirely to be charged with statutory rape. When she had the tape, all Emily had to do was tell Dean how old she was when he'd made it, and that was the end of that. It was mutually assured destruction.'

'Which presumably she did?'

'Just to make sure, I suggested she get one of those gizmos you can use to record calls. That way she could also get proof that he'd filmed her secretly when she didn't know it was happening.'

I positioned the last semi-inflated ball. What the hell did people do with them? Whatever it was, I had more pressing questions for Davina Jackson.

'And that was the end of that?' was the first.

'Seemed to be. A few weeks later I got a card from Em saying that everything was sorted out and that she was grateful for my help.'

'What did she do with the recordings?'

'That was the odd thing. She wrote that she'd given them to Humphrey to look after, as though I knew who Humphrey was.'

'Which you didn't?'

Davina shook her head.

'Didn't you ask the next time you met?'

'We didn't meet again. A week after I received the card, a half-blind pensioner knocked me down on a zebra crossing. I spent six weeks in traction and two months in rehab.' Davina pulled the band of her leggings down to reveal a thick surgical scar on her hip. 'Pilates was part of the therapy, so I guess it's an ill wind . . .'

'You realise what this means?' I asked. 'If Emily had something that could disgrace Dean and send him to jail then it gives him a motive to murder her.'

'I thought about that when you said that her body was found. But didn't Dean have a strong alibi when Emily went missing? And what happened to Castor?'

'Maybe Dean killed him too. If the police knew what you've just told me . . .'

Davina's jaw tightened. 'I've got two young boys and my husband's just been signed off work with depression,' she said. 'The last thing I want is a crowd of reporters camped outside the house.'

'Won't happen. The cops would give you anonymity.'

'You can't guarantee that. And what proof is there? Without the tapes, everything I say is just anecdotal.'

She had a point. Shaheen would listen to Davina's story – she was a credible witness, after all – and he might even go so far as to pull Dean Allison in for a chat. Without actual evidence, though, all the sick fuck had to do was deny everything and it was conversation over. Unless the tapes were still around . . .

'You've absolutely no idea who Humphrey was?' I asked.

'None whatsoever,' she replied.

The door opened and Andy the receptionist was with us again. 'The natives are restless, Dav. Can I send them in yet?'

'Whenever you like,' Davina replied.

'Did Emily ever talk about her relationship with Castor?' I asked, making the most of the last moments of our interview.

'Only that she was worried about his health and that touring and writing were putting him under a lot of pressure.'

'What about Cas and the other band members?'

'She said that he'd been arguing with Chop Montague a bit, but that it was just creative differences about the new album.'

'Nothing about a dust-up with JJ Freeman?'

Davina shook her head, and the class began to enter the studio.

'Thanks,' I said. 'I appreciate you talking to me.'

'Will you share it with the police?'

'If I can find the tapes then I won't need to reveal the source of my information. And if I can't, then there probably isn't much point.'

'Well, good luck. Em was special. Whoever killed her deserves to—'

A woman in a pink tracksuit interrupted Davina with news of a knee ailment. My options were to hang around and see what use the blue balls and the rubber bands were put to, or call the one person who might know who Humphrey was.

Two minutes later, I was on the phone to Pam Ridley.

TWENTY-SEVEN

'*Humphrey?*' Pam said. 'Did Em know someone called *Humphrey?*'

'That's right,' I said. 'Humphrey.'

'Old-fashioned name, ain't it?'

'Yes, I suppose it is,' I said. 'Perhaps it was a neighbour . . .'

'No Humphreys round our way,' Pam said. 'Not that I knew of, anyway. There was a Harold who ran the allotment association. Couldn't have been him, could it?'

'Did Emily know Harold well?'

'She might have met Harry when he came round to get the monthly subs off her dad, but why would she be friendly with him?'

Why indeed. Allotments had become trendier, but Naomi Campbell had never appeared on *Gardeners' Question Time*. And the idea that an eighteen-year-old model would entrust rape footage to her father's gardening buddy was risible.

And the guy's name was Harold.

'It's not him,' I said. 'Did Emily ever mention anyone at work called Humphrey? A photographer or a booking agent, perhaps?'

'Hold on,' Pam said. 'We're going through another tunnel . . .'

The sound of the train doing exactly that came through the speaker for the next ten seconds.

'Em definitely didn't mention no Humphrey,' Pam said when she came back on the line. 'Who is this bloke and why are you so interested in him?'

'The name came up in a conversation I had with Davina Jackson. There's a chance that whoever it might be could have some information.'

'What kind of information?'

I opted not to relay Davina's story. There wasn't much point unless I could contact the mysterious Humphrey. And Pam was impetuous. If she knew what Dean Allison had done to her daughter, who knew how she might react?

'I'm not entirely sure,' I said. 'It might be something and it might be nothing. Davina just said someone called Humphrey was close to Emily at that time.'

'She's got it wrong,' Pam said. 'I'd have known about it.'

'Fair enough. But if anything does occur, Pam, do give me a call. How long are you staying with your sister for?'

'Until they release Em's body. Then I'll need to come back and arrange the funeral. They reckon it shouldn't be much more than a few days.'

'How are you bearing up?' I asked.

'Not too bad. I gave Em's stuff to the charity. I know it might sound daft, but I got one of my mates to drive it up to Finchley where he lives. I didn't want to see no one round here wearing her clothes.'

'That's perfectly understandable, Pam.'

'What about you, Kenny? Sorted out the stuff we talked about?'

I recalled Pam's advice about saying the things you needed to say to the people you needed to say them to, in case you didn't get the opportunity again.

'Not yet,' I admitted. 'But I'm working on it.'

195

Two things caught my eye when I entered the Vesuvius: the first was the huge bouquet of roses on the bar; the second was Whispering Nick balancing on a chair while attempting to change a light bulb. Only a quick grab for the fixture saved him from going arse over tit when I made my presence known.

'For fuck's sake, don't you ever knock, Kenny?' he said.

'To enter a boozer?'

'Well, make some kind of noise at least.'

'Who are the flowers from?' I asked.

Nick stepped off the chair. 'Jake sent them. I think he and Stephie had a bit of a—'

The office door opened. Make-up partially concealed the bruise on Stephie's cheek. It also drew attention to it. On seeing me, her hand went reflexively to her face. The silence was deafening. Nick reacted first. 'Wrong type of fitting, Steph,' he said, holding the bulb up. 'I'll see if I can borrow one from upstairs . . .'

Connecting Stephie's injured face and the flowers was a simple enough equation.

'Now d'you believe me?' I asked after Nick had left.

She dropped her hand and jutted out her chin.

'It wasn't Jake's fault. I went to see him last night and we had a row. He doesn't like me drinking and I stank of booze.'

'And that merits a punch in the eye?'

'It was a slap.'

'Oh, well, if it was only a slap . . .'

'You wouldn't be so bloody sanctimonious if you knew how upset he was afterwards. And that I'd lost my engagement ring.'

I took the velvet box from my pocket and laid it on a table.

'Why the hell didn't you call me?' Stephie asked, snatching it up.

'Because you told me that you never wanted to see me again, and because I knew I was coming in here today.'

'Jake's got a lot on his plate,' she said, pushing the box into her jeans pocket. 'He's under an incredible amount of pressure.'

'You'll be telling me you deserved it next,' I said. 'You're not stupid, Steph, you know that when men hit women it's never a one-off. This might not happen again for a while, but it will happen again, and it'll probably be worse.'

'Jake might kill me – is that what you're saying?'

'I'm saying you need to leave him and I think you know it.'

We stared at each other like a pair of gunfighters. Stephie drew first.

'That's not happening, Kenny,' she said. 'Jake might not be perfect but he wants to spend the rest of his life with me, and I want to spend the rest of my life with him. Whether you approve or disapprove is completely irrelevant.'

Before I could respond, Whispering Nick re-entered carrying a small cardboard box. 'I think this is the right type,' he said before stopping in his tracks. 'Er . . . Should I go outside and have a fag or something?'

'No need for that, Nick,' Stephie said. 'Kenny and I have said everything that we need to say to each other and I'm pretty much done here for today.'

Stephie picked up her coat from the rack and walked out without putting it on. Nick stared at me as though he half-expected me to self-combust.

'D'you want a drink, Kenny?' he asked when that didn't happen.

'Yeah,' I said. 'A drink would be good.'

◆ ◆ ◆

As most people do on entering the V for the first time, JJ performed a double take. As Stephie had left, Nick had relaxed the no-smoking rule. The nicotine haze could only have added to JJ's sense that he had somehow left 2017 at pavement level and descended to 1976.

'Can I get you a drink?' I asked when he approached my table.

'No. Let's get on with it.' JJ was wearing a biker jacket over a T-shirt featuring Buster Keaton. Bristles studded his jaw like tiny black nails and his eyes looked like chunks of bulletproof glass. I smiled. He didn't. I got on with it.

'I met up with Sweat Dog yesterday.'

'So you said.'

'He was telling me a bit about the old days.'

No comment from JJ.

'Including your relationship with Castor. Apparently the pair of you had an argument and you laid him out.'

'We were in a rock band. Shit happened.'

'And then you went missing for a few days.'

'I was pissed off with Cas.'

'Any particular reason why?'

'None of your business. Are we done?'

'Not entirely. Sweat Dog said that Cas stayed at his flat for a while when he was in the States. He left a lot of stuff behind, including some old tapes and books . . .'

The left corner of JJ's mouth twitched a couple of times.

'Dog said that he gave the stuff to you when he cleared his place out a few years ago,' I continued. 'He felt that you were the closest Cas had to family.'

'So what?'

Time for my first shot in the dark.

'On one of the tapes were a few songs Cas had been working on.'

'Dog told you that?'

My shrug was non-committal. If my theory wasn't correct then hopefully it left me room to extricate myself. JJ shifted in his seat and ran a hand over his chin.

Encouragement enough for me to try shot number two.

'You sold the tapes to the *People's Inquisitor*,' I said. 'They put them up on their website along with the story that Castor had taken the Golden Road.'

JJ's right hand shot out and fastened itself around my neck. If I hadn't had my back against the wall, I'd have gone flying over backwards. As it was, I had to gasp for breath.

'I did not tell that pack of jackals Cas was still alive,' he said.

'Urghhhh,' was all I could manage.

'And I didn't tell them that he'd been taken by the Golden Road either . . .'

JJ's fingers were fastened around my windpipe like a nest of baby pythons. My attempt to pull his wrist away only made things worse.

'The fuckers just printed all that shit and there was nothing I could do about it,' JJ said, his voice tightening with his grip. 'They made me sign a contract that gave them full licence to do what they wanted to with the tapes.'

The noise in my ears sounded like water gushing through storm drains. In a few seconds' time I would either pass out or proceed directly to death with *Strangled in a drinking club* as my unfortunate epitaph.

'I know Kenny can be a pain in the arse. But he's got two hundred quid on his slate and I'll get a bollocking if he doesn't pay it off.'

Nick was holding a four-pound lump hammer at shoulder height. He kept it behind the till in case things ever got too lively in the Vesuvius. I wasn't sure that he'd actually hit JJ over the head with it, but then neither was JJ.

The grip loosened and air rushed into my grateful lungs.

TWENTY-EIGHT

JJ downed the Jack in one and looked into the empty glass as though it still held something interesting. Judging by his expression it was a triple shot of regret with a twist of bitterness. I was sipping my waga with greater restraint, not least of all because my bruised trachea was still recovering.

'D'you want another one?' I asked.

JJ thought about it and decided against.

'Why not take me through what happened?' I suggested.

'What's the point? You've already worked it out.'

'Actually, that was a bit of a punt. Sweat Dog had no idea the cassettes had Castor singing on them. He thought they were compilation tapes.'

JJ gave me a sharp look. My head bobbed back reflexively.

'What made you think I'd sold them to the *Inquisitor*, then?'

'Saskia Reeves-Montgomery said that Cas worked his ideas out on tape before bringing them to his sessions with Chop. It made sense that he'd have a few hanging around.'

'I honestly didn't know they'd print that he was still alive,' JJ said.

'You won't be the first person the *Inquisitor*'s had over and you won't be the last,' I said. 'Why did you approach them in the first place?'

'I needed the money. The Junction was doing badly and I'd been through a tough divorce. It wasn't a fortune but it was enough to keep us open.'

'What about the Mean royalties?'

This brought a mirthless laugh from JJ.

'What royalties? A few grand comes through from time to time, but Castor and Chop hold all the writing credits. That was why I laid him out in Manchester. When the Spiders started, the agreement was that all the members would split everything equally. Of course we were a covers band then so it didn't really matter. But when Chop and Cas started writing, it made a hell of a difference.'

'Because there was a lot more cash coming in?'

'Yep. I didn't have a problem with them having the bigger slice of cake. But Cas was suggesting that he and Chop pretty much take all of it.'

'And that's why you decked him?'

'Not just because of the cash. By then Cas was a complete pain in the arse on just about every front. God knows how Chop put up with it bearing in mind that—'

JJ was interrupted by the fruit machine paying out a jackpot. As the last time this had happened was during the Wars of the Roses, it caused quite a commotion.

'Did you know much about Cas's financial situation in general?' I asked when the excitement had died down. 'He seems to have put more or less everything into a single numbered account a few months before he disappeared.'

'He didn't mention it to me,' JJ said, 'but we weren't talking much by that stage.'

'Dog said Cas was very close with money.'

JJ laid his empty glass on its side and spun it around.

'Cas's old man had a gambling problem. After his wife died he went through cash like no one's business. One day Cas came home from school to find he'd sold all their furniture. It ain't surprising he felt insecure about money all his life.'

JJ span the glass again. It came to rest with the rim facing in my direction. I picked it up and put it on another table. 'Didn't your manager take care of the money?'

'We didn't have one. The label paid us directly.'

'D'you think you were ripped off?'

'Chop's accountant kept on top of the unit sales. The label fucking hated him but at least we were paid our due.'

JJ folded a beer mat in half. Without a guitar to play or someone to throttle he was quite the fidget. Maybe that was why the skin on his knuckles was barked.

'You must have had an interesting few days,' he said. 'It was all over the place when you found Em. How'd you know she was in the air vent?'

'Lucky guess,' I said. 'Have the police interviewed you?'

'Some guy called Shaheen said he might want to go over my statement from '95. I told him that I'd be happy to do that, but I couldn't remember anything else.'

The beer mat was now being systematically torn into pieces.

'Did you know Emily had been in a relationship with Dean Allison before she met Castor?' I asked.

'What?' JJ said. 'No way . . .'

'He told me about it, as did a friend of Emily's. I take it Cas knew nothing?'

'Christ, no. He'd have had Dean's guts . . .'

'Not Dean's fault he met her first.'

JJ gathered the beer mat fragments into a small pile. 'Wouldn't have made no difference.'

He leant back in his chair and stared at a point a few inches above my head. I'd seen the same body language in interviews before. It meant someone was thinking about disclosing something privileged or marginal. Usually it was simply a matter of waiting. It took less than ten seconds in JJ's case.

'The reason I decked Cas in Manchester wasn't just because he was gypping me on the money,' he said eventually. 'He was trying to turn Em on to heroin.'

'She told you that?'

JJ nodded.

'Did she try it?' I asked.

'Em said not and I believed her, but I could see she was thinking about it. Smackheads are a nightmare. All they do is nod out when they're using, and all they can think about when they aren't is their next fix. Only way you can get close to them is by joining them. Which is why I said Em should get out.'

'But wasn't Cas clean on the night of the Emporium gig?'

'Doesn't mean shit. Contrary to popular belief, addicts can go a day without using and not climb the walls. It's only after a few days they really start hurting. Anyway, Em made me promise not to say anything to Castor. That's why I put some extra on the punch in Manchester. Made me feel a whole lot better, if you know what I mean.'

The revelations were coming so thick and fast from JJ that I needed a few moments to collect my thoughts before asking my next question.

'What might have happened at the Emporium is that Castor found out about Dean and went completely ballistic. He killed Emily, hid her body in the air vent and then somehow left the club without anyone seeing him. Does that sound possible?'

'He was sober enough,' JJ said. 'And if he'd found out beforehand then he could have prepared. Castor was a druggie but he wasn't stupid.'

'I don't think Dean told him,' I said. 'So how could he have found out?'

'Maybe Em said that she wanted to break up and he lost it.'

'And where d'you think Castor is now?' I asked.

'Like I told you in the Junction. He took a hot shot and killed himself.'

'Apart from there's no body.'

'That's what they said about Em 'til you found her. Maybe you'll turn Cas up as well. But if you don't then what does it matter? Sometimes it's best to let things in the past stay in the past. Speaking of which . . . you're not going to tell anyone about the *Inquisitor* business, are you? It's the last thing I need in my life right now.'

'I've no reason to,' I said.

JJ nodded his thanks. 'I know I've badmouthed Cas but that's only because of what the smack and the fame turned him into. If he'd never met Chop Montague and we'd just kept playing blues in clubs for couple of hundred quid a night . . .'

He stared at the table as though a film of what might have been was flickering across its surface. He wasn't the first person to do that in the V and he wouldn't be the last.

'Sorry again for the way I reacted, Kenny. It's just that the *Inquisitor* thing really got to me and, well, you already know I've got a bit of a temper.'

'No problem,' I said, and we stood up and shook hands.

For a moment I thought JJ was going to add something. Then he turned abruptly and departed the club.

TWENTY-NINE

As the V is pretty much a dead zone for mobile signals it meant resurfacing after my interview with JJ to pick up my messages and emails. There were three voicemails from Odeerie asking me to call, each tetchier than the last. His line was engaged and I turned my attention to my emails. The only thing requiring immediate attention was from a previous client asking whether I was available to go undercover at his amusement arcade in Brighton. I was tapping out an apologetic response when the screen lit up with an incoming call.

'I've had a message from my agent saying that you want to talk to me about a photograph,' Chop Montague said. 'Is that correct?'

'It is,' I said. 'When's a good time?'

'Now.'

'Actually, it'd be better if I showed you the photograph. Any chance I could come and see you, Chop? It would only take five minutes . . .'

The opening bars to a Shirley Bassey song began playing. Chop must have put his hand over the phone's microphone as he shouted something I couldn't make out. The music ended and he was back with me.

'At least give me an idea what the thing is.'

'I found it on Saskia Reeves-Montgomery's houseboat,' I said. 'She was the journalist murdered yesterday. You may have heard about that.'

A few seconds of dead air.

'Can you be at Encore Studios in an hour?' Chop said.

'No problem,' I replied.

◆ ◆ ◆

I called Odeerie from a cab on my way to Camden. After letting him vent his considerable spleen, I covered off the conversations I'd had that morning with Davina Jackson, Pam Ridley and JJ Freeman.

'So in summary,' the fat man finally said, 'there's a video of Dean Allison having sex with Emily Ridley when she's underage and a voice recording in which she confronts him about it. This gives him a motive to murder her but someone called Humphrey was handed both tapes twenty-odd years ago and no one has any idea who the hell he is, including Emily's best friend and her mother. That about right, Kenny?'

'Pretty much,' I said.

'JJ sold the demo tapes to the *Inquisitor* because he needed the cash to keep his club open and they invented the story about Cas taking the Golden Road because they're an immoral set of shits who'd do anything to make a few quid?'

'Right again.'

'You seem very excited about all this.'

'Aren't you?'

'Not really. For one thing Dean seems to have a very strong alibi for the night Emily Ridley was murdered, and for another, tracking down the right Humphrey is next door to impossible. At least I think it is.'

'Can't you find a list of Humphreys in the Tooting Bec area around that time?'

'Possibly. But let's say there's fifty. What do we do then?'

'See how many are still alive.'

'And after that?'

'Get in touch with them.'

'To say what? Did Emily Ridley happen to give you a couple of tapes for safekeeping that might implicate Dean Allison in her murder?'

'Something like that.'

'How long's all that going to take? And don't you think that Humphrey might already have given the tapes to the police when he heard that Emily had gone missing? Not to mention her body being recently found.'

'Maybe he's forgotten he has them.'

Odeerie's sigh was more eloquent than words.

'Okay,' I said. 'How about you go through the records at the school Emily went to and see if there were any kids called Humphrey attending at the time.'

'Because it'll take just as long. And wouldn't Davina Jackson have remembered him? It's not the kind of name you're likely to forget.'

'At least it's something to go on.'

The cab turned from Camden High Street into Delancey Street.

'Look, Kenny,' Odeerie said, 'we agreed last night that you were going to quit the Ridley job and focus on your health and going into hospital. Have you been in touch with the consultant to make a date for your operation yet?'

'It's on my to-do list.'

'Between what, picking up a new ballcock valve and getting your curtains dry-cleaned? You've got a brain tumour, for fuck's sake.'

'I'm getting somewhere with this, Odeerie.'

'No, you're not. All this Dean Allison business adds up to is absolutely bugger-all. If you won't tell Pam Ridley we're quitting then I will.'

'Do it tomorrow. I'll speak to the consultant first thing.'

During the silence I could almost hear the cogs in Odeerie's mind turning. The cab had just pulled up outside Encore Studios by the time he made his decision.

'Okay, but you ring the hospital and you get things moving.'

'Scout's honour.'

'What are you doing now?'

'About to talk to Chop Montague about the photograph.'

'Anything left to follow up after that?'

'Only the email I forwarded. Could you trace where it came from?'

'Nope. Looks like it was sent via an onion router.'

'A what?'

'Multiple layers of encryption.'

'Who would go to the trouble of doing that?'

'Trolls, criminals and nutters, usually.'

'But not always?'

Odeerie paused. 'Something just doesn't feel right about this, Kenny.'

'Which bit specifically?'

'All of it.'

◆ ◆ ◆

Encore Studios had originally been built in the 1930s as a cigarette factory. What with people lighting up pretty much on exiting the womb back then, Sphinx Tobacco hadn't needed to skimp on the budget. A pair of the mythical creatures cast in bronze stood either side of a portico decorated in fancy brickwork, and a burnished rising sun had been suspended over a wrought-iron door inlayed with art deco panelling. Its rays warmed my face as I entered the building. At least it felt that way.

A man in a tight suit was eating a Cornish pasty behind reception. He surreptitiously shoved it under the desk and asked if he could help. I told him that I had a meeting with Chop Montague, after which the guy checked a clipboard and seemed surprised that this was indeed the case. I was issued with a visitor's badge and instructed to go through the double doors and follow the signs to Studio 4.

The corridor had been decorated with pictures of artists who had used the building since it was repurposed in the sixties. I passed black-and-white photos of The Who, Jimmy Tarbuck, Bonnie Langford, the Chuckle Brothers and Lee Evans before arriving at my destination. The recording light was off, although I could hear a James Bond theme blasting through the woodwork.

I knocked and heard no response. I opened the door and entered. A blonde in early middle age was standing on a low stage. Her T-shirt bore the Rolling Stones logo studded with rhinestones and her jeans were tucked into pink cowboy boots.

Chop had his back to me and was stationed beside a pair of speakers connected to an iPhone. A backing track was rattling out and the woman was singing the lyrics into a mic. Neither she nor Chop registered my arrival.

He killed the music.

'Why've we stopped?' the woman asked plaintively. 'I did it like you said.'

'No, you didn't, Yvonne,' he replied. 'You need to put more emphasis on the lines as they reach the climax. They still sound flat.'

'Are you sure?' she asked.

'I'm sure,' Chop said. 'Let's go again. I'll rewind and you come in on cue. Try to remember the song is about seduction and excitement.'

If Chop had wanted more emphasis, he got it. Yvonne screamed into the mic and the mic screamed back. When the feedback had stopped reverberating around the studio, Chop killed the music again.

'Why did you choose me to be your mentor, Yvonne?' he asked.

'Cos I'm a big fan of your work, Chop.'

'Are you also a fan of the work of Shirley Bassey?'

'Yeah. I love her?'

'Well then, let's hope Shirley doesn't tune in for the final.'

'Why not, Chop?' Yvonne asked.

'BECAUSE THEN SHE WON'T HAVE TO LISTEN TO YOU MURDER THE SONG SHE MADE FAMOUS, LIVE ON NATIONAL TV.'

Yvonne dropped the mic and exploded into tears. Ten seconds later she was clacking past me on Cuban heels with her considerable bosom heaving.

◆ ◆ ◆

While Chop consoled his distraught mentee, I booted up my tablet and brought Saskia's photo up on the screen. My plan had been to shove it under Chop's nose and ask about the extraordinary resemblance his onetime girlfriend bore to Emily Ridley. But in light of recent events, I was wondering if confrontation was the ideal strategy.

My phone rang. Given that Chop was likely to be a while, I opted to answer it.

'Is this *Kenneth* Gabriel,' a man who sounded like a minor member of the royal family asked, 'the private investigator?'

'Who's calling?'

'My name's Angus Glazier, I'm the MD of Billingsgate Publishing. We were talking to Saskia Reeves-Montgomery about the republication of *Play Like You Mean It*. I believe she discussed a collaboration with you . . .'

'She might have done,' I said. 'How do I know you are who you say you are?'

'Why not google the switchboard number and call me back?'

'No need,' I replied. 'How can I help?'

'Did you receive our offer of a contract to work on the book? We sent it yesterday to the email address Saskia gave us.'

'Yeah, I got it. Sorry not to reply, but I've had quite a bit on my plate.'

'You're still engaged on the Emily Ridley murder . . . ?'

'Only until the end of today.'

'Ah, right,' Glazier said. 'How is it progressing?'

'Confidentially.'

'Yes, of course, but if things are drawing to a close today then presumably you'd be able to start on the book immediately afterwards.'

'Apart from Saskia's dead,' I pointed out.

'Absolutely, and we're all terribly upset about that at Billingsgate.' Glazier's tone adjusted to reflect the shift in subject matter. 'Sas was a very well-regarded friend and colleague who had the respect and admiration of —'

'You must be completely devastated,' I interrupted, 'because you don't seem to have worked out that I can't collaborate with a corpse.'

'Yes, of course,' Glazier said, his manner flipping again. 'However, the copyright now resides with us and a co-author can revise the original text.'

'But you still need my input?'

'You would be integral to the project. So much so that we'd be prepared to pay you the bulk of the advance. Fifty thousand on signing and thirty thousand on publication. I appreciate the hastiness might appear unseemly,' Glazier said as Chop re-entered the studio, 'but if the book is to be a success it would need to be on the shelves as soon as possible. Time and tide wait for no man, I'm afraid . . .'

I made a signal to Chop that I wouldn't be long.

'What d'you say, Kenny?' Glazier asked. 'Do we have a deal?'

'I'll think about it,' I said, and cut the call.

Chop looked more fried than when I'd interviewed him at Mickleton Lodge. You could take your weekly shop home in the bags under his eyes, and his complexion had the consistency of putty. He replaced the mic in its stand and tapped it a couple of times. Miraculously it was still operational.

'How's Yvonne doing?' I asked.

'In the ladies putting her face back on.'

'D'you think she'll be back?'

'Sadly, yes. So whatever it is that you couldn't wait to show me, Kenny, you'd better show me now.'

Chop jumped off the low stage and landed on the concrete floor with a dull clump. His outfit matched his demeanour: grey V-neck sweater, dark-blue shirt, heavily creased chinos and black suede brogues. It's not often that I have the sartorial advantage in life. I felt like David Bowie standing beside Chop.

My tablet was in sleep mode. It took a few seconds to bring the photograph back. Chop pushed his glasses on to his forehead and stared at the screen.

'Where did you get this?' he asked after a few seconds.

'It was published in the *Essex Courier* in 2001. I found a hard copy on Saskia Reeves-Montgomery's houseboat. She said that she had something important she wanted me to see. I think this may have been it.'

No response from Chop.

'Look at the woman,' I said, and enlarged the picture using thumb and index finger. 'Don't you think she looks exactly like Emily Ridley?'

'Yes, you're right,' he said after a few more seconds scrutinising the tablet. 'Lydia bore a remarkably strong resemblance to Emily back then.'

'You remember her name?' I asked.

'Of course.'

'And are you still in touch?'

'We had supper two weeks ago.'

'Who is she?' I asked.

'My sister,' Chop replied.

THIRTY

Several million coffin nails had probably been manufactured in Studio 4 before it became Studio 4, making it ironic how many No Smoking signs were on the walls. I was so desperate for a nicotine hit that I could barely focus on Chop's account of the Mickleton Lodge fire. Sitting on the stage, his trousers had ridden up to reveal unexpectedly hairy shins above a pair of argyle socks.

'Thank God it didn't properly take hold,' he said after explaining that the fire had broken out in the kitchen. 'Otherwise I'm not sure how it would have turned out for Lydia and me. Even so, if Diego hadn't acted as promptly as he did then we might well not have made it out.'

'Diego being your gardener?'

'That's right. During summer he occasionally stays in the guest cottage at the rear of the property. Fortunately he was up before dawn and raised the alarm. If he'd decided to go home the previous day . . .'

Chop pursed his lips and shook his head.

'As it was, we got off lightly,' he continued. 'Several items in my memorabilia collection were destroyed, and Diego had to be treated for smoke inhalation.'

'The investigators were certain it was an electrical fault?' I asked.

'Positive,' Chop said. 'Some of the wiring was seventy years old. It was an accident waiting to happen.'

'What was destroyed in your collection?'

'Posters, photographs, T-shirts. Nothing of any great monetary value.'

'No suspicions at all surrounding the fire?'

'Not according to the incident report. Although, having said that . . .' Chop scratched the back of his neck. '. . . there had been a burglary two days before.'

'What did they take?' I asked.

'A few hundred pounds and some jewellery.'

'Did you report it?'

'Only to get a crime number. The police thought it was probably kids.'

'Why?'

'They spray-painted graffiti on the walls and one of them . . . one of them defecated on my bed. Not the kind of things professionals do, apparently.'

Chop was right. Your career burglar likes to get in and out with as little fuss as possible. Taking a dump and tagging walls takes time and leaves DNA behind. The kind of person who does that is usually high . . . or bears a grudge.

'Was there anything personally abusive about the graffiti?' I asked.

Chop thought about it and shook his head.

'Not that I can recall. Mostly it was just four-letter words.'

'Could whoever broke in have interfered with the wiring?'

'Wouldn't the investigation have indicated that?'

Fair point.

'And why do all the damage if arson was your motive?' he added.

Another fair point.

'And why would anyone want to burn me alive?'

Fair point number three. The only reason I could think of that anyone might want to immolate Chop was that he knew something they wanted kept quiet. Even if he didn't know he knew it.

Someone like the Golden Road.

'Are you quite sure this photograph is the one Saskia wanted to show you?' Chop asked. 'Admittedly it's quite dramatic, but that aside . . .'

'I'm not sure, no,' I said. 'It was left under the lid of the copier.'

'Possibly by accident?'

'Possibly,' I admitted.

'Then why do you think it's so significant?'

'Your sister looks incredibly like Emily.'

'Not anymore. Two divorces and three children take a toll.'

'But at the time . . .'

'Lydia was a big fan of Emily's look, although your photograph makes her appear more like her than she actually did.'

Chop frowned as though something had just occurred to him.

'Do you think Saskia might have thought it was proof she was still alive?' he asked.

'No idea,' I said.

'What do the police think?'

'About what?'

'The photograph. I'm assuming they've seen it.'

'They haven't. I took it from the copier before they arrived on the scene.'

'Does that mean you found the body, Kenny?'

I nodded. Chop winced.

'That must have been awful.'

'It was. I'd only met Saskia a couple of times but I liked her very much. And no one deserves to be put through the ordeal she was. Someone held an electric iron to her face before they killed her.'

'Christ, why do that?'

'Either to find out something she knew or for kicks. The consensus opinion seems to be that it was to see if she had any valuables on the boat.'

'You don't seem convinced.'

'I'm not. The way Saskia lived it must have been pretty clear to anyone that she didn't have a lot of cash. It was either a sadist or someone
who wanted to find out information she had before they killed her.'

'Connected to Castor and Emily?' Chop asked.

'That'd be my guess,' I said.

Yvonne entered the studio. Her eyes were a little red but little else
indicated that she had just been comprehensively bollocked. Her coach
was on his feet immediately.

'Yvonne, I'm incredibly sorry,' he said. 'It's just that you're the stron-
gest finalist by a country mile and I want to get an amazing performance
from you.'

Bullshit, although it played well with Yvonne.

'I know you're trying your best for me, Chop,' she said. 'I was
thinking in the ladies that maybe we should try a different number. I
sang "River Deep, Mountain High" at the audition, don't you think it's
better suited to my vocal range?'

Mime was best suited to Yvonne's vocal range. Judging by the way
Chop flinched as though she'd thrown a glass of ice water in his face,
he shared my opinion.

'Huge mistake to switch songs at this stage,' he said. 'Why don't
we give it another half-hour and call it a day? Don't want to strain the
cords . . .'

Yvonne beamed. 'You're the boss,' she said.

The first thing I did on leaving Encore Studios was google *Chop
Montague sister*. Three images came up. In two, Lydia Montague was
with her brother – an awards do and at their mother's funeral. In the
third she was wearing riding gear and standing next to a horse called
Fruit Fly. Lydia Montague was prominent in her own right as a three-
day event equestrian on the verge of the British Olympic team.

Had Emily Ridley lived to bear three children and spend a lot of time riding over open country in all weathers, she may have ended up looking like Lydia Montague. Chop's sister had a ruddy complexion and sturdy shoulders. The elfin look was long gone, although at a stretch it was possible to imagine Lydia as the girl in the photograph. Her brother and Odeerie had been right: I'd made two and two add up to five, or more specifically a random photo add up to a conspiracy.

I called St Mick's and arranged an appointment for the following morning. By noon I'd be scheduled to have my operation, always assuming that the surgeon didn't saw my skull open there and then.

My cabbie's genial banter and wry sense of humour added up to the best case for self-driving cars I'd ever heard. By the time we pulled up at Brewer Street, I was on the point of strangling the cockney git.

My plan for the rest of the day was to chain Marlboros, eat junk food and drink Monarch until I passed out. Shortly after instructing Dominos to bike round a cheesy chicken, bacon and chorizo pizza, my phone buzzed with a message.

We are in the grey van. Open the rear door and get in. Leave your phone behind.

According to my watch it was 6 p.m. exactly.

Life often hinges on choices that seem insignificant at the time. Should I take this job offer? Ask Jill from accounts out? Take the 3.15 from Waterloo or the 4.18 from Victoria? Climbing into a van on the instruction of an untraceable email and an anonymous text message does not fall into that category. You know that it's not something you'll barely remember a month afterwards. There will be consequences.

I stared out at the vehicle on the opposite side of the street for at least a minute. Tinted windows made it impossible to see the driver. Apart from that it was a standard Transit – the kind of thing plumbers and electricians drive around on a daily basis. On the other hand it had also been the vehicle of choice for serial killers, rapists and terrorists for over fifty years. My phone bleeped again:

60 seconds.

I grabbed my jacket from the back of the chair and took the stairs two at a time. Crossing the road, I almost collided with a Deliveroo cyclist.

The handle on the back door was stiff and took some opening. The interior of the van was empty and dimly lit. If I got in then I was taking a journey to who knew what and who knew where. If I didn't then I would probably never know the fate of Castor Greaves. There was another possibility, of course, but I put that out of my mind as I closed the door behind me. The engine started up and the driver put it into gear.

And off we went.

THIRTY-ONE

The first thing I noticed was the empty van's astringent smell; the second that its doors had been centrally locked. For twenty minutes I sat with my back against the side and tried to envisage our destination. Would Castor's whereabouts be revealed in a cosy bistro over a rack of lamb and an agreeable Bordeaux? Probably not. Likelier scenarios were deserted woods, lock-up garages or remote farm buildings.

The sounds of the city faded and the Transit picked up speed. The temperature dropped. I jammed my hands in my pockets to keep them warm. The resin smell became more pungent, as though the van had been used for transporting recently felled pine logs. Odds shortened on the woods as our final destination.

After we'd been travelling the best part of an hour, the van slowed. It took several turns, suggesting we were negotiating roundabouts, and came to a halt. I heard the driver's door open. Moments later, so did mine.

I was looking at Donald Trump.

The latex mask was the kind you buy at joke shops with holes for the eyes and a slit for the mouth. It was disturbing in and of itself. When worn by a bulky man in a donkey jacket, doubly so.

'Get out,' he ordered. I swung both feet on to the tarmac road on which the vehicle was parked.

My legs were weak and it wasn't entirely due to the cramp and the cold. The guy indicated that I should raise my hands and then patted me down. In the gloom I could make out three buildings. The largest was two storeys high. All the windows had been boarded up. Bits and pieces of twisted metal were strewn over a concrete forecourt, through which weeds had broken at irregular intervals.

A shove in the back sent me stumbling forward. A second helped me further along the way. 'Keep fucking going,' the guy instructed. The closer we got to the units, the more evident it became that they'd been derelict for a considerable time. Corrugated roofs had oxidised, and even the tin sign that read UNSAFE STRUCTURE: KEEP OUT had begun to buckle away from the brickwork.

The entrance doors to the largest unit had been secured with a padlock. My companion – or 'abductor' might be the more accurate description – removed a bunch of keys from his jeans and selected one.

'Watch your step inside,' he said. 'There's all sorts of crap lying around and the electricity's live.'

It was dark, cold and damp inside the building. Water flowed steadily through a ruptured pipe somewhere, its sound magnified by the silence. The door closed and the blackness became so profound that I could almost reach out and grab handfuls of the stuff. A lever was thrown and the interior flooded with light.

The place was the size of a car showroom. Beyond that, all comparisons ended. Its rough cement floor was strewn with broken glass, chunks of masonry and what looked like a rusted engine. To my left were a couple of small brick enclosures, to my right a channel about six foot wide constructed from two low concrete walls.

Halfway down the channel a piece of orange-painted machinery had been mounted, with cables that fed into its rear. A few yards further down, a winch had been bolted into the ceiling. From it hung several lengths of chain. A large metal drain had been set into the floor. Not a deserted farm building, not a lock-up garage, and not a deserted wood either. I was standing in a derelict slaughterhouse.

◆　◆　◆

Trump led me to a wooden chair and forced me on to it. He positioned my wrists behind my back. I felt a nylon tie click into place around them and waited for a bullet to the back of the head and a split-second journey into oblivion.

'How are you, Kenny?'

The question emerged from an ancient tannoy speaker attached to one of the walls. It had been digitally disguised in the same way the guy claiming to be Castor's had when he warned me off the case in his late-night call. Presumably vocal synthesisers were standard-issue at the Golden Road.

'I've felt better,' I managed to say. 'Who are you?'

'Call me George. Who knows, it might even be my real name. The driver's Alex, by the way, and as far as you not feeling too great is concerned . . . sorry, but you did accept our invitation.'

'Whose invitation?'

'We'll discuss that later,' George said. 'For the moment, let's focus on your surroundings. Any idea what this place used to be?'

'A sherbet-dip factory?'

'Try again.'

'It's an abattoir.'

'Correct. To be specific, you're currently in the dispatching shed. Cattle would be led through the door opposite you and into the slaughterhouse. A bolt would be fired directly into their brain, after which the carcass would be taken to the rendering plant next door. All very humane and efficient, wouldn't you say?'

'Tip-top,' I said. 'Can I leave now?'

'Except that description omits a lot of detail,' George continued. 'They say animals can sense danger, which may well be true. The one thing they must have been able to do was smell the blood and hear the terrified bellows. It had to be an appalling place to work. Have you ever met a slaughterman, Kenny?'

'Not that I recall.'

'Most only do the job for a few months and then leave. Those who last longer either become desensitised to the work or actually enjoy inflicting pain. They're the ones undercover journalists find playing baseball with live chickens or blinding calves with hook knives to watch them stumble around the yard for an hour or two.'

'Any specific reason you're telling me this?' I asked.

'Merely to emphasise that you're in a place where bad things have happened,' he said. 'And a place in which bad things can happen still. Clear on that?'

'Crystal,' I replied.

'Good, then let's proceed to the matter at hand. You were employed by Pamela Ridley to find her daughter Emily. You succeeded in that endeavour and now you're trying to discover the whereabouts of Castor Greaves. Is that right?'

I confirmed it was.

'The organisation I represent would like you to cease doing so immediately. In return we are prepared to tell you what it is that you want to know.'

'What happened to Castor?'

'Correct, although the information is for your edification only. Continue to search for Castor and the next time we get in touch will be the last time we get in touch. Does this make sense, Kenny? It's important there are no misunderstandings.'

'Perfect sense,' I said. 'What's the name of your organisation?'

'As far as its members are concerned, it doesn't have a name,' George said. 'Although inevitably people have invented something to call us by.'

'The Golden Road?'

'Indeed. Although everything you've heard is almost certainly nonsense.'

'So tell me the truth.'

'I don't think so, Kenny. What you're interested in is what happened to Castor Greaves on the night he was last seen in Soho.'

'And where he's been for the last twenty-two years,' I added.

'I can help on both counts,' George said. 'Castor left the Emporium club at one forty-five. He got into a van, not unlike the one you arrived in tonight, and two days later departed the country.'

'Why didn't the security cameras pick him up leaving the club?'

'They were doctored. A relatively easy procedure in those days.'

'Did Castor kill Emily Ridley?'

'He did not,' George said.

'Who did?'

'I can't help you with that.'

'Because you don't know?'

'I can't help you,' he repeated. 'Ask a different question.'

'Where was Castor taken?'

'Initially, a remote part of Algeria. Two years later he was moved to an island near the Philippines, where he spent nearly a decade. For the last eight years he has been living in a South American country. You'll forgive me if I don't supply its name.'

'Why did he take the Golden Road?'

'The usual tedious reasons.'

'What do you get out of it?'

'We're drifting towards a reef of specifics, Kenny. Let's just say there are financial as well as philanthropic compensations for the organisation.'

'And that's where Castor Greaves is now? Hiding in South America?'

'Correct. Although you almost certainly wouldn't recognise him. A different lifestyle plus extensive cosmetic surgery have altered Castor's appearance.'

'What if he tells someone about the Golden Road?'

'Who would believe him if he did?'

'I'm guessing you haven't managed to alter his DNA. All it would take is a drop of blood to prove who he really is.'

'Which is one of the reasons he's closely monitored. However, Castor is one of our more successful candidates and presents virtually zero flight risk.'

'If Castor is so well tucked away, why's the Golden Road concerned about me finding him? Surely there's no danger of that happening.'

A pause before George answered.

'As you can imagine, the organisation is publicity-averse and you've created quite a bit of publicity over the last few days. We're currently working with another candidate. It's important nothing jeopardises her transit.'

'Does that mean I get to go home now?'

'Not before I'm absolutely happy that you have appreciated the gravity of your situation. Alex, would you please take Mr Gabriel to the chute?'

◆ ◆ ◆

Alex secured my legs with a thicker version of the nylon tie constricting the blood supply to my hands. He hauled me over his shoulders, carried me across the floor and laid me between the walls of the chute. The rough concrete reeked of the shit and blood of the animals that had met their ends there. The winch chain lowered and something hooked around my ankles. I was hoisted until my head was parallel with the tops of the walls. Coins fell out of my pockets and clattered over the floor.

'Sorry about this, Kenny,' George said. 'But I have to be entirely convinced that you really are going to stop looking for Castor Greaves. Otherwise I'll have no other option than to . . . Let's just say that I have to be absolutely sure, shall we?

'The orange contraption you've probably noticed is a static bolt gun. It hadn't been used for over a decade and the mechanism had become rusted. Fortunately Alex is a savant when it comes to repairing mechanical instruments. Sourcing the bolts for such an old model turned out to be the difficult part. Thankfully, eBay came to our rescue. Alex, could you give Mr Gabriel a demonstration, please?'

A small watermelon was balanced on a wall about eighteen inches from my head. Alex dropped something into the gun's chamber and positioned it. The air was filled with flying flesh and black seeds, several of which spattered against my face.

'Of course, the result is different on a cow or a horse,' George said. 'The bolt remains in the brainpan of the beast. Exactly what it would do to a human head, I'd prefer not to find out. But that's entirely up to you, Kenny.'

Alex wiped the sticky gunge from my face. He replaced the used cartridge and positioned the muzzle of the gun three inches from the centre of my forehead.

'Have you ever come across visual accessing clues, Kenny? It's a method psychologists have developed to tell whether a person is lying or not.'

'All that NLP stuff is psychobabble bullshit,' I said, echoing Odeerie's sentiments. 'As far as I'm concerned, the search for Castor Greaves is over.'

'Maybe you're right and maybe you aren't,' George said. 'Although I'm afraid it's all I have to go on right now, so I'll ask you the question and Alex will decide whether he believes you. *Are you going to stop searching for Castor Greaves?*

I couldn't remember whether looking left or right constituted a constructed truth (aka a lie) or whether it was the other way round. And of course I was upside down, which meant that the positions might be reversed. Not that I could be sure that Alex would take this into account anyway. I stared directly into Donald Trump's face and tried to sound as sincere as possible. Not hard under the circumstances.

'I have zero intention of looking for Castor Greaves.'

The next few seconds were the longest of my life. If Alex didn't believe me then they would also be the last.

'No fucking way,' he said eventually.

And then he pulled the trigger.

◆ ◆ ◆

I screamed and writhed on the end of the clanking chain. Still breathing. Still alive. Either the bolt had missed, which seemed improbable, or the gun had misfired. Death delayed rather than denied. Alex would reload, make a couple of adjustments, and then it would be lights out for real.

George put me right on that.

'Congratulations, Kenny,' he said. 'Most men would have soiled themselves in similar circumstances. You appear to have avoided that indignity.'

'Fuck you!' I shouted, although there was barely any volume to it. The pressure in my head was so great that it felt as though my eyes were about to pop out.

'In case you were wondering,' George said, 'Alex used a blank cartridge. However, fail to keep your word, and next time you won't be invited to your own murder. The job will be done as it's usually done: efficiently and anonymously.'

I attempted another obscenity. All that emerged was a croak.

'No need to thank me, Kenny. It's been a pleasure, but hopefully for your sake we won't meet again.'

The tannoy screeched and fell silent.

◆ ◆ ◆

Alex slashed the nylon tie around my legs with a knife that looked as though he'd borrowed it from Tarzan. My wrists he left bound. Being suspended upside down for ten minutes and taken to the brink of death isn't great for your mental or physical well-being, with or without a brain tumour. It took five minutes for the shock to subside and the blood to redistribute around my system before I could be frogmarched out of the building.

Darkness had properly gathered, although there was a full moon. Trees surrounded the slaughterhouse on both sides. It wouldn't take long to identify its location online, although would there be any point? No doubt George and Alex had taken every precaution not to leave any evidence behind.

I lay in a foetal position in the freezing Transit and tried to keep warm. I also tried to process what had happened. Was Castor Greaves living in Paraguay courtesy of the Golden Road, or had the story and the night's events been specifically concocted to stop me looking for him? The van began to slow fifteen minutes after leaving the abattoir. It came to a halt and the engine was turned off. It hadn't been nearly enough time for us to get back to Brewer Street. Fear blossomed in my stomach like a malign flower. Alex pulled the back doors open, still wearing the Trump mask.

We were in a layby on a deserted country road. In the distance I could hear the sound of fast-moving traffic. Alex's knife was out. He scraped its edge first against my left cheek and then my right before holding its needle-sharp tip against my throat.

'You're lucky to get a second chance, arsehole,' he said, and allowed the point to sink in for emphasis.

A trickle of blood slalomed down my neck. Then the knife was removed and used to cut through the nylon tie around my wrists. My hands were numb from the cold and the paucity of blood. I held them under my armpits in an attempt to warm them up.

'M25's over there,' Alex said. 'You can hitch into town.'

He walked around the side of the Transit and got into the driver's side. The engine started up and the van eased out of the layby. Within seconds its tail lights had disappeared from view. I stomped around on the track, swore loudly to combat the encroaching pain in my fingers, and vomited into a nettle patch.

Then I began to trudge towards the motorway.

THIRTY-TWO

I'd only been on the motorway fifteen minutes when a Dutch guy delivering a lorry-load of cut flowers picked me up and took me as far as Greenwich. From there I took a taxi to Brewer Street. The first thing I did was pour myself a quintuple Monarch; the second thing I did was call Odeerie. No answer, which was peculiar as the fat man tends to stay awake until at least two in the morning. I texted him to give me a call as soon as possible, and then settled down to try to drink myself to sleep.

While the finest Scotch a tenner can buy did its best to calm my jangling nerves, I reviewed the last few days in an effort to identify who I'd seen or what I'd done that would warrant someone dry-firing a stun gun at my head in an attempt to warn me off. Whatever it was hadn't surfaced by the time I stumbled to bed.

I woke at seven thirty with the kind of headache only whisky and brain tumours provide. Had the vision in my left eye not been quite so terrible, I'd have gone back to sleep. As it was like peering through frosted glass, I opted to keep my appointment at St Michael's and hauled myself out of my pit.

Odeerie rang while I was outside the hospital's main building having a Marlboro prior to checking in at reception.

'Where were you last night?' I asked.

'In bed,' he said. 'I'm trying to get into a better sleep routine.'

'Remember the mysterious email?' I said.

'The one saying you'd get more info at six p.m.?'

'That's the one.'

I ground out my fag end and took the fat man through the previous night's events. He interrupted a couple of times to make sure that he'd heard correctly, but I had the story covered off by the time I was due to enter the building.

'You need to go to the police,' was his verdict.

'And say what? That I willingly accepted the invitation of a mythical organisation to find out the whereabouts of a rock star who's been dead for twenty-odd years?'

'That whoever it was threatened to murder you.'

'Shaheen thought I was nuts when I told him someone tried to drown me at Pegler's Wharf. If I start banging on about Donald Trump masks and disused slaughterhouses, he'll have me arrested for wasting police time.'

Odeerie breathed heavily. 'Maybe you're right,' he said. 'But why would someone want us off the job so badly?'

'Because they think we're close to something.'

'Which means they could come after me next.'

'They're not stupid, Odeerie. Harming you would bring attention.'

No response from the fat man.

'If I text you the van's registration, can you run a search?' I asked.

'Yeah, but why bother? I called Pam Ridley and told her that we've done as much as we can.'

'You're not curious, Odeerie?' I asked.

'Of course I am, but the plates are going to be false and you'll be in hospital for quite a while, so what's the point? And it sounds as though the Golden— as though these guys aren't mucking around, Kenny. Maybe safest to let it slide.'

'Are you sure about tracing the email? There's no way to do it at all?'

'It's not completely impossible but it takes time, effort and luck.'

'And could you take a look at disused abattoirs as well?' I said. 'It was within a fifteen-minute drive of Junction 5 on the M25. Place looked as though it had been abandoned for at least ten years, maybe longer.'

'You're not thinking of going back?'

'Probably not, but it would be interesting to know where it is at least.'

'Why?'

'Because two wankers strung me up and put a bolt gun to my head like I was a fucking animal, that's why. And if there's any way I can pay the bastards back then I'm taking it, regardless of the consequences.'

An elderly gent in a chair and the medic who was wheeling him towards the main doors looked round at me. My angry rant had taken all three of us by surprise.

'Okay, Kenny,' Odeerie said. 'Leave it with me.'

They say that the older one becomes, the younger policemen appear to be. The same applies to consultant neurologists. Alison (call me Ali) McDonald didn't seem to be much into her thirties. Curly dark hair fell as far as the collar of her jacket, and when she smiled a couple of dimples manifested in her cheeks. She was taller than me by a couple of inches and her Irish accent was easy on the ear.

'You were out for about a minute on the roof, then?' she said after I'd filled her in on my symptoms and the Emporium incident. I confirmed that was the case. 'And there haven't been any fainting incidents since?' was her second question.

'I've felt dizzy in the mornings, although I haven't lost consciousness,' I said.

'But the vision in your left eye's been affected?'

'Only for about half an hour or so. And I could still see out of it.'

'Did you have the same issues this morning?'

I nodded.

'Any nausea at all?'

'A little, but it passed.'

Ali reviewed the notes she'd made on her laptop. A wall clock with a loud tick read 10.18, which meant that we'd been in her consulting room almost fifteen minutes. I ran a finger around the inside of my collar. In common with the rest of St Michael's Hospital, the room was stiflingly warm.

Opting not to confess that the nausea might well have been due to having consumed half a bottle of Monarch the previous night, I told Ali that I'd been hearing, seeing and feeling things that almost certainly weren't there.

'Okay,' she said. 'That's actually quite rare but not unheard of.'

'Is it due to the size of the tumour?' I asked.

'Probably. Here's the image we took during your scan.'

The wall-mounted screen above her head flickered into life. I'd expected Ali to slap a piece of film against it. Instead she pressed a couple of keys on her laptop and a monochrome image appeared that resembled a Rorschach inkblot.

'If you look here you can see the mass,' she said. 'It's benign, which is one of the reasons it has such well-defined borders.'

The bleached white area stood out from the frogspawn grey.

'Still looks pretty big,' I said.

'That's why I'd like to operate as soon as possible,' Ali said. 'Although the tumour isn't malignant, it will continue to grow. That's going to mean increased pressure and could result in a stroke. To be honest, you've been fortunate to avoid that up to now. I'm going to increase the medication Dr Arbuthnot prescribed. That should cut down on some of the more unusual symptoms you've been having. Just to emphasise that you need complete rest, though, Kenny. No exertion whatsoever . . .'

Did exertion include undergoing a mock execution in a disused abattoir by a guy wearing a Donald Trump mask? Probably.

'When d'you suggest I come in?' I asked.

'Before the end of the week. You have comprehensive medical insurance, so that shouldn't be a problem.'

'How long will it take?'

'Usually four to six hours. You'll need a few weeks to recuperate and we may elect to do some radiotherapy pending the biopsy results.'

'What's the best outcome?' I asked.

'That the tumour is removed without complications and you make a successful and speedy recovery.'

'And the worst?'

'There's a degree of bleeding.'

'What would that mean?'

Ali clicked the screen off and leant forward in her chair. 'Partial or total loss of vision in your left eye, or even both eyes, might be a possibility,' she said. 'And there may be some physiological issues including fits, seizures and difficulty speaking.'

'What about the *absolute* worst outcome?'

'You're asking me whether it could prove fatal?'

'That's what I'm asking.'

'I won't lie to you, Kenny, this type of procedure is complex and it's difficult to predict how it will unfold with any certainty. The chances of you not regaining consciousness are significant, although each case is unique to itself.'

'My doctor said there was a ten per cent chance I wouldn't make it.'

I'd hoped that Ali would raise her eyebrows to indicate that Arbuthnot's assessment had been wildly pessimistic. They remained neutral.

'Mortality is less likely than likely, although there's a chance it may occur. It might be an idea to make the appropriate arrangements before you come into hospital, if you haven't done so already.'

'Put my affairs in order, you mean?'

Ali gave me a sympathetic smile. I stared at a large cowrie shell on her desk and wondered what would be left behind when I was gone. A wardrobe full of budget clothes, a few dozen records and a mermaid cigarette lighter whose nipples lit up when you depressed the tail. Except her batteries were flat.

'What d'you want to do, Kenny?' Ali prompted.

'What choice do I have?' I replied.

Nothing quite like seeing an image of your brain to make a philosopher out of you. Particularly when it looks as though a chunk of it has been Tippexed over. Had Ali not expressly forbidden alcohol, I would have left St Michael's, headed to the nearest pub and sunk a waga or six. Mercifully, she hadn't said anything about cigarettes.

I lit a Marlboro and considered my situation. Three days until I went under the knife. They might represent my final seventy-two hours on earth. How best to use them was the question. What were my chances of tracking down the abattoir twins? Not sensational, and Odeerie hadn't exactly sounded certain about cracking the email. He'd be able to locate the slaughterhouse, though. If I could find out who owned it then at least I could make a few enquiries, beginning with how and when the electricity had been restored.

However careful they think they've been, people make mistakes. It's usually just a matter of looking hard enough and long enough. Chances were that I'd be no wiser in three days' time, but at least it would give me something to do until my skull was shaved and the anaesthetist instructed me to start counting back from a hundred.

Outside St Mick's, I picked up the *Standard*. There were a couple of columns about Emily Ridley's murder on page seven. DCI Shaheen claimed to be following a 'number of potential leads', which was police-speak for *I haven't got a clue.*

I left the paper on the back seat when I got out of the taxi. My plan was to take a nap for a couple of hours, by which time Odeerie would hopefully have some information for me to begin to work with. As I was putting the key into the front door, a man emerged from the entrance to the Parminto Deli.

'Your name Kenny Gabriel?' he asked.

'Who wants to know?' I replied.

Fiftyish, my height and build and wearing a burgundy V-neck and a pair of grey chinos, the guy didn't look like a contract killer.

'My boss wants a word with you.'

'Who's your boss?' I replied.

'Jake Villiers,' he said.

The traffic was relatively light. While the driver concentrated on getting us to Fulham, I sat in the back seat and wondered what his boss wanted to speak to me about. I also wondered what I wanted to speak to him about. Since he'd lied through his teeth to me in his office, I'd heard about how Jake Villiers had compelled Pauline Oakley to commit fraud. He was almost certainly responsible for the deaths of Arnie Atkinson and Pauline, and I'd seen what he'd done to Stephie. She still thought the sun shone out of his arse and there wasn't a thing I could do to stop the pair of them getting married. Safe to say that we wouldn't be discussing QPR's back four, or how best to combat climate change.

We pulled up outside the Duck & Unicorn. If you can count on a murderer to have a fancy prose style, then you can also rely on him to come up with a bloody stupid name for a pub. Not that the D&U was a pub in the strictest sense.

A plate-glass window had both creatures stencilled across it. Inside were several rows of tables covered with pristine white tablecloths and shining cutlery. A large notice on the door indicated the place would be opening for business in two days' time. Jake's chauffeur opened up and ushered me inside.

Whitewashed brick walls had huge photos of cityscapes hanging on them. The floorboards had been stripped, and distressed industrial lights were suspended from the ceiling. Jake was sitting at a table at the furthest end of the room, by a picture of the Ponte Vecchio.

'Kenny,' he said, looking up from his laptop. 'How are you?'

'Fine,' I said.

He offered me his hand. I didn't reciprocate.

'Would you mind handing your phone to Lucien?' Jake said, with no apparent change in demeanour. 'He'll return it when we're finished.'

I gave my mobile to the driver, who looked questioningly at his boss. Jake nodded. Lucien patted me down and found nothing of interest.

'I'm thinking of banning phones in here,' Jake said after he had left. 'Make people actually talk to one another.'

'Will your customers get a body search too?'

He smiled. 'I might not go quite that far.'

A navy polo shirt emphasised Jake's lean torso and toned biceps. It also contrasted nicely with his lightly tanned features. A lack of conscience might send him straight to hell one day but it hadn't affected his complexion. He closed his laptop and indicated that I should occupy the chair opposite his.

'Fancy a drink?'

I shook my head and said, 'You've got two minutes.'

'Are you usually this direct, Kenny?'

'Pauline Oakley told me about how you forced her to falsify your tax return twenty years ago. But you must know that, otherwise I wouldn't be here.'

A muscle twitched in Jake's jaw. He put his hands behind his head and sat back in his seat.

'Actually, I wanted to offer you a job.'

'A job?'

'Apparently you used to run a members' club in Soho.'

'Half a lifetime ago.'

'I'd be employing you for your personality rather than your experience. What somewhere like this requires is a manager who can get on with the clientele and make sure the crew are well motivated. It pays sixty grand a year.'

'I've already got a job.'

Jake frowned. 'Shame. It would have made all of this an awful lot easier . . .'

'All of what?'

'I'm aware that Pauline was indiscreet about my tax affairs, Kenny. I also know that you don't have a copy of the papers she was using to blackmail me. You could go to the police, but without evidence what would be the point?'

'If you're not worried then why are we talking about it?'

'Because there's an outside chance they might follow up, which could be a little inconvenient for me, not to mention bad for business.'

'Speaking of which, how are things going at the Emporium?'

'I'm sorry?'

'You own the place.'

'I know.'

'Why did you buy it?'

'Because the lease came up for sale and it makes money. And thanks to you, Kenny, it'll make even more money now. Nothing like an unsolved murder to create a bit of notoriety.'

'Especially when it's a body on the roof that no one's noticed for twenty years because the new owner doesn't like people nosing around.'

'What's your point?'

'Ever heard of the Golden Road?'

Judging by Jake's blank expression the answer was no. I leaned forward and accidently-on-purpose knocked the Mac off the table. It landed with a clatter that echoed around the room. He didn't so much as blink.

'Is that how you sleep at night?' I asked. 'Put the murders of three people into the box marked "Business" and get yourself a solid eight hours? Because if it is then you'd better keep the lights on. What goes around comes around.'

'I didn't murder anyone.'

'Bullshit. You faked Pauline's suicide and you either got rid of Arnie Atkinson personally or had someone do it on your behalf. And what you did to Stephie was disgusting. If you ever do anything like that to her again . . .'

'Are you threatening me, Kenny?'

We stared at each other for a few moments. Jake chuckled softly. 'Of course you aren't,' he said. 'Not the type for threats, are you?' He shook his head as though he couldn't quite believe he'd taken me seriously. 'Arnie Atkinson needed stopping and I stopped him. Other way round and he'd have done the same.'

'What about Pauline Oakley?'

'What about her?'

'Did she have to be stopped too?'

'Pauline put everything I've created at risk.'

'So you hanged her and made it look like suicide?'

'I did what had to be done. That's the difference between you and me. It's also why I've got thirty million in the bank and I'm engaged to your ex-girlfriend.'

Jake leant further forward.

'The reason Stephie's with me is because I'm strong, Kenny. If she steps out of line then she needs to know about it. All the hearts-and-flowers stuff is great in the early stages, and it pays to sound unconcerned about ex-boyfriends. Be advised that's all going to change, though.'

'What if she steps out of line again?'

Jake shrugged. 'Women are like animals. They can usually be controlled if you apply sufficient force in the correct manner.'

He checked his watch and made a disappointed face.

'Looks like my two minutes are up,' he said. 'Thanks for your time, Kenny. Lucien will take you wherever you want to go.'

A solid ball of anger ricocheted around my nervous system like a pinball machine. Buzzers buzzed, bells rang and digit counters multiplied. And then everything became serene, as though the plug had been yanked from the wall.

'Thank you, Jake,' I said. 'And good luck with the opening.'

A V-shape formed on Jake's forehead as he looked at my outstretched hand. He accepted it, though with a grip that was less pneumatic than usual.

Thirty seconds later, I departed the Duck & Unicorn.

Traffic had thickened in London's arterial system. It took Lucien twice as long to drive back to Soho as it had to travel in the opposite direction. By the time he dropped me off on Brewer Street, the guys in the Parminto Deli were washing down steel trays and office workers were beginning to make for the Tube.

Angus Glazier's voicemail advised me to contact his mobile number if my call was urgent. He answered in person thirty seconds later.

'Angus, it's Kenny Gabriel,' I said. 'Sorry to bother you after hours, but I've been thinking about our conversation yesterday afternoon. Basically, I'd like to accept your offer.'

'Fantastic,' Angus said. 'May I ask what caused you to reconsider?'

'It's a great story and it deserves to reach the public. And I think it would be a fitting memorial to Saskia. Could we dedicate the book to her?'

'Of course,' he said. 'It would be a very fitting gesture. Any chance we could chat about this tomorrow, Kenny? I'm on my way to an important meeting.'

'Absolutely. There's just one small thing . . .'

A note of concern entered Angus's voice. 'What's that?' he asked.

'I need the advance in my account within twenty-four hours.'

'That simply isn't possible, I'm afraid. Even with a boilerplate contract it'll take at least a fortnight. And of course we need to find a writer for you to work with. Nothing so slow as publishing, I'm afraid . . .'

'Okay, I'll take what I know elsewhere.'

Angus's suavity died. 'Hold on a moment,' he said. A brief silence followed. 'It sounds as though you need the cash quickly for some reason.'

'Can you arrange it?'

'Not the whole amount, but I might be able to manage ten thousand at short notice. You'd have to sign a contract before anything could be done, though.'

'When could you have it with me by?'

'First thing tomorrow.'

'And the cash?'

He took a deep breath. 'Couple of hours after you sign.'

'Sounds great, Angus. I'll let you get off to your meeting.'

An hour later I dug out a number that I hadn't rung in over six months. Had hoped never to have to ring again. Before doing so, I poured out the rest of the Monarch bottle and drank it while watching dusk turn to night. The neon sign flickered on at the Yip Hing supermarket and a parking warden slapped a ticket on a Range Rover.

When the darkness was complete, I called Farrelly.

THIRTY-THREE

I spent ten minutes dry-retching into the lavatory. The vision in my left eye was so diminished that for half an hour all I could make out were vague outlines. Factor in a headache that felt as though someone was banging a six-inch nail into my temple and you have a good idea as to how I felt circa 8 a.m.

The contract from Billingsgate Publishing had arrived in my inbox. Five pages of close type made my head swim even more. The important clause was that ten thousand quid would be transferred into my account as soon as the document was returned. I signed it electronically and sent it back with my banking details.

Just when I'd decided to cancel Farrelly, the pain began to subside. Ten minutes later and my sight sharpened. I flipped a coin as to whether I should keep our appointment or tell the imp of death that I was too sick to see him. It came down tails. Once I was confident that I wouldn't barf all over its interior, I summoned an Uber to take me to Victoria Park in the East End.

Farrelly had been the chauffeur to my old boss Frank Parr. We'd first met in the seventies when Farrelly had taken an immediate and sustained dislike to me. Forty years hadn't improved his opinion. When Frank hired me to search for his missing daughter, Farrelly hadn't been inclined to let bygones be bygones.

The relationship had mellowed slightly when I employed his son as a bodyguard, although saying that Farrelly was your friend was like saying that you kept a pet crocodile. The relationship was subject to change without prior warning.

As arranged, he was sitting on a bench by the Chinese pagoda. It represented the juxtaposition of two philosophies: reflective spiritual harmony; focused and intense violence.

'You look like shit,' he said as I sat beside him.

'That's because I've got a brain tumour,' I said. Most people would have expressed a modicum of sympathy. Farrelly wasn't most people.

'Ain't no surprise,' he said. 'Crap you put into yourself.'

Farrelly was teetotal and worked out every day. Had he been born seven hundred years earlier, he could have been a Shaolin warrior. Although it was difficult to see him wearing saffron robes instead of a black Harrington jacket over a Ben Sherman polo shirt and sta-press trousers.

'That why you want a weapon?' He put a finger to his shaven temple and mimed blowing his head off. 'Save the aggro of going through chemo.'

'It's benign. At least they think it is.'

'You want to do someone?'

I nodded, and Farrelly began to laugh. It was a bit like listening to a komodo dragon attempting to gargle. A disturbed swan hissed at him from the safety of the water.

'Don't think you're the type, son,' he said when the hilarity had subsided.

'Okay, if you can't help, then I'll sort something else out.' I began to get up from the bench.

Farrelly's arm forced me back down. 'Tell me who it is.'

'Won't that make you an accessory before the fact?'

'Just bleedin' tell me.'

It took fifteen minutes to cover off how Jake Villiers had disappeared Arnie Atkinson, killed Pauline Oakley and blackened Stephie's eye. Farrelly stared at the horizon throughout and didn't make a single interruption.

'So basically you want to top this bloke because he's marrying your girlfriend?' he said when I'd finished.

'Didn't you hear what I said about the murders?'

'There's fuck-all proof he's killed anyone,' Farrelly said. 'And this Arnie geezer weren't no angel, from the sound of it.'

'What about Pauline Oakley? Scaring her shitless would have done the trick.'

'He couldn't have been completely sure.'

'Look, bottom line is that I don't want Stephie marrying a man whose default position when it comes to conflict resolution is murder.'

'All he's done is given his bird the back of his hand,' Farrelly said. 'That's a long way from putting her in the ground. And she can always walk away if he gets too rough. It's a free fucking country.'

'Stephie's got a serious temper, Farrelly,' I said. 'She's not the kind to walk away. If he does max up the violence, there's a chance she'll go for him.'

'Sounds like they were made for each other.'

'Apart from Jake will take it all the way. He thinks women should be treated like animals. And you know what happens to dogs that can't be house-trained . . .'

Farrelly sniffed a couple of times and pursed his lips.

'Why d'you give a shit?' he asked.

'Let's just say I do.'

'Okay, how about you drop me a monkey and I give him a hiding? Tell him that if he don't dump her, then I'll be back with an angle grinder.'

'It's a generous offer, Farrelly, but it's personal.'

Farrelly nodded. In his world, real men did it themselves, be that wallpapering the landing, changing the oil on a Jaguar Mark 2, or pumping four bullets into a love rival.

'You won't be picking him off from a hundred yards,' he said, nevertheless. 'You'd have to get right up to be sure.'

'Does that mean you'll sort me out?'

'What will you do if I don't?'

'Find someone else.'

'You don't bleedin' know anyone else.'

'I'll go to the Dark Web . . .'

Farrelly rolled his head and sighed. 'Well, then you might as well get it from me or you'll be nicked before you know it's happened.'

'How much will it cost?'

'Three grand. Two back if everything goes okay and you return the shooter.'

'What if it doesn't?'

'I keep the cash and you do life.'

The money I'd asked Angus Glazier for would easily cover the amount Farrelly wanted.

A lurcher retrieved a tennis ball that had rolled in front of the bench. Farrelly waited until the animal had raced back to its owner before speaking again.

'Still wanna do it?' he asked.

'Yeah,' I said.

'I'll be in touch.'

◆ ◆ ◆

While I was on my way back to Soho, Odeerie called with an update as to his attempts to trace the number plate of the Transit van, the source of the email and the address of the slaughterhouse. The news was mixed. 'The plate does link to a Transit van,' he said. 'But it belongs to a sixty-year-old tree surgeon who lives in Dumfries. There's no reports of it being stolen, so it sounds as though whoever it was knocked up false plates registered to a Transit in case they were pulled over.'

'What about the email address?' I asked.

'Still working on that. There's a ton of encryption on it.'

'You will be able to crack it eventually, though?'

'Maybe and maybe not. It'll take time before I know.'

'How much time?'

'Could be a couple of days.'

'Okay, and what about the slaughterhouse?'

'It's a few miles outside Sevenoaks. Belongs to a property company called Gifford-Wicks. They bought it off a wholesale meat business that went bust eight years ago and have just put it on the market. I gave them a call to see what the deal was with the power and they said it was disconnected.'

'Who did you say you were?'

'Someone from the utility company checking account information. Don't worry, Kenny, the woman who took my call didn't ask questions.'

'Okay, so that means whoever took me there knew how to reconnect the supply, which means they had some expertise as far as electricity is concerned.'

'Sounds as though they were quite sorted in general,' Odeerie said. 'What are you going to do now?'

'Not much I can do until you crack the email encryption.'

'*If* I can crack the email server,' Odeerie reminded me. 'You're going into hospital the day after tomorrow, aren't you?'

'That's right.'

'And you're likely to be in for a while?'

'Probably.'

Odeerie's silence was freighted with meaning. What was the point in pursuing something that I wouldn't be able to follow through?

'Let me know as soon as if there's any news on the email,' I said.

'No problem,' Odeerie replied. 'But to be honest, I wouldn't hold your breath. What have you been doing this morning?'

'Nothing important,' I said.

◆ ◆ ◆

I was about to make an omelette that I didn't particularly fancy eating when the call came through. 'Is that Kenny?' a half-familiar voice enquired.

'Speaking,' I said.

'It's Davina Jackson. You came to see me at City Stretch . . .'

'Of course,' I said. 'How are you?'

'I'm well, thanks. After our meeting I had a look to see if I could find the card that Emily sent when I was in hospital. I'm a bit of a hoarder when it comes to that kind of thing. And it was the last time that I had any contact with Em . . .'

'Did you find it?' I asked.

'Actually, I did. It was in the loft with a load of photographs. I'm not sure if this is going to be much use to you – in fact I think it might just make things even more confusing. Anyway, you know I said that Emily wrote that she'd given the Dean Allison tapes to Humphrey?'

Excitement welled in my chest.

'Well, I think I might have got it wrong. It looks more like *Humpty.*'

'Humpty?' I said.

'That's right. Emily's handwriting wasn't that clear but I'm ninety per cent sure that it's Humpty and not Humphrey.'

'Did you know anyone called Humpty?'

'I'm afraid not. It's an even more unusual name than Humphrey, isn't it?'

'It is a bit,' I said.

'I'm sorry, Kenny, I probably shouldn't have bothered you with it but you did seem to think that it was important.'

'You did the right thing,' I said. 'And it could prove useful. I'll check to see if there was anyone Emily knew who went by that name.'

Asking Pam Ridley if her daughter had known anyone called Humpty wasn't something I fancied on an empty stomach. I opened the fridge to find there was a single egg left in the rack. I was putting my coat on to pop out to the Yip Hing when suddenly I was back in Emily's room staring at the large cuddly toy on her shelf.

Thirty seconds later I was praying her mother would answer my call.

THIRTY-FOUR

The car gained ten yards. It had been a toss-up whether to take the Tube or a cab to Finchley. When we hit roadworks it became clear that I'd chosen poorly. I asked the driver if there was another route we could take. There wasn't another route we could take. I called the Worldwide Aid head office for the ninth time in thirty minutes. On the other eight occasions I'd been routed to voicemail. Having already left two messages asking that someone return my call as a matter of urgency, I was preparing to leave a third when an actual human being answered. 'Worldwide Aid Direct, Jeremy speaking, how can I help you?'

'Could you give me the number for your Finchley shop?'

'May I ask what it's in connection with?' Jeremy asked.

'Someone donated several items recently on behalf of a woman called Pam Ridley. One of them was an egg-shaped cuddly toy. I need to get it back as soon as possible.'

'Sorry, I didn't catch that,' Jeremy said. 'The signal broke up.'

The car advanced another ten yards.

'What's the number of your Finchley shop?' I almost screamed at him.

'May I ask what it's in connection with?'

I took a deep breath and repeated the bit Jeremy had missed, adding that the item was of huge sentimental value.

'I'm afraid we don't return items once they've been donated,' he said.

'I'll buy it,' I said. 'In fact, I'll pay ten times the price you've got on it. All I want to know is whether it's still in the fucking shop.'

The driver changed lane and we picked up speed.

'Worldwide Aid has a zero-tolerance policy when it comes to foul and abusive language,' Jeremy said. 'I'm putting the phone down.'

'Please don't do that! I'm sorry about the swearing. It's just that the toy used to belong to someone who's deceased and it'll break her mother's heart if we can't get it back. All I need is the number of your Finchley shop.'

Jeremy sighed. 'Hold a moment, please . . .'

While I was listening to a message that explained Worldwide Aid's mission to irrigate the poorest parts of the planet, the car stopped abruptly. 'Sorry, mate,' the driver said. 'Might clear up a bit after the next roundabout.'

We gained another ten yards. Jeremy came back on the line.

'Okay, this is the Finchley number,' he said. 'Although you might be unlucky, I'm afraid, as all our UK shops shut at two o'clock today.'

I wrote the number on the back of my hand. My watch read 2.05 p.m. The number rang for about twenty seconds before the bastard message kicked in.

'This is the Finchley branch of Worldwide Aid Direct,' a female voice intoned. 'I'm afraid no one is available to take your call at the moment. Items can be donated directly to the shop and we offer a collect service for larger items such as household or garden furniture. For legal reasons we are no longer able to accept electrical items such as washing machines, televisions, hair dryers, refrigerators, radios or cookers. If you want to leave a message, please do so after the beep.'

No beep. I called the number and suffered the message again. This time there was a beep. 'Please pick up if there's anyone there,' I said. No one picked up. 'My name is Kenny Gabriel, there's something in the shop that was donated in error and I need to get it back urgently. If you get this message in the next few minutes then could you please return my call?' I left my number and rang off.

The car gained ten yards.

◆ ◆ ◆

We pulled up outside the shop at 2.28 p.m. The chances of it being open half an hour after it was due to close were next to zero. If the Humpty Dumpty toy was in the window then I could call Jeremy and ask if someone could let me into the shop, or put a brick through it and snatch the toy. The latter option was the favourite, apart from there being no sign of the thing. I put my face to the grimy glass and peered into the gloomy interior.

There was a dining room table with a balsa-wood toucan perched on top in the centre of the room. To its left were two armchairs upholstered in lime-green cloth and to its right several racks of unmatched pots, pans and plates. Also present were two shelves of paperback books, what had to be at least a hundred DVDs, and five racks of assorted clothing. Contrary to its position on accepting electrical goods, there was an old upright vacuum cleaner. Absolutely no sign of a large egg-shaped toy.

A door opened at the end of the room. Through it walked a woman in her sixties wearing an anorak and a green bobble hat. I banged on the window and she started. I pointed to the door. The woman walked towards it in what seemed like slow motion. She flipped the latch and opened it cautiously.

'Can I help you?'

'Someonedonatedaneggtoyacoupleofdaysago,' I said. 'Haveyoustillgotit?'

'I beg your pardon?'

I repeated the sentence, leaving gaps between the words. Recognition dawned on the woman's face. 'Oh, yes,' she said. 'A couple bought it for their boy. The little chap saw it in the window as I was closing up.'

'What couple?'

'I'm sorry?'

'Who were they?'

The woman frowned. 'I've no idea.'

'Which way did they go?'

'Oliphant Road car park,' she said. 'They were complaining about the council putting up the charges.'

'Where's Oliphant Road?'

The woman pointed to my right. 'Just after you pass the garden centre,' she said. 'Can I ask what this is about?'

I was already running.

◆ ◆ ◆

By the time I reached Corrigan's Home & Garden, my heart felt as though it was attempting to batter its way out of my chest and my head was pulsating with pain. Chances were the family who had bought Humpty were already halfway home. The last thing I'd see before suffering a seizure was a sign offering Supastrength Weedex at £9.99.

A guy carrying a sack of potting soil asked if I was feeling okay. Between pants I assured him I was and asked how far down Oliphant Road the municipal car park was. He pursed his lips and decided about half a mile. I felt disappointed and relieved in equal measure. Given they had a fifteen-minute head start, my chances were zero that I'd be able to catch Humpty's new owners. The best thing I could do was return to the shop and ask the woman for a description of the family.

And then Humpty went past in a Nissan Pulsar.

Specifically, he was in the back seat wrapped in the embrace of a kid who looked as though he'd met his soulmate in corduroy form. The car stopped at the traffic lights. I took as deep a gulp of oxygen as my lungs would permit and began running again, to the amazement of the Samaritan gardener. I was almost within touching distance of the Nissan when the lights turned green and it began to move off.

The kid noticed me out of the back window. I've no idea what he said to his father, although I'd imagine it was along the lines of *Daddy there's a funny man running behind us waving his arms around.* The car pulled to a halt at the side of the road. A tall guy in black jeans and a denim shirt got out of the driver's side. I approached him like a ship-wrecked sailor staggering on to a deserted beach.

'Were you following us?' he asked.

All I could manage was a brief nod.

'Is there something wrong?' Although broad and athletic, the man had the unsettled look that people tend to get in the presence of the deranged.

'The . . . doll,' I managed to say. 'Need . . . Humpty . . .'

He looked at the back of the car. 'Robbie's toy?'

I nodded.

'I . . . just want . . . to examine it.'

Robbie's dad looked through the rear window and back to me. His partner was craning around in the passenger seat, looking equally perplexed. For a moment I thought that he was about to get into the car and start the engine. Instead he opened the back door and addressed his son. 'Robbie, could I borrow Noggy a moment?'

Reluctantly the kid handed the rechristened Humpty over.

'What's all this about?' his father asked me.

'Something . . . inside. Won't take . . . more than . . . a . . . minute.'

The man handed me the toy. It was in good condition, largely as it had sat undisturbed in Emily Ridley's bedroom for over twenty years. Inside was something that had remained secret for the same amount of time. Or maybe it wasn't.

I felt the oval toy for any bulges and found none. The zip running around Humpty's midriff refused to budge. I tried to force it and the kid began to cry.

'He's hurting Noggy, Daddy. He's hurting Noggy.'

'What d'you think you're doing?' the man asked.

'I'll give . . . it back . . . in a bit,' I said.

'You'll bloody well give it back now!'

He grabbed one end of Humpty and I held on to the other. As we both pulled, the toy elongated to the point that it was no longer obese but severely anorexic. The kid began to wail. His father released his left hand, took a swipe at me and narrowly missed. He would probably have repeated the action were it not for a tearing sound and a ragged five-inch gash appearing around the toy's circumference.

The guy lost his hold and careered backwards into the car. I plunged a hand into Humpty's guts. By now the kid had been shocked into dumbfounded silence.

'Right, you asked for this, mate,' his father said.

He balled and raised his fist at around the same time my hand encountered something hard. Out of Humpty came a polythene bag.

'What the hell's that?' the bloke said, lowering his hand.

THIRTY-FIVE

Odeerie made several calls before he could locate a contact who had equipment capable of playing both the cassettes I'd found in Humpty's guts. While waiting for a Handycam and a Dictaphone to be biked round, we handled the tapes like a pair of archaeologists poring over ancient artefacts.

'They look okay,' I said. 'And they can always be re-spooled if necessary, can't they?' The fat man dunked a digestive into a mug the size of a small Jacuzzi and pursed his lips.

'Depends whether they've been near any strong magnetic fields. That could wipe the content or make it unwatchable. We'll have to see . . .'

He dropped the soggy biscuit into his mouth and swallowed it after a cursory chew. I popped another couple of Nurofen and dispatched them with a gulp of water. The pain in my head had dissipated since the roadside drama, although the vision in my left eye was blurry around the edges again.

'What did the kid's old man do when you pulled these out?' Odeerie asked.

'Looked a bit taken aback,' I said. 'I told him the tapes were evidence in a cold case investigation and that I'd need them and the doll as evidence.'

'Was he okay with that?'

'He was when I told him that I was a plain-clothes Met officer and gave him twenty quid to buy his kid a new toy.'

Odeerie levered another biscuit free and offered me the packet. I shook my head. Along with the presence of blurry vision, my appetite had disappeared. More alarmingly, there was a buzz in my left ear that sounded as though a fly had become trapped inside it.

'So you think it's footage of Dean Allison and Emily having sex when she was underage?' Odeerie asked.

I nodded. 'It was Davina Jackson's suggestion that Emily ask for a copy of the tape. If Dean showed it to Cas, then she could show it to the police.'

'Which effectively made it a standoff?'

'That Dean resolved by murdering her.'

Odeerie put aside what remained of the biscuits and brushed the crumbs that had collected on his chest to the floor.

'Didn't Dean leave the club while they were both alive?' he asked. 'And I thought he had an alibi . . .'

'None of the evidence pointed to Dean being a suspect at the time, so his alibi probably wasn't tested that rigorously. And don't forget this didn't become an official murder inquiry until a few days ago.'

'D'you think he did it, Kenny?' Odeerie asked.

I stared at Humpty propped up on the sofa. Quite a bit of his stuffing had been left on the road, causing him to sag as though he was a victim of a pernicious wasting disease. The crooked grin was still in place, though, even if it did resemble a smirk.

'I think he's capable of it,' I said.

'Not what I asked,' Odeerie said. 'And what about the business in the abattoir? If Dean's our man, what the hell was that all about?'

'I don't have a clue,' I admitted. 'But we're assuming Castor's disappearance is connected to Emily's murder. It doesn't necessarily follow that's the case.'

'You think Dean killed Em at the same time Castor took the Golden Road?'

'*If* he took the Golden Road. Maybe Dean cooked up the slaughterhouse bullshit because he doesn't want us to find Castor.'

'Apart from he's got a busted jaw and he can barely walk. Not to mention he's a total loner and would have needed accomplices to set the whole thing up. And the fact that we're nowhere near finding Castor Greaves—'

The intercom interrupted Odeerie. He looked at the unit and then stared at me expectantly. I rolled my eyes and got out of my chair. 'I have a package for a Mr Odeerie Charles,' the messenger said. 'Can someone sign for it, please?'

'Be right down,' I told him.

◆ ◆ ◆

Odeerie's hands may look like two bunches of sausages but he's dexterous enough when it comes to anything digital. Within five minutes of removing the Handycam from its box, he had inserted the tape and connected the cables to the larger of the two monitors in the office. It would have been easier to play the audio cassette first, but we had opted to watch the video before listening to the tape. Hopefully . . .

Odeerie squinted at the control panel and prodded it with a fingertip. The monitor flooded with static. After twenty seconds my heart began to sink. It seemed that two decades had indeed degraded the tape. And then suddenly we were looking at a bed covered in a black duvet on which Dean Allison was lying naked.

His pale body was slim and his cock semi-erect. He stared directly at the camera for a few seconds, perhaps wondering if it was working properly. The loud bebop we could hear was presumably there to mask the sound of the mechanism.

Emily came into shot wearing a T-shirt and knickers. She removed both and Dean pulled her on to the bed. For the next fifteen minutes the pair had sex that would have been unremarkable had Dean not persistently engineered positions for the benefit of the camera. And the date showing in the bottom right of the screen.

According to Wikipedia, Emily Ridley had been born on the tenth of April 1977, which meant that she was two months short of her sixteenth birthday in the video. This, combined with the fact that Dean was clearly aware of the camera's presence and Emily had no idea it was there, would have added up to a slam-dunk prosecution in court.

The tape made for very uncomfortable viewing, above and beyond its voyeuristic nature. I reached for the remote and switched the monitor off before the event reached its conclusion.

'We've seen enough,' I said.

The sound recording began with the electronic parp of a ringing phone. Emily hadn't skimped on the equipment. The quality was loud and crisp.

Dean Allison answered groggily as though roused from a heavy sleep – ironic, bearing in mind that he was about to receive an even bigger wake-up call.

'It's me,' Emily said with a hardness that Dean couldn't have failed to notice.

'Everything all right?' he asked.

'Your video arrived. I played it last night.'

'Okay, so what's your decision?'

'I'm taking it straight to the police.'

'You're doing what?' Dean asked.

'You heard.'

'Why?'

'Because you're blackmailing me.'

'You've got no proof of—'

'And I'm being raped.'

Dean chuckled. 'I don't know what tape you've been watching, Em, but I think it's fair to say that you weren't being raped in that video. More the other way round, if anything. You were always enthusiastic in the sack, I'll give you that.'

'Actually, I think the term is statutory rape,' Emily said, mispronouncing the word slightly. 'It means having sex with someone under the age of consent.'

A three or four-second pause on the tape followed this revelation. 'But you weren't underage,' Dean said, all humour purged from his voice.

'I was fifteen when we were seeing each other.'

'You lied to me about how old you were?'

'No, I didn't, Dean,' Emily said for the benefit of any third party who might subsequently listen. 'Remember, I told you how old I was when we met and you said that it wasn't a problem as far as you were concerned.'

'I said no such thing,' Dean snapped. 'And anyway, how can you prove that you were underage? It'll just be your word against mine.'

'Oh no, it won't,' Emily said, beginning to enjoy herself. 'I don't know what tape you've been watching, Dean, but the one you sent to me has the time and date on it.'

There was another hiatus in the conversation, during which Dean presumably considered his next move.

'Take it to the police and it'll come out that you were seeing me. Castor will drop you immediately.'

'You're right there,' Emily conceded.

'So does that mean you aren't going to show them?'

'As long as you don't send a copy to Cas. If he gets to hear that we were ever together, then I'll be in a police station within the hour.'

'You're bluffing.'

'Try me.'

Even twenty years after she had made her threat, it was clear that Emily was serious. Dean could have drawn no other conclusion at the time.

'You stupid bitch,' he said. 'You think that moron's going to stay with you? If he doesn't OD then he'll find some other brainless slut to fuck.'

'That's rich coming from a man who can barely hold a pair of drumsticks,' Emily snapped back. 'If it weren't for Cas and JJ, you'd be working in a call centre.'

It took several seconds for Dean to reply.

'You think you've been so clever, don't you, Em?' he said. 'But you and the junkie had better watch out. I might not be the greatest drummer in the world, but I have other talents.'

'What's that supposed to mean?' Emily asked.

'Wait and see,' Dean said.

THIRTY-SIX

The audiovisual suite in West End Central had all the bells and whistles. A large oval table could have seated at least a dozen people. Each place came with its own microphone and operating console. The screen attached to the wall was the size of a pool table and the ozone tang in the air was reminiscent of the seaside.

Despite the hi-tech wizardry (or more likely because of it), DCI Shaheen had to summon someone from IT to connect the Handycam to the screen. While we waited, I filled him in on how I'd come across the footage. I also told him about my interviews with Dean Allison and suggested that he might want to look at his alibi again.

Shaheen made notes and asked a few questions about Davina Jackson and her relationship to Emily Ridley. I thought about recounting my trip to the slaughterhouse and decided against it. Shaheen would probably have grilled me for a couple of hours and might have insisted we visit the site. None of which I had time for.

The DCI's face was passive throughout the video, although he was quick to switch the unit off after the film had finished. He laid the remote on the table next to his pad and frowned.

'Does Dean Allison know you've got this?'

'Nope. As soon as Odeerie and I saw what it was, I brought it straight to you.'

'Who?'

'Odeerie Charles. He's my business partner.'

Shaheen jotted down the information.

'So, what you're claiming is that Emily Ridley had no idea she was being recorded?'

'What do you think?'

Shaheen shrugged. 'It looks that way,' he said. 'But we don't know for sure.'

'Yes, we do,' I said. 'And here's the reason why . . .'

I played the recording Emily had made on the phone. Afterwards, Shaheen tapped his teeth with his pen for a few seconds and delivered his verdict. 'Fair enough, it sounds as though Dean Allison probably did rape Emily.'

'Probably? You can see the date on the tape.'

'Okay, definitely raped her, then.'

'And there's the comment about waiting to see what other talents he has.'

Shaheen rubbed his hands over his face as though attempting to wipe away the tiredness etched into his features. I hadn't expected him to dance with joy but I had anticipated a slightly more effusive reaction.

'It's not exactly a death threat, is it?' he said.

'Sounds like one to me.'

'That's because you're hearing what you want to hear. You don't like Allison, and after watching that I can understand why. Saying that he's got "other talents" isn't enough to bring a murder charge, though. The CPS wouldn't look at it twice.'

'At least check his alibi again.'

'You think I haven't already done that? Nine witnesses saw Allison in Chester's bar at the time he says he was there. And the woman he met confirmed they spent the night together. No way could he have murdered Emily. Not unless one of his other talents was being in two places at the same time.'

'You're doing fuck-all, then?'

'I'll have him in and ask if he's got any comment to make. Don't get me wrong; if Emily Ridley were still alive then we'd almost certainly bring an historic rape charge against Allison. As things stand, though . . .'

'He gets away scot-free?'

Shaheen shrugged.

'How often does that happen?' I asked.

'Guilty people walking? All the time.'

'Doesn't it piss you off?'

'Of course it does, but I'm not God, Kenny, I'm a copper. And if you can't take losing a few then it's time to hand your card in.'

Shaheen's buzzing phone punctured the silence. He made an apologetic gesture and answered it. 'When will he arrive?' he asked, and looked at his watch. 'Okay, give me a call after he's processed and book an interview room. We'll need to brief Sue Behan as well. When this gets out the press'll go berserk.'

He killed the call and put the phone in his jacket pocket.

'Thanks for bringing this to me, Kenny. I know it wasn't the outcome you were looking for, but I hope you understand why.'

'Was that call connected to the case?' I asked.

'What call?'

'Oh, come on! I've bent over backwards for you. And it sounded as though you're going to make whatever it is public soon, anyway.'

Shaheen ran a hand through his hair. 'Okay, but you don't say anything to anybody, Kenny, otherwise I'll have your nuts on a stick.'

I made a zipping motion across my lips.

'Forensics put someone in the frame.'

'Do I know them?' I asked.

Shaheen nodded. 'Kristos Barberis.'

◆ ◆ ◆

They say the only two sure things about the future are that it will be different and that it will surprise you. That Whispering Nick's Uncle Kris was being hauled into West End Central as a prime suspect held true on both counts. For one thing the guy had looked genuinely shocked when I uncovered Emily's body on the Emporium's roof, and for another I couldn't imagine him murdering a hamster.

Shaheen pointed out that most killers would be fairly stunned if their victims were produced in front of them after twenty years, and that judging anyone by the face they present to the world is usually a mistake. He added that Kris hadn't been charged, let alone convicted. Despite this, I could see that Shaheen was excited at the prospect of spending time in an interview room with him.

He refused point-blank to tell me what the forensic evidence was, although he pointed out that Kris was the only person who had both access to the CCTV and keys to the building. This meant that he was capable of returning to the club to hide Emily's body at leisure and could have doctored the tapes to conceal the fact.

Except he hadn't. The forensic evidence would turn out to be flawed and it was protecting the real culprit: Dean Allison. The more I thought about the tapes, the more I became convinced Dean had killed Emily and probably Castor. The problem was proving the fact before I was admitted to hospital in less than forty-eight hours.

I took a detour on my return from West End Central to pass the Emporium. Flowers had been heaped against the walls of the building, as had photographs of Emily Ridley and Castor Greaves. Judging by the messages scrawled across them – *rip sweet angels, together 4 eternity, true love never dies* – most fans were convinced that Castor was kicking back in the great dressing room in the sky where the Jack Daniel's flows like water and the rider never ends. They might think differently if they knew about my experiences in the slaughterhouse two days ago.

Continuing my journey to Brewer Street, I wondered whether Dean Allison really was capable of setting up something as elaborate as the slaughterhouse business to cover his tracks. Odeerie's dismissal on the grounds that he had a busted jaw and was Johnny No-Mates had sounded convincing. But that was before we played the tapes. Dean's 'other talents' claim had been so malevolent that I could believe him capable of anything, including mock execution by proxy.

The question was pushed to the back of my mind as I mounted the stairs. Someone was moving around the flat. My stomach backflipped and I was about to clatter back down to street level and call the cops when I remembered that my brother Malcolm was due back from Hong Kong that day. It made sense that he would come round ASAP and had let himself in when I hadn't answered my doorbell.

As there were no signs of forced entry, and the lock was a Banham, there could be no other explanation. Nevertheless, I opened the door as quietly as I could. The sounds stopped immediately. Brandishing the snooker cue I kept for emergencies, I pushed the sitting room door open. Farrelly was sitting on the sofa peeling an orange.

'Where the fuck have you been?' he said without looking up.

The white towel was draped over the coffee table. On it were two pieces of hardware. Largest was the body of a handgun. Next to it was the magazine that I'd just watched Farrelly load with bullets taken from a small cardboard box.

'It's a Beretta M9,' he said. 'The US army uses 'em so they're reliable, but you gotta know what you're doing otherwise you could fuck up and you can't afford that.' He picked up the gun. 'First of all, insert the magazine. Then close the slide.' He performed both actions. 'Safety's up by your thumb here,' he said, holding the weapon at an angle in order that I could see it. 'Make sure it's on release. These things hardly ever jam, so if it ain't workin', chances are the safety's on. This is on and this is off.' He repeatedly clicked the catch back and forth, saying metronomically, 'On, off, on, off, on, off, on, off, on, off', as he demonstrated the mechanism.

'I think I've got that bit, Farrelly,' I said.

'Just make sure you have, because once this thing's in sight he's gonna know what's coming and you need to be fast. For fuck's sake don't try and shoot it with one hand and don't hold it down here. You ain't Humphrey Bogart.'

Farrelly elevated the weapon from his waist and held it at arm's length. Both gnarled hands were folded around the grip.

'Keep it up at eye level with your arms stretched out,' he said. 'Don't be too tight or too loose. Make sure that you're ready for the recoil. You want to be about this distance away from him. Any closer and he might grab you; any further and there's an even chance you'll miss the fucker.'

Farrelly pointed the gun at the mirror. The fact that he appeared to be involved in a duel with himself only served to heighten the demo's surreal quality.

'That's only eight feet,' I said.

'Don't make no difference,' Farrelly replied. 'He'll be begging for his life and your hands are gonna be shaking like fuck. Put two into his chest. And then, no matter what, put another pair in his nut. There'll be all kinds of shit flying around when you do him in the head. You gotta be prepared for that.'

'I'll bear it in mind.'

Farrelly put the gun on safety and lowered it.

'Shouldn't I be using a silencer?' I asked.

'Nine millimetres don't make much noise,' Farrelly said. 'Better take a couple of practice shots in the woods to get used to it, though. Speaking of which, where are you planning on doing it?'

'Not sure,' I said.

Farrelly released the magazine and pulled the slide back. He checked the well and chamber were clear before releasing the slide and putting the safety on. Then he put both magazine and gun back on to the coffee table.

'Best thing is to stake him out for a couple of weeks and see what his habits are. That way you can make a move when there's no one around.'

'It has to be tomorrow.'

'What?'

'I'm in hospital the day after.'

'Can't it wait until you get out?'

I shook my head. 'I might not get out.'

'Why's that?'

'The tumour's huge. There's a chance I won't make it through surgery.'

Farrelly's lips pursed like an art expert asked to ratify an old master of doubtful provenance. 'Still a hundred per cent?' he asked. 'Because you could always farm it out to a pro, or just forget the whole fucking thing, which would be a better idea.'

'No way. I want Jake to know it's me.'

'You can call it off right until the last moment.'

'I'll bear that in mind.'

'Last bit of advice,' he said, reaching for his jacket. 'Once it's done, stick the shooter in your bag and walk away as though you haven't got a care in the world. Do not run unless you know for sure someone's after you. And don't call me afterwards; I'll get in touch with you. Any questions?'

'Only one,' I said, handing over a brown envelope full of cash. 'D'you think I can do it? Only you've always seemed to think that I'm a bit of a . . .'

'Useless twat?' Farrelly suggested.

'Pretty much.'

The imp of death stroked his chin.

'Thing you've got to watch out for is bottling it,' he said. 'Once you point the gun at this geezer then you can't choke. Otherwise he'll send someone after you. Don't let nothing or no one change your mind. Understood?'

'Understood,' I said.

It was nearly nine when I bought four five-kilo bags of rice from the Yip Hing. Hauling them out of my bedroom window and on to the roof was a pain. But if I was going to check the gun was working before tomorrow then it was my only option. An L-shaped brick construction sheltered the ventilation fans from the elements. More importantly, it meant no one could see what I was doing from the other buildings.

After arranging the bags against a wall, I loaded as Farrelly had demonstrated, slotting the flat end of each round against the flat end of the magazine. A voice in my head played a running commentary: *You're seriously doing this? You're out of your mind. Murdering a sack of basmati is a lot different to murdering Jake Villiers. You're a skip-tracer, not Carlos the Jackal. Stop it, Kenny. Stop it now!*

The last two sentences were courtesy of my mother. They were the kind of instructions issued when I was pulling a wheelie on my bike or tormenting my brother in the back of the car. Although Ma was no longer around, I was confident that rehearsing an execution on a Soho rooftop would have inspired similar orders.

And yet what did I have to lose? There was a good chance I'd die under the knife. Even if I didn't, I might as well be in a prison hospital as a regular one. Sure, I'd found Emily Ridley's body, but she would have been discovered eventually. The real challenge had been to track down Castor Greaves and I'd failed to do that.

One positive thing I could do with whatever time I had left was take Jake Villiers out of the game. Stephie would never thank me but if I planned things well enough then she'd never know I was responsible.

Fuck it, as Confucius probably once said.

I levelled the pistol at the bags in the same way Farrelly had demonstrated an hour earlier. The weapon jumped and made a sound like a cracking whip. Dry rice cascaded from one of the bags. My grip was steadier second time round.

THIRTY-SEVEN

That an arrest had been made in connection with Emily Ridley's murder dominated the morning news. All the police would reveal was that the man was in his sixties and an employee of the Emporium club. Reporters named Kristos Barberis as the man of the moment. Kris's picture flashed up on the screen every three minutes with rolling text informing viewers that he'd been detained at West End Central police station overnight and that questioning would continue today. In other news, the pound had continued its downward trend against the dollar, a man from Perpignan had received a successful face transplant, and I was partially deaf in my left ear.

On the plus side, my headache was within acceptable limits and I didn't feel like puking into the loo. My call was answered promptly.

'Jake Villiers speaking.'

'Hi Jake, it's Kenny.'

If Jake was surprised to hear from me he didn't sound it.

'Hello, Kenny, what can I do for you?' he asked, as though the last time we'd spoken I'd been trying to sell him life insurance instead of accusing him of murder. Nevertheless, what had been said had made it important to play things carefully.

'Jake, I just wanted to . . . Actually, forget about it. Sorry to bother you.'

'Hey, hang on,' Jake said. Judging by the background noise, he was driving. 'There must have been something you wanted to speak about . . .'

I left a calculated pause.

'I've been thinking about the other day . . .'

'And?'

'I flew off the handle.'

'Just a touch. I had to buy a new laptop.'

'I'm sorry about that. And I'm sorry about the other things I said.'

Jake changed gear and I heard the car accelerate.

'I did what I had to do, Kenny,' he said. 'Simple as that.'

'I get that now. And that's why I wanted to apologise.'

'Okay, apology accepted.'

'The other thing I was thinking . . . You said that you might be prepared to offer me a job managing the Duck & Unicorn. This investigations thing isn't going anywhere and the happiest time in my life was when I was running the Galaxy.'

For a few moments all I could hear was the hum of the car's engine.

'Let's not piss about, Kenny,' Jake said. 'We both know that the job offer was contingent on you keeping certain unverifiable information to yourself. How about I make it easier and pay you the cash as a one-off consultancy fee? Then we can forget all about it.'

'I'm not threatening you, Jake,' I said. 'And I'm not looking for a handout. I really want to work. But if you don't think it's feasible . . .'

'Hang on, hang on,' he said. 'Why don't you swing by the office tomorrow lunchtime and we'll have a chat?'

'Actually, I wondered if there's any chance we could meet today,' I said, trying to minimise the tension in my voice. 'You know what it's like when you get the bit between your teeth . . .'

'Can't be done,' Jake said. 'I'm scouting a place in Folkestone.'

'I could be in Richmond this evening. That's where you live, isn't it?'

Jake's satnav advised him there was a turn coming up in eight hundred metres.

'Can you be there by six?' he asked.

'No problem.'

'I'll text you the address.'

'No need for that,' I said quickly. 'Just give me your postcode and house number.'

He obliged with the details.

'Great,' I said. 'Oh, and Stephie won't be around, will she? It might be a bit, you know . . . awkward.'

A pause, and then Jake said, 'Steph won't be there.'

'See you later, then,' I said, and ended the call.

◆ ◆ ◆

The best advice I can give you when it comes to executing someone is to pretend that it isn't happening. I put Farrelly's gun and the ammunition under my mattress and focused on the day ahead. The first thing was to call Whispering Nick and see what information he had about his uncle being taken into custody.

The answer was not much. Kris had been interviewed after we'd found Emily's remains and then asked for a 'routine' DNA sample a day later. His arrest had come out of the blue and the police weren't giving the family any more information than they were to the public. I told Nick that I was sure that his uncle was innocent and to get in touch if there was anything I could do to help.

My conversation with Odeerie mostly concerned his ongoing search for the source of the email used to lure me to the abattoir. He'd tried various methods to break the encryption. None had succeeded and he sounded as though he was losing hope. I asked him to give it another day and then give it up as a bad job. The rest of the call was spent discussing Shaheen's suspicion that Kris was implicated in Emily's murder.

'It's not Kris,' I said. 'He's a roly-poly Greek guy who wouldn't harm anyone.'

'*Now* he is,' Odeerie said. 'But twenty years is a long time, Kenny. And a lot of people thought Ted Bundy was a very charming guy.'

'For fuck's sake, he's not Ted Bundy.'

'All I'm saying is that you have a tendency to be impressed by superficially charming people. And if the police have DNA evidence and have held him overnight, then they must be fairly sure that he has something to do with the murder.'

'It's Dean Allison. You saw the movie and you heard the tape.'

'Shaheen wasn't that impressed.'

'Yeah, well, we'll see.' A lame way to end the discussion, but I couldn't think of a snappier line.

'What time are you going into hospital?' Odeerie asked.

'Ten o'clock tomorrow.'

'Why don't you come round tonight for a drink?'

'Actually, I've got something on.'

'Like what?'

'Er . . . My brother's having me for supper.'

'Oh, right, well I guess you should be with your family.'

The disappointment in Odeerie's voice made me bite my lip. 'That's fairly early, though,' I said. 'I might come round afterwards . . . depending on how I feel.'

'Be good to see you, Kenny,' the fat man said. 'Obviously I'd visit you in St Mick's if I could, but you know how it is . . .'

'I know, Odeerie,' I said. 'I'll call you later.'

◆ ◆ ◆

My brother rang from Hong Kong while I was packing my hospital bag. He'd taken a tumble in a restaurant while entertaining a client and broken his arm. As a result he'd missed his flight and wouldn't be back in the UK for another forty-eight hours.

Malcolm said the things that big brothers say to little brothers even when their combined age is well north of a century. He asked if there was anything I needed. I told him there wasn't. He promised that his would be the first face I saw when I woke up. I told him that brain surgery was punishment enough.

I'd just pulled the zip closed on six boxer shorts, twelve socks, a twenty-year-old pair of pyjamas, and some carpet slippers that I'd forgotten I owned, when my phone rang again.

Pam Ridley got straight down to it. 'It's just been on the news that they've charged someone,' she said. 'Is that right, Kenny?'

'I don't think they've charged Kristos, Pam. He's just being questioned.'

'Did it have anything to do with that toy you were so excited about?'

No point in telling Pam about the tapes. She would insist on playing them, and viewing her daughter's rape would serve no useful purpose.

'Just a hunch that came to nothing,' I said. 'The arrest was made after DNA screening. Kristos was the premises manager at the Emporium. He still works there. At least he did.'

'Wasn't he there when you found Em?'

'That's right.'

'But you didn't suspect him?'

'I didn't then and I don't now. But the police must think they have some fairly compelling evidence. They wouldn't have held him so long otherwise.'

'How long can they keep him for?'

'Forty-eight hours with an extension.'

There was a silence, during which Pam digested this information.

'I spoke to Swami Hari again before I left,' she said. 'He reckoned that you'd be the one to find out who killed Em, and if you don't think it's him then it isn't him.'

'Maybe the swami's wrong on this one,' I said. 'I'm going into hospital tomorrow morning and I won't be doing anything for several weeks at least.'

Always assuming that I came out at all, that was – or didn't get arrested for murdering Jake Villiers before I went in.

'Everything's going to be fine, Kenny,' Pam said.

I had my doubts about that.

◆　◆　◆

In the afternoon, I realised that what I intended to do was insane. Instead I should treat myself to a decent meal, have a nightcap with Odeerie, and get what sleep I could before setting off for St Mick's the following morning. Farrelly could have his 'shooter' back, and God, karma or random chance could deal with Jake Villiers in whichever way it chose. I wasn't a cold-eyed dispenser of justice; I was a bloke with a growth in his head and a stupid tattoo on his arse. Jake would probably end up taking the gun and using it on me.

And then I changed my mind again. Leaving things to God, karma or random chance wasn't an option. Jake Villiers could easily go on to murder anyone else who got in his way. The pendulum swung to and fro, and could have done so indefinitely had Stephie's bruised face not edged into my memory. At 3 p.m. I left the flat carrying a loaded Beretta.

THIRTY-EIGHT

From Richmond station to Jake Villiers's house took ten minutes by taxi. Instead I chose to walk, ensuring that my baseball cap was pulled down low over my face when exiting the barriers. All that the CCTV cameras would record was a man in a black jacket and jeans whose face wasn't visible and who had a rucksack over his shoulder.

I'd arrived two hours before I was due to meet Jake, in order that I could take a circuitous route. Many of the buildings I passed were a couple of hundred years old and most likely owned by stockbrokers and fund managers who wanted to live in a leafy Georgian town within a few miles of Central London.

Gresham Street was lined with mature plane trees coming into bud. The houses in the terrace were three storeys high and each front door was painted navy blue. A couple in their thirties were too involved in an argument to take any notice of me, and an elderly woman walking a portly golden retriever didn't give me a second glance.

I walked past number 17 three times before pressing the bell. Jake answered the door wearing jeans and a pink shirt with the sleeves rolled up to the elbows. On his head was propped a pair of reading glasses.

'God, is it that time already?' he said, checking his watch. 'Come in . . .'

The study looked out on to the back garden. A teardrop chandelier provided the light and a large Oriental rug protected the floorboards.

An oak bookcase held what looked like a complete set of Wisden, and a pair of leather sofas faced an exquisitely moulded fireplace. By the window was a pale-green cactus as tall as I was.

'Didn't know you were an Arsenal fan,' Jake said.

'What?'

He pointed at my cap.

'Oh, right. I'm not. Just bought it to keep the chill out.'

I took the cap off and stuffed it into my jacket pocket. My breathing was so shallow and rapid that if I didn't slow it down I would start to hyperventilate.

'On your own?' I asked.

Jake nodded. 'Chance to get an early night for once. Fancy a drink, Kenny? You look like you could use one.'

'That would be great,' I said. 'Scotch if you have it.'

Jake opened a cabinet to reveal at least a dozen bottles of spirits and several tumblers. 'I've got some vintage Ardbeg,' he said.

'Fantastic,' I said. 'Any chance I could use your loo . . . ?'

'Out of the door, second on your right.'

I splashed cold water over my face and took deep and regular breaths. My hands were shaking so much that it could have been minus ten in Jake's downstairs lavatory. I used the towel, opened the rucksack and removed the gun. I released and reinserted the magazine. Then I checked the safety was definitely off.

Jake was holding a tumbler and staring out of the window. He'd put some jazz on the sound system and didn't hear me enter the room. It would have been relatively simple to fire a couple of rounds into his back. Instead I powered off the system. The music slurred as the turntable slowed. Jake turned. His eyebrows rose in mild surprise. And then he started to laugh. 'Is that thing real?' he asked.

'It's real,' I said.

'You're going to shoot me?'

I nodded.

'Wow! Do I get to know why?'

'You murdered two people and there's every chance you'll do the same to Stephie when she realises what a piece of shit you are.'

Jake took a hit on his Scotch and sighed. 'We've been over this already,' he said. 'If people threaten me, they need to be dealt with. As far as Steph goes, what can I tell you? I've got a temper and sometimes it gets the better of me. But if you're worried about her, Kenny, then let me put your mind at rest. She's perfectly—'

The tumbler fell to the floor. A blackbird in the garden made a skittering cry. Jake looked down at his right leg and looked at me. A moment later he collapsed. 'You shot me,' he said, clutching his thigh with both hands. 'You fucking shot me!'

Indeed I had. The tension in my hand had increased to the degree that I'd pulled the trigger involuntarily. Not that Jake knew that. As far as he was concerned I'd put a bullet in his leg for taking the piss. I took a couple of strides forward and levelled the gun again. Jake groaned. It might have been the pain or it might have been the fact that he was seconds away from oblivion.

'Stephie and I broke off the engagement last night,' he said.

'What?'

'You heard.'

'She did or you did?'

'She did.'

'You're making it up.'

'Call her.'

'That's not really an option, Jake.'

'See that cabinet . . .' Jake released one bloodied hand and pointed at an escritoire next to the bookcase. 'Open the drawer and take a look inside . . .'

I followed Jake's instructions. Nestled amongst a few folded documents and envelopes was a diamond engagement ring. As far as I could tell it was the same one I'd returned to Stephie in the Vesuvius.

'Now do you believe me?' he asked.

'Why did she do it?'

'Does it really matter?'

'I want to know.'

'She said that she didn't want to be with someone who thought it was okay to hit women. All of which means that you don't have to do anything stupid. Just give me my phone so I can call for help, and fuck off.'

I replaced the ring and shut the drawer.

'If you're worried about me telling the police, don't be,' Jake said. 'The last thing I want is them hearing your claim that Pauline's suicide wasn't really suicide. I'll make some story up about . . . how I answered the door . . . to an intruder . . .'

Jake's face was the colour of putty and his teeth were beginning to chatter. The damp patch on his leg was widening and darkening.

'Let me tell you why you're really doing this,' he said. 'You know full well that I'd never really harm Stephie . . . What's pissing you off is that I was with her and you weren't . . .'

'Bullshit.'

'No, it isn't. You can fool yourself that you're doing something noble and self-sacrificing . . . but you aren't. If you . . . if you kill me, you're doing it for one person and one person only . . . You're doing it for you . . .'

Was Jake right? Was the real reason I was standing in front of him pointing a gun essentially envy? No time to think about that now. There was a more important question I needed answering. 'Are you connected to the Golden Road?'

'Jesus, not that again.'

'Are you?'

'Why . . . would I be?'

'How about the Road paid you to buy the Emporium in case some-one else bought the place and decided to develop it?'

'What?'

'Then Emily's body would be discovered.'

'The Golden Road's . . . just a . . . conspiracy theory.'

'You said in the Duck & Unicorn that you'd never heard of it.'

'Which is why I checked it out. Kenny, are you sure . . . this Golden Road thing hasn't unbalanced . . . you mentally?'

I tightened my grip on the gun.

'I'm going to ask you again, Jake. Lie to me and I'll kill you.'

'For fuck's sake . . . I'm telling—'

'Are you connected to the Golden Road?'

Jake looked me straight in the eyes.

'I swear I'm not,' he said.

I squeezed off three rounds in quick succession.

All three hit the target.

◆ ◆ ◆

I sauntered down Gresham Street as though taking a late-evening con-stitutional. Heavy rain meant that it was ten minutes before I passed the first person who might be able to ID me to the police afterwards. It was the best part of an hour before I walked on to Richmond Bridge, and even then I found it more by accident than design.

First, the body of the gun descended into the dark water swirl-ing beneath me. Seconds later the magazine followed. If one day the river deposited them on to the shore then they would be unusable and untraceable. For some reason I couldn't move, as though a hypnotist had commanded I remain rooted to the pavement.

What seemed like a flash case of the flu set in and my body ached and shivered. Tears began to course down my cheeks. I was wondering if I might have to remain on the bridge until someone arrived to lead me off it, when the weeping stopped and my feet seemed capable of shuffling forward. Ten minutes later I called Odeerie.

THIRTY-NINE

A bottle of brandy usually lasted Odeerie six months. He was now on his third glass in twenty minutes. The curtains in his sitting room were drawn and the lighting muted. Odeerie occupied a brown leather sofa next to a shelf of classical vinyl. I was slumped in the corduroy armchair by the door.

'Christ, Kenny,' he said after I'd reached the end of my account. 'The guy could have bled out.'

'I wrapped a towel around his leg before I left. The flow had stopped and if Jake called an ambulance straight away then he'll be fine.'

'What about the cactus?'

'The cactus was fucked.'

'I meant why did you shoot it?'

'Things were a bit tense,' I said. 'It was either the cactus or Jake.'

'What if he tells the cops?'

I shrugged.

Odeerie knocked back the rest of his brandy and picked up his phone. He tapped it a few times and scrutinised the screen. 'There's nothing online.'

'Maybe the news services haven't picked it up yet.'

'Unlikely. They get hold of this kind of thing almost straight away. Jake could have passed out after you left and been unable to make the call. That would mean he's lying dead in his house right now.'

'Thanks, Odeerie.'

'Just being realistic, Kenny.'

'The police could be delaying the release for operational reasons.'

'Or Jake didn't call an ambulance.'

'Why wouldn't he?'

'He might have gone private.'

'BUPA?'

'Someone prepared to take care of it without informing the police. You know, a GP who's been struck off or a dodgy vet.'

'Oh, yeah,' I said. 'See what you mean.'

Taking the train from Richmond had felt like taking an acid trip. My anxiety levels were so high that everyone seemed to be staring at the whey-faced damp bloke in the corner of the carriage and muttering about him under their breath.

No way was I convincing Odeerie that I'd just returned from a quiet supper with my brother. My attempt to explain events had been so incoherent that the brandy had been produced. Currently the fat man was outdrinking me at a ratio of 3:1.

'Nope. Jake's either dead or used a hooky doctor,' he said, having found no information on his phone. 'Why didn't you tell me about this earlier, Kenny?'

'Because it would have implicated you.'

Odeerie looked at the ceiling and shook his head.

'Where did you get the gun?' he asked.

'Farrelly.'

'Farrelly, the guy who tortures people for fun?'

'Yeah,' I said. 'That Farrelly.'

'It just gets better and better. You've shot a prominent businessman with a weapon supplied by a stone-cold psychopath. What are you doing for an encore, Kenny?'

'Going into hospital and having my skull opened.'

The line stopped Odeerie in his tracks.

'That was another reason I went after Jake,' I said. 'There was a decent chance there wouldn't be any comebacks.'

'I don't understand.'

'The operation's not quite as straightforward as I told you. The tumour isn't malignant but it's bloody big. Getting it out isn't going to be an easy job. If things go well then I'll need a few weeks to recuperate.'

'And if they don't you'll need a few more weeks.'

'It's not that simple. I might be blind or physically incapacitated. If it goes really badly then I might not come out of hospital at all.'

A car drove past with the dull repetitive thud of bass cranked to the max. After twenty seconds or so, its pumping beat was swallowed by the night.

'I'm sorry, Kenny,' Odeerie said.

'Yeah,' I replied. 'So am I.'

For the next hour or so Odeerie did his best to be positive. We talked about the statistics I'd been given and the fact that hospitals tend to err on the side of caution. The fat man opened up a box of Krispy Kremes and began to plough through them while I collared what remained of the brandy. We kept the TV tuned to BBC News in case something came up about a shooting in South West London.

There's only so much you can say about a brain tumour before it gets samey, and the conversation drifted. Odeerie still hadn't cracked the encrypted email and wasn't particularly hopeful it could be done. In his opinion, whoever had taken me to the slaughterhouse had been well prepared and knew what they were doing. He bit into his third doughnut and chewed thoughtfully.

'Let's review the whole thing. You're convinced that Dean Allison killed Emily but he's got an unbreakable alibi, according to the police.

JJ Freeman and Castor were best mates, right? So close they were essentially brothers.'

I nodded.

'So if Castor did murder Emily in a fit of rage after finding out that she had a thing with Dean Allison, then he could have gone to JJ for help afterwards.'

'Apart from they were having huge barneys about money.'

'What brothers don't have arguments? Doesn't mean they aren't going to be there for each other when the shit hits the fan. JJ could have smuggled Castor out of the country and he doesn't want you or anyone else to know where he is.'

'Why would he think we were even getting close?'

In lieu of an answer, the fat man introduced another name to the conversation.

'Chop Montague.'

'What about him?'

'He and Castor were writing hit songs but Castor was getting himself wired on drugs and writing less. Chop could have got pissed off that his career was going down the toilet and decided to do something about it.'

'Apart from Chop's gone from strength to strength.'

'He didn't know that would happen at the time.'

'Fair enough, but why kill Emily?'

Odeerie thought about this for a few seconds.

'What if the two events aren't connected? What if someone killed Emily and someone else killed Castor?'

'Hell of a coincidence.'

'So we come back to Castor murdering Emily and escaping under his own steam, or more likely with the help of a third party . . .'

'You really think a shadowy group called the Golden Road disappears rock stars and makes a fortune off their royalties?'

The fat man spread his palms. 'I'm just saying that's where the evidence is pointing, Kenny. And if the Golden Road doesn't exist, who made the phone call to you and arranged all that business in the abattoir?'

It was a question to which I had no answer. Odeerie stared at the doughnut in his hand for a few moments, as though it were a tiny crystal ball instead of a globe of deep-fried pastry. Then he popped it into his mouth and ate it.

◆　◆　◆

By 2 a.m. there hadn't been any reports about a shooting incident. It looked as though Odeerie's theory about Jake's unregistered doctor had been right. Our hug was awkward. My arms couldn't span Odeerie's circumference and he patted my back as though winding a baby. I'd felt more comfortable pulling a gun on Jake Villiers.

The streets served as a decompression chamber following a long dive. The familiarity of buildings I'd known for thirty years helped neutralise the emotion of the last few hours. It would be a while before I trod the cobbles of Berwick Street, set my watch by Bar Italia's clock, or smoked a fag with the doormen outside Sunset Strip. All of which I did before returning to the flat.

There were no police officers. Waiting was the bag I'd packed for St Mick's, a half-empty bottle of Monarch and an unopened pack of Marlboros. Every New Year I had promised myself that life would be different. I'd join a gym, quit smoking and get a proper job. It had never happened and now it probably never would.

After settling into the chair to get some sleep, I roamed through dreamscapes littered with guns, supposedly dead rock stars, and giant eggs. Pauline Oakley hung from a tree on Hampstead Heath and Farrelly gave me a bollocking for not following through. By the time the alarm on my phone woke me at seven thirty, I felt more knackered than when I'd drifted off. A long shower and a pint of coffee went some way to making me feel better. While waiting for the taxi, I sat down and read a week-old copy of the *Guardian*.

The paper's lifestyle guru detailed an exercise in which people were asked to look for everything brown in a room and told to close their eyes. When asked what was green they hadn't a clue. The point was that we see what we expect to see, not necessarily what's there – particularly if someone misdirects us. Was Castor Greaves still alive and writing music? Of course he was.

I'd just been looking in the wrong place.

FORTY

The bungalow was a converted stable constructed from the same granite blocks as Mickleton Lodge. There was about a hundred yards between the buildings. A skylight and a solar panel had been set into the roof, and a decking area was home to several potted shrubs, a barbecue station and a bench with a propane heater above it.

I used my binoculars to switch from the house to the bungalow and back several times. No one around. I clambered over the dry-stone wall and deposited my rucksack under an oak tree. The damp from the grass penetrated my Hush Puppies long before I'd reached the decking. My feet squelched over the planks as I approached the door.

I knocked. No answer. I knocked again. Still no answer.

The window to the left served a kitchen. A few dishes had been left in the sink and a pair of muddy wellingtons lay on a sheet of newspaper. Curtains had been drawn across the window on the right, although I could make out a TV and the edge of an armchair. I passed a gleaming steel septic tank on my way to the rear of the building.

A beaten-earth path led from the bungalow to a nearby copse, above which a parliament of rooks circled and cawed. There was only one window and one door. I peered into a small bedroom. Lying on the bed was a battered acoustic guitar along with an A4 pad. On the bedside table, next to a clock radio, was a copy of the iconic picture of Emily Ridley with her head on Castor Greaves's shoulder.

Had I taken a couple of photos and left, it would have been enough. Instead, I tried the door. It was locked. An expert could have cracked the single-lever mortice with a paper clip. Even I took less than a minute using a tension wrench and a pick.

The door to the left opened on to the bedroom. Opposite was the bathroom. After establishing this, I entered the sitting room and switched on the lights. Five shelves contained what had to be a couple of thousand records and CDs. An electric guitar was propped against the TV and a keyboard lay on a waist-high stand.

The wardrobe was filled with jackets and boots. What looked like a balaclava had been draped across the rail. I reached in and pulled it out. Peering up at me was the rubberised face of the forty-fifth president of the United States. I'd just transferred the mask to my pocket when I heard the click. Chop Montague was pointing a shotgun in my direction.

'You took another look at the photo, didn't you, Kenny?' he asked.

'Yeah,' I replied. 'I took another look at the photo.'

The nylon tie had been looped around the cooker's gas pipe. Had I been strong enough to wrench the thing free, I'd still have risked blowing the building sky-high. The only thing I could do was sit on the kitchen chair and stare at Chop, who was leaning against the fridge with the shotgun cradled under his arm.

'Who else did you tell you were coming here?' he asked.

'Fucking everyone,' I said. 'If I'm not checked into St Mick's Hospital in the next half-hour then they'll know exactly where to look for me.'

Chop smiled. 'I don't think so, Kenny. You couldn't have been sure that the guy in the picture was Castor and you wouldn't have wanted to look stupid.'

He was right. The first time I'd seen the press photograph of the blaze at Mickleton Lodge I'd focused on the woman who was Emily Ridley's doppelgänger. What I should have been doing was checking out the guy who had raised the alarm.

'When you showed me the photo on your tablet at Encore I thought it was the end of the line,' Chop said. 'And then you started going on about my sister being Emily Ridley. I didn't know whether to laugh or cry. I was all for killing you, but after what Castor did to Saskia Reeves-Montgomery I thought it a trifle risky.'

'Castor killed Saskia?'

Chop nodded. 'She called and asked how long my heroic gardener had been working for me. Of course there wasn't much doubt as to why she wanted to know, which is why Cas had to pay her a visit.'

'Why torture her?'

'We had to know if she'd told anyone else.'

'That was Cas's idea?'

'Actually, mine, but there isn't much people won't do to preserve their freedom. Particularly if they're reminded of the alternative from time to time.'

'Which is what you've been doing for Cas all these years?'

Chop's smile answered my question.

The radio attached to his belt loop buzzed. 'Hello, Cas,' he said, holding it to his mouth. 'Yes, unfortunately it turns out that, despite our best efforts, I was right about Mr Gabriel . . .'

I heard the indistinct buzz of a male voice.

'Well, I think there's only one solution, don't you?' Chop looked directly at me. 'Probably the woods. If anyone hears they'll assume that we're shooting rabbits . . . I've got the gun here, so there's no need to go back to the house . . .' Chop's radio clattered on to the kitchen table.

'Anyway,' he continued, 'not wanting to draw too much attention was why we went to the enormous inconvenience of arranging the drama in the abattoir.'

'You pretended to be the Golden Road?'

Chop chuckled. 'Of all the theories as to what happened to Castor, that was the most absurd. But when the *Inquisitor* got hold of those demos, suddenly it became rooted in the public imagination.'

'Why didn't you just kill me and Saskia at the same time?'

'Too risky. You'd blabbed in the *Post* about how you thought the Golden Road was involved in Castor's disappearance and that he was still alive. If we'd killed you then it would have been seen as proof you were right.'

'And that would have meant even more publicity?'

'Indeed. Unfortunately, now you've left us with no other option . . .'

Chop ran a hand over the blued-steel barrels of the shotgun. The action caused my stomach to contract and my bowels to loosen. The story in the *Post* had both kept me alive and condemned me to death. Thank you, Danny Abbott.

'What happened in the Emporium that night?' I asked.

'I can't tell you, Kenny,' he said.

'Why not?'

'Because it would mean . . .'

Chop's brow furrowed. He laid the gun carefully on the table and approached the sink. From a holder containing Fairy Liquid and other cleaning sundries, he selected a dishcloth and scrunched it into a ball.

'Open wide.'

'What?'

'You heard.'

'You're not serious.'

'Kenny, you'll be dead in fifteen minutes. What does it matter?'

The grey rag had congealed fat and particles of food clinging to it. The idea of letting it anywhere near my mouth was repellent. But then so was having a twelve-bore discharged into my face. Chop inserted the cloth.

'Spit it out,' he said.

Impossible. The cloth had wedged my jaws open to a degree that I'd lost the ability to manipulate them. All I could do was try not to vomit and choke to death.

'Good,' Chop said. 'Now you can know what happened to Cas and Em. Even if you will be taking the story to a shallow grave.'

He settled into one of the kitchen chairs and crossed his legs.

'When Castor and I began writing together it became clear that he had a gift. Cas could barely read music and had absolutely no idea as to the principles of composition, but that wasn't a problem. Having been to the Royal College, I could introduce those elements to the mix easily enough. What I lacked was raw talent.

'Unfortunately, the more Cas learned, the more he realised that all I was doing was transcribing his ideas. If he left the band, I would have gone from being one half of the most exciting writing partnership in a decade to applying for teaching jobs.

'Cas got disastrously into heroin, as you know. With everything that entailed, it looked as though my writing days were numbered. Which was when fate provided the kind of opportunity that you either take or regret not doing so for the rest of your life. I believe there's something in *Henry V* about it . . .'

There is a tide in the affairs of men, which, taken at the flood, leads on to fortune was probably the passage Chop was referring to. It was from *Julius Caesar*, but no way could I put him right about that with a dishrag stuffed in my mouth.

'Pure luck led to me trying the door to the roof,' he continued. 'Had it been locked, things would have turned out very differently. Castor had been trying to turn Emily on to smack, and in the end he succeeded. Be careful what you wish for, isn't that what they say? Anyway, she was carrying the stash and they'd agreed to take it together under the stars. Unfortunately the gear was abnormally pure. Cas still had the needle in his arm when I found the pair of them out cold.'

Chop took a deep breath.

'And that's when I made my choice, Kenny,' he said. 'I pinched Emily's nostrils and held my other hand over her mouth. Two minutes later she was dead. Then I slapped Castor's face and brought him round. He assumed that Emily had died because of the junk he'd pumped into her veins.

'Cas panicked until I told him there was a way out. He would need to stay on the roof with Emily's body until the following day, when I'd arrive to supervise the removal of the band's equipment. Cas wasn't officially missing and it wasn't too hard to get him out unrecognised. The real problem was what to do with Emily.

'The heating ducts had just been capped off and I thought it was where we should temporarily conceal the body. When no one discovered it after three months, leaving her there seemed the safest option. And then you turned up, twenty-two years later.

'All I wanted was for Castor and me to keep writing together. Everything would have to be released under my name, but that didn't bother him unduly. It was more about creation for Cas than it was the cash or the glory.

'That wasn't the case for me. I'd grown too accustomed to the praise and the plaudits to say goodbye to them. Have you ever been so envious of someone that you did something you ought to be ashamed of?'

Of course the answer was yes. Our motives may have been different but when it came down to it there wasn't much difference between Chop and me. We'd both been prepared to kill to get what we wanted. He'd just been more successful at it.

'Cas is so very grateful that he'll do my bidding no matter how repugnant he may find it, which is why he agreed to torture Saskia,' Chop continued. 'Poor chap was so distraught he threatened to kill himself afterwards. You see, Kenny, Cas may have a genius for composition, but he's terribly weak, I'm afraid.'

Chop's facade had first slipped in Encore Studios when he'd bawled Yvonne out. Should I have connected the dots then, and did any of it really matter now? I'd come to the conclusion that it probably didn't when the front door opened.

◆ ◆ ◆

Castor's scalp showed through a buzz cut and his complexion was ruddy from working outdoors. He was wearing a pair of stained jeans and a faded lumberjack shirt. On his hands were a pair of uPVC gloves; the twin of Chop's radio protruded from his pocket. The snake-hipped frontman had been subsumed by middle age, and yet his blue eyes retained the intensity that had stared out of posters back in the day and out of the Trump mask back in the abattoir.

'Hello, Cas,' Chop said. 'I'd introduce you to Kenny Gabriel, but of course you've met before. He became a little shouty, which is why I gagged him. I think it's best we get this over with as soon as possible, don't you?'

Chop's apprehension was understandable. If the cloth slipped out of my mouth then I could reveal the secret he'd kept from Castor for over twenty years. But even if that happened, Cas would just assume it to be the fabrication of a desperate man.

Basically, I was doomed any which way you sliced it.

Castor stared at me and breathed heavily through his nostrils. He slipped his gloves off and removed the radio from his pocket. When he laid it on the table it emitted a shriek like a snared animal. He frowned and quickly switched it off.

'Why don't you do it, Chop?' he said. It was the voice that I'd first heard ordering me around in the abattoir.

'I don't think so,' Chop muttered. 'You're far better at this sort of thing than I am, Cas. I'll happily watch, though. Then we can either bury the body in the woods or take him out to Spashett Lake and dump him there.'

Castor nodded. Either method, it seemed, was acceptable.

◆ ◆ ◆

Chop cut through the wrist tie and released my hands. I thought about grabbing a knife from the block by the cooker, but with Castor training the shotgun on me there was only one way it would have ended. My wrists were bound once more, and Chop led me through the hallway to the rear of the bungalow.

A fine mist had descended and deepened the silence. A couple of muntjac deer looked on from the edge of the copse as we proceeded along the path to the trees. Soon the world would draw to a close in a deadly spray of lead pellets, and my corpse would be consigned to the loamy earth or the chilly depths.

The deer ran when we were within twenty yards. I was first into the woods, followed by Chop and then Castor holding the gun. The ground was covered in a mulch of dead leaves and rotting acorns. Branches exuded renewal in the form of tiny bumps from which pale shoots would emerge in the next few weeks. A huge tree had been felled by lightning, sickness or age; its roots protruded in a redundant tangle.

'Over there,' Castor said, gesturing with the gun. As instructed, I stood with my back to the gnarled and mossy bark of the horizontal trunk. The three of us formed an equilateral triangle, with Castor to my right and Chop to my left.

'Get on with it, Cas,' Chop instructed. 'We don't have much time.'

Castor swivelled and pointed the gun at him.

'Shut the fuck up.'

Chop's mouth opened and closed like a gaffed trout's. Castor took a few steps closer.

'You let me think I killed her, you piece of shit,' he said. 'Have you any idea what it was like to spend the night alone with her body thinking I was responsible? I said, HAVE YOU GOT ANY FUCKING IDEA WHAT IT WAS LIKE?'

Castor's shouting caused the rooks to take to the air cawing. It also jolted Chop out of his bewilderment. 'What are you talking about, Cas?'

'You left the radio on, Chop. I heard every word you said to Kenny about what happened that night in the Emporium.'

Which was why the handsets had reacted when placed next to each other and presumably why Castor had been so quick to switch them off. I could almost see the calculations flashing behind Chop's eyes as to how to get out of this nightmare.

'Emily would have died anyway, Cas,' he said. 'As it is, you've had twenty years of freedom and we've written some amazing songs together.'

'*We've* written them?'

'I meant you did, Cas. They're your songs. You wrote them.'

Taking credit for the only thing that had ever mattered in Castor's life apart from Emily Ridley was Chop's second big mistake of the morning.

'For God's sake, don't put it all at risk, Castor,' he said. 'All you have to do is finish this idiot off and we can carry on as normal.'

'You call this normal?'

'Cas, I'm *ordering* you to shoot him. Do it *right now*.'

The gun was lowered and Chop exhaled heavily with relief. Presumably Cas had needed to build up his nerve, which was why he hadn't shot him in the bungalow. Now it looked as though he was about to lose it again. The gun would be redirected at me and Castor would pull the trigger. That was the way it looked.

Right up to the point he blew Chop's head off.

◆　◆　◆

If I could make open ground then Castor would only have one shot to bring me down. That said, he was fifteen years younger and ten times fitter. He also didn't have his hands tied behind his back and wasn't wearing a pair of disintegrating shoes.

Escaping was a tall order, but having seen Chop's skull explode in a miasma of blood and brains, I wasn't hanging around to let it happen to me.

Castor's feet were thumping behind me and he was shouting for me to stop. I tripped on a root and went sprawling. At least the impact with the ground dislodged the cloth from my mouth and allowed more oxygen into my starved system.

I scrambled to my feet and began running again.

My efforts were encouraged by the sound of sirens. Not just one vehicle but a couple at least. I was within a few yards of daylight when the earth gave way and my right ankle snapped. The pain was phenomenal. I rolled on to my back to see Castor standing above me with the gun pointing down at forty-five degrees.

'I'm sorry, Kenny,' he said.

'Sorry for what?' I asked. Keeping Cas talking until the police arrived on the scene looked like being my only hope. *Was* my only hope.

'Everything that's happened,' he said.

'Was it you who made the call warning me to give up the case?'

He nodded.

'Was that Chop's idea?'

'No. He didn't know anything about it. I just wanted you to stop . . . wanted all this to stop. *Why didn't you fucking listen to me?*'

Cas's last sentence was delivered almost as a wail. His head appeared to shimmer as though printed on a silk sheet rippling in the breeze.

'I had to know the truth,' I said through a wall of pain.

'Why? Why did it matter so much?'

First one siren died, and then the other. Doors opened and slammed shut. Hopefully the officers attending were armed to the teeth.

'Doesn't it matter to *you*, Cas? At least you know what happened to Emily now, and that you didn't kill her.'

'What good does that do me? Em's still dead. All I ever wanted to do was carry on writing. Now they'll lock me up for life.'

Our conversation sounded muffled, as though it were taking place underwater. Also I was blinking every couple of seconds and unable to stop.

'Then what's the point in shooting me?' I managed to say.

'Because you're the only one who knows about Saskia. If you're dead then I can say Chop killed the pair of you and that I shot him in self-defence.' Castor's hands stiffened around the gun. 'I'm really sorry, Kenny. But if you'd done what you were told then none of this would have happened.'

The inside of my mouth tasted wooden and salty, as though I'd been eating smoked almonds. A bright light flashed, leaving Castor's image imprinted on my retinas. He mouthed something that I couldn't understand. Not that it really mattered.

A blanket of darkness had rolled over the world.

FORTY-ONE

Nurse Bevan ushered DCI Shaheen into my room. She explained that he had twenty minutes, after which time she'd be back. The speech was as much for my benefit as it was for the DCI's. Since regaining consciousness, I'd been trying to convince her that reading the papers and watching daytime TV weren't likely to return me to the induced coma I'd been in for the last nine days. Eventually she had succumbed.

The Mickleton Lodge incident was still in the news. Some of the story had been pieced together correctly; most of it hadn't. The assumption was that Castor Greaves had killed Emily Ridley and concealed her body in the heating duct. He had then gone to Chop Montague for help and been sheltered for over twenty years.

No one was aware that Chop had murdered Emily, that Castor had written virtually all of Chop's songs and that he had also killed Saskia Reeves-Montgomery. I was the only person who knew that, just as I was the only person who knew what had taken place in Mickleton Woods. An account Shaheen was eager to hear.

'Christ,' he said after I'd finished. 'So all those hits were really Castor Greaves's and not Chop Montague's?'

I nodded.

'And Castor was okay with that?'

'What was important to him was being able to write. Also he felt indebted to Chop for keeping it that way, and guilty for what he'd done to Emily.'

'And if it weren't for the business with the radio then all this would still be going on,' Shaheen said, looking down at his notes.

Which of course was true. Chop had spent God alone knew how much time and money protecting Castor. The only thing that had got in the way was a random electrical fire, a moment's carelessness with a walkie-talkie and an overwhelming need to confess a story that he'd kept secret for years.

Not for the first time since he'd entered the room, the DCI took a look at the dressing on my head. 'Did the operation go well?' he asked.

'They haven't removed the tumour,' I said. 'They just eased some of the pressure that built up after the stroke. I've got your officers to thank for getting me to hospital in time. How did they know where I was?'

'A hiker saw you acting suspiciously outside Mickleton Lodge. When you jumped the wall, he called three nines and reported a burglary in progress. Otherwise you'd have died in the woods and we'd be none the wiser.'

'Particularly as you had Kris Barberis as your prime suspect.'

The DCI reddened. 'Forensics isn't an exact science.'

A meditative silence followed.

'Why d'you think Castor didn't finish you off?' he asked. It was a question I'd pondered myself, usually in the watches of the night when sleep wouldn't come.

'Maybe he thought he'd killed enough people for one lifetime. Or perhaps he was just in too much of a hurry to get away. Have you caught him yet?'

Shaheen shifted on his chair. 'Matter of time,' he said. 'How far can you get with the entire country on the lookout for you?'

Nurse Bevan looked in and told Shaheen his time was up. He screwed the lid on to his pen and placed the notebook in his briefcase.

'When d'you get out of here?' he asked.

'End of the week, hopefully.'

'What'll you do?'

'Lead a quiet life.'

The DCI chortled. 'Are you serious? You're almost as famous as Castor Greaves. Every newspaper in the country wants to interview you, and they only know half the story. You'll be able to charge what you like for PI work.'

'There won't be any more PI work.'

'Why not?' Shaheen asked.

'I'm retired,' I said.

◆ ◆ ◆

My mobile had been lost in Mickleton Woods. The only way that anyone could contact me was by calling the hospital and being transferred to the ward. As DCI Shaheen had predicted, most of the calls were from media agencies requesting interviews, although Odeerie had rung half a dozen times and left messages.

I'd postponed returning the fat man's call, as I wasn't looking forward to telling him I was quitting.

'You feel like that now, Kenny,' he said when eventually I bit the bullet. 'But when you're on your feet again, things'll be different.'

'No, they won't, Odeerie. I'm done.'

'You've said that before.'

'This time I mean it.'

'Why?'

'When Castor Greaves had the gun at my head, I swore that if I got out alive then I'd do something useful with my life.'

'Aren't you already doing good work, Kenny?'

'Photographing dodgy window cleaners?'

'Wielding the sword of righteousness. And you won't have to do bread-and-butter stuff any more. It'll all be missing tiaras and corporate retainers.'

'You're breaking up, Odeerie,' I said, and cut the call.

I stayed with Malcolm for a week. His townhouse was large and sufficiently protected to keep the media at bay. Castor hadn't been found and theories were already springing up. Favourites were that he had committed suicide in a remote spot or made it out of the country in a private boat. The *People's Inquisitor* even had definitive photographic proof that he had visited a Warsaw karaoke bar.

On the third day of my stay, Malcolm introduced me to his company lawyer. Bettina's opinion was that my contract with Angus Glazier at Billingsgate Publishing was invalid, as I'd made it when the tumour was affecting the balance of my mind. Despite this being completely untrue, I signed a document giving her full authority to negotiate on my behalf and she promised to get back to me with revised offers.

I visited St Mick's to see Ali, who seemed happy enough with my progress and said that the operation should go ahead as soon as possible. After the stroke I had difficulty gripping with my right hand and had lost peripheral vision on the left side. Bearing in mind how bad it could have been, I'd got off incredibly lightly. Now it was time to cross my fingers and roll the dice a second time.

In the waiting room, I flicked through a copy of *Chat*. A double-page spread featured a photograph of Jake Villiers holidaying in Barbados. Following a freak gardening accident – a bandaged thigh being proof of this – Jake had decided to take some time off from his busy schedule to recuperate. A few times I'd picked the phone up to call Stephie, but on each occasion had decided against it.

When I entered the flat for the first time in over a month it was early May. Malcolm had arranged for the place to be redecorated. A vase of flowers stood in the sitting room where the Monarch usually waited, and the fridge was full of fresh vegetables. Among the accumulated mail was a letter from Pam Ridley thanking me for finding her daughter's killer. A photo from the album showing Emily celebrating her birthday had been tucked into the envelope.

Recently signed as a model, her entire future had lain before her. And then she had met Dean Allison and Castor Greaves. Had she been slightly less exquisite, Emily's life may have run like those of the majority of others: work, marriage, children, retirement, varicose veins, dementia, death. I wedged the photo into the corner of the sitting room mirror to serve as a reminder, although I wasn't entirely sure of what.

I roamed the parish by night when fewer people were around. The flowers outside the Emporium club stretched almost thirty yards along the pavement. In addition to the wilting daffodils were tiny teddy bears, satin hearts, electric candles, miniature bottles of Jack Daniel's; the usual detritus of remembrance.

Pictures of Cas and Em in plastic sheaths had been taped to the walls of the club and nestled amongst the bouquets. That Castor had indirectly murdered his girlfriend and tortured and killed Saskia Reeves-Montgomery didn't seem to bother everyone, if indeed it bothered anyone. I collected an armful and dumped them in a nearby bin.

It was three thirty when I got back to the flat. I was turning the key in the newly installed lock when the window of a car on the opposite side of the street slid down.

'Oi, shithead,' a horribly familiar voice said. 'Get your arse over here.'

Farrelly's ten-year-old Toyota was immaculate. Hanging from the rear-view mirror was a pair of tiny boxing gloves. There were no other clues as to the owner's identity, like a corpse stretched out on the back seat or a knuckleduster peeping out of the glove compartment. Farrelly didn't appear to be in a good mood, but then Farrelly never did. Perhaps the imp of death was smiling on the inside.

'What the fuck did I tell you in your flat?' he said when I'd settled into the passenger seat. 'If you pull a gun, you've got to do the business.'

'I did the business.'

'You put one in his fucking leg. And what did you do with the bleedin' shooter afterwards? Have it framed and stuck up in your front room?'

The vein in Farrelly's temple had engorged, as it so often did during our conversations. If he didn't watch it then he'd be stroking out himself before too long.

'I broke it up and dropped it in the river,' I said.

'Anyone see you?' Farrelly asked.

'Don't think so.'

'Did they or fucking didn't they?'

'No, they didn't. It would have come out by now. And I think Jake was treated by someone off the books. There haven't been any reports about it.'

'Yeah,' Farrelly said. 'He used Lonnie Murphy.'

'Who?'

'Quack who got struck off for writing snide prescriptions.'

'How do you know?' I asked.

'Villiers told me,' Farrelly said.

'You went to see him?'

'What option did I have after you ballsed everything up? If we didn't have a straightener then chances were he'd have come after you.'

A 'straightener' usually had only one outcome where Farrelly was concerned. As Jake Villiers was grinning from the pages of a celeb magazine, that clearly wasn't the case in this instance.

'What did you tell him?' I asked.

'That I sold you the shooter and any comeback was on me.'

'Aren't you worried?'

Farrelly shook his head. 'Ain't nothing in it for him. Only reason he does anything is to keep what he's got or get more of what he has.'

'You came to a gentlemen's agreement, then?'

'I said that I'd have his knackers on toast if he came anywhere near you or me. He said that wouldn't happen and we shook on it.'

I believed Farrelly when he said that Jake only killed for profit. Jake probably believed that Farrelly would eat his knackers. The world was a safer place.

'Although that means Jake gets away with killing Pauline Oakley,' I said.

'This time he does,' was Farrelly's verdict. 'Jake's got more front than Margate, but someone'll fuck him over eventually. It just ain't gonna be you.'

A fox trotted into the middle of the road. It stared in the direction of Regent Street for a couple of moments, the streetlight making its eyes look like a pair of opals. Then it nosed the air and disappeared in the direction of Golden Square.

'What happened to this bird, then?' Farrelly asked.

'Stephie? She broke up with Villiers before I went round.'

'And you shot him anyway?' Farrelly looked impressed.

I opted not to confess that I'd pulled the trigger accidentally.

'Back together?' he asked.

'Nope. I haven't seen or heard from Stephie since I went into hospital.'

'Why not?'

'Obviously she doesn't give a shit.'

Farrelly exhaled heavily. 'You go after a dead bird so hard your nut explodes, but when it's flesh and blood you chuck the towel in at the first hurdle.'

It was neither the time nor the place to point out to Farrelly that he was mixing his sporting metaphors. 'You may have a point,' I said.

'Get your feet off the fucking dashboard,' he replied.

◆ ◆ ◆

In the run-up to my op, I stayed off the smokes, drank smoothies and ate my first-ever tofu fillet. I also left nine messages on Stephie's phone, all of which she completely ignored. Bettina kept me in touch with how the book negotiations were progressing. The eventual amount was enough to keep me in alfalfa-shoot salads and beetroot zingers for life – assuming I was still around to eat them. DCI Shaheen called to say that the CPS had decided to prosecute Dean Allison for historic child abuse. Even if unsuccessful, the nature of the charge meant that everyone would vilify Dean and not just the JFA – who may, or may not, have given him a good kicking.

It was late Friday afternoon when I pressed Odeerie's intercom. Spring was in full flood. Not that it meant much to a man with less vitamin D in him than a coelacanth.

'What d'you want?' he asked.

'Just fancied a chat.'

'I am *very* busy, Kenny,' the fat man said.

'That's a shame, because I've got a cheesecake from Maison Bertaux. But if you're snowed under then I can always come round another time . . .'

The lock buzzed open.

While we demolished the cake, I filled Odeerie in on the news about Dean Allison. He wasn't quite as jubilant as I'd been, but then he hadn't met the guy face to face.

'What about JJ Freeman?' he asked. 'Did he know anything about Dean and Emily?'

'Don't think so,' I said. 'JJ would have done something about it.'

'Must be hard for him,' the fat man said. 'After all, Castor was his best mate when they were growing up. Ever think about going to see him?'

As a matter of fact, I'd visited the Junction club two nights previously and sat at the bar. JJ had encored with 'Crossfire Alley', its piercing notes slashing through the gloom. It was a torch song for another place and another time.

I'd left before JJ noticed I was there.

'I'll catch up with him eventually,' I said. 'Meanwhile there's something I need to give you . . .' I reached into my jacket and handed Odeerie a white envelope. He frowned, wiped his hands on a kitchen roll and opened it up.

'What's this?'

'What does it look like?'

'A cheque for a hundred and ten grand.'

'That's because it *is* a cheque for a hundred and ten grand.'

Odeerie's bushy eyebrows knitted together.

'Only you can't cash it,' I said.

'Kenny, are you okay?'

'But you will be able to present it in a couple of weeks. Hopefully.'

The fat man looked no less concerned.

'It's half the advance I got from agreeing to write a book about the search for Cas and Em.' I took Odeerie through the discussions I'd had with Billingsgate. 'And that's just the publishing end. The movie rights won't be sorted for a few months, although they're already talking to Idris Elba about playing you.'

'Seriously?'

'Well, you never know. It all depends on me surviving the operation, though. If I can't write the book then all bets are off.'

'You haven't changed your mind about coming back?'

I shook my head. 'If I get through okay I'm doing something else with my life. The book money should give me a good start.'

'You'll be fine, Kenny,' Odeerie said. 'Just one thing, though . . .'

'What's that?' I asked.

'Wouldn't Denzel Washington be a better choice for me?'

◆ ◆ ◆

A couple of kids found Castor's shotgun beside a railway track near Hastings. It provoked a huge police search and God knows how many column inches of media speculation. My best guess was that Castor had had a flight stash in case his cover was ever blown, and probably a fake passport or two as well. Photographs would begin to emerge online of a Caucasian guy who answered Castor's description and was allegedly living on an Indian ashram or a Kenyan sugar plantation.

Two days before my operation I'd fallen into a late-night doze when the intercom went. It was two in the morning. Although Farrelly had sorted Jake Villiers out, I put both security chains on the door and peered through the crack.

'Don't say a word,' Stephie said. 'Do not say a fucking word.'

Our naked bodies told different stories. Stephie's taut skin and sleek muscles were a tale of early-morning runs punctuated with Pilates sessions and a diet rich in protein and essential nutrients. Mine was a far less wholesome physical narrative. Not for the first time, I thanked God for the forgiveness of women. We were sharing the cigarette that I kept with a miniature of Monarch in my sock drawer in case of dire emergency. The last twenty minutes scarcely counted as that, but I'd made an exception.

Stephie sent a jet of smoke towards the bedroom ceiling before handing the Marlboro back to my side of the bed.

'Here we are again, then,' I said.

'Thought I told you not to say anything,' she replied.

'Yeah, but now that we've . . . Isn't it okay?'

'Not if you come out with shit like *here we are again then* it isn't.'

I took a final toke from the cigarette and extinguished it on the heel of one of my shoes. 'So, why are you here?' I asked.

'Wasn't that obvious?'

'I meant why did you change your mind?'

'About what?'

'Marrying Jake.'

Stephie took so long to answer that I thought she'd either decided not to or had fallen asleep.

'Don't try to make this anything other than it is, Kenny,' she said.

'Of course not. Er . . . What is it, exactly?'

'A never-to-be-repeated trip down memory lane that I'm already beginning to regret.' More silence. 'Look, maybe what you said about how I felt about you and how I felt about Jake was true. Despite how much I sincerely wish it wasn't.'

'Then what's stopping us from carrying on where we left off?'

'I was gutted when you didn't show up in Manchester. What have you ever done for me, Kenny? What have you ever put on the line?'

Not a lot I could say.

'Exactly! Sod all, that's what.' Stephie levered herself out of bed and started to dress. 'Are you back working yet?' she asked. 'You and Odeerie must be flooded with stuff after all that publicity.'

'Actually, I've decided to try something new.'

'Like what?'

'I'm co-writing a book about the search for Emily and Castor.'

'How long will that take?'

'Six months or so. I haven't started yet.'

Stephie squinted at me suspiciously.

'I'm going on a trip,' I added.

'Where to?'

'Not sure.'

Stephie pulled on her jeans. 'Yeah, well, that's probably not a bad idea. You need to get some decent rest after your operation and I'm glad you're turning over a new leaf. It's about bloody time. When d'you get back?'

'Soon, hopefully.'

'Okay, well, *maybe* we'll have a drink when you are.'

'I'd like that,' I said.

◆ ◆ ◆

After Stephie left, I couldn't get to sleep. I gave it up as a bad job around 4 a.m. and threw the living room curtains open. A cleaning van trundled past in the street below. A man took a piss in the doorway of the Yip Hing, two women ran past in day-glo Lycra tracksuits, and a helicopter hovered over Oxford Circus.

Dawn would break in half an hour and another day would begin in earnest. All over Soho, people would be swindled, delighted, heartbroken, promoted, abused, bored, educated, appalled, diagnosed, bewildered and caught red-handed.

Further afield, Pam Ridley would get out of bed and go to her first cleaning job of the day. Perhaps she would imagine what her daughter might be doing had Castor Greaves not introduced her to heroin and Chop Montague killed her. Davina Jackson would begin limbering up at City Stretch, Sweat Dog would load up his ink gun in Muswell Hill and DCI Shaheen would interview another suspect on Savile Row.

Perhaps Castor had made it out of the country and this time really was living anonymously in some distant part of the world. However pointless life may seem, it's still the only game in town.

The sun had fully risen by the time the intercom buzzed. 'Taxi for Kenny Gabriel to go to St Mick's Hospital,' my driver said.

'On my way down,' I told him.

ACKNOWLEDGMENTS

Thanks to:
    Kiare – as always.
    Jack Butler and the Thomas & Mercer team.
    Veronique Baxter at David Higham Associates.
    Russel D McLean.

ABOUT THE AUTHOR

Photo © 2016 Kiare Ladner

Born in Liverpool, Greg Keen got his first job in London's Soho over twenty years ago and has worked there ever since; his fascination with the area made it a natural setting for his books. *Soho Dead*, the first in the Soho Series of urban-noir crime novels, won the CWA Debut Dagger in 2015. Greg lives in London.